Prayer in Time of War

David Clensy

ISBN: 9798872551997
Prayer in Time of War, published 2024

www.davidclensy.com

© 2024 David Clensy. All rights reserved.

Interior pictures: Author's family archive

David Clensy asserts the moral rights to be identified as the author of this work in accordance with the Copyright, Designs and Patents Act 1988. A catalogue record for this book is available from the British Library.

All rights reserved. No part of this publication may be reproduced, stored in a retrieval system, or transmitted in any form or by any means, electronic, mechanical, photocopying, recording or otherwise, with the prior permission of the publishers. This book is sold subject to the condition that it shall not, by way of trade or otherwise, be lent, re-sold, hired out or otherwise circulated without the publisher's prior consent in any form of binding or cover other than that in which it is published and without a similar condition including this condition being imposed on the subsequent purchaser.

This is a work of fiction. Names, characters, businesses, events and individual incidents are the products of the author's imagination. Any resemblance to actual persons, living or dead, or actual events is purely coincidental.

Also by the author:

Walking the White Horses
Island Life: A History of Looe Island
The Mole of Edge Hill
Walking The Wolds Way
As Wide As All The World

In loving memory of my grandad,
Harold James Barr
and all the so-called "D-Day Dodgers"
"Dove andare domani?"

Prayer in Time of War

Chapter one
1993

Ernie Green's life had been hollowed out by love, and the loss of it. He had spent his years tiptoeing through a minefield of emotions, but found it was easier to tread carefully when walking alone.

The sun's rays filtered through the stained-glass fanlight that stretched above the front door. Ernie walked through the distinctive hues. These patterned clouds of colour, familiar to him since childhood, had never changed, though now they moved across the age spots on his hand as he reached down to pick up the post from the door mat.

"Bill, bill, bill," Ernie counted the envelopes out, placing them down on the slim mahogany console table. He was left holding a postcard. On one side a slightly dated, Technicolor picture of the Bay of Naples, with the word NAPOLI marked out in a bold font. The old eyebrows raised, and Ernie shuffled to the kitchen to find his glasses.

"Can never find them when I need them," he grumbled. Then patting his head, he remembered they were perched on his balding scalp, where he had left them as he puzzled over a crossword clue just a few minutes earlier. "Silly old fool," he whispered to himself, taking a seat at the kitchen table. "Now who's been visiting my old stomping ground?" He turned the postcard over to find just a few words written in an elegant sloping cursive. The colour immediately drained from Ernie's face. The old hand started to shake a little. He pushed the glasses back on to the top of his head and his watery eyes turned to look out at the sunlight dappling the garden.

"*Jesus Christ*," he whispered.

1943

Torre Annunziata, like all the other war-husked towns clustered around Naples – from Torre del Greco to Resina and Portici – was a landscape of shattered streets, where petty larceny ran wild within the squalor to the point of kleptomania, but Ernest's unit felt perfectly able to turn a blind eye. After all, the Italians had their own police to keep them in check. It seemed beneath the dignity of the British Army to fuss too much about every misdemeanour in a city such as this.

With boots crunching across the glass-strewn streets, he walked with his fellow soldiers, Patterson, Smudge and Mouse, as they jostled their way through a crowd of GIs, formed excitedly around a lorry carrying American Army supplies. The American soldiers swayed like rushes as they peered over each other's shoulders, keen to get a sight of what was in the lorry's stacked boxes.

Ernest stopped and looked through the gaps between jostling shoulders, to see across to the little square beyond. In the corner of the square stood a butcher's shop with empty windows, but a queue forming that must have been 30-strong. The Italians queued surprisingly neatly as they waited for their share of the unspecified meat that the butcher had got his hands on.

But Ernest's eyes were drawn through the scene, through these two very different crowds, drawn to another pair of eyes that had caught his attention from a great distance. Leaning against the doorway of the butcher's shop, counting customers inside four at a time, a girl of no more than 17 or 18 years was standing with her arms folded and her unsmiling face tilted a little to one side. Despite the grim surroundings, despite her dour dress, despite the piteous aura of misery that creased into the lines around her dark olive brown eyes, she was, Ernest quickly realised, a thing of celestial beauty.

Her cheeks flushed ever so slightly, and her delicate tilted face seemed to betray a greater suffering, with all the subtlety of a Titian Madonna. And as he gazed at her, the world came to a sudden, jolting stop around him. No more did he hear the American soldiers with their bustling and bantering. No more did he hear the elderly Italians chattering expressively. Even the water in the fountain at the centre of the square seemed to freeze its motion. Not a muscle in his whole being moved, the air seemed to vacuum in his lungs, and then they turned straight towards him, those dark brown, almost amber eyes. They locked with his eyes and in so doing, released the world around them once again. The voices re-emerged. The pigeons flapped out of their lofty freeze-frames. Even the water in the fountain began to trickle once more.

But in that moment, every fibre in Ernest's body and soul had been transformed; transfigured. He instinctively knew he had become another being altogether. The old Ernest was gone, evaporated in that moment of magic, reborn, radiant with a confidence that he had never before experienced.

His limbs acted independently of his mind, and he found himself being carried across the square. The Yanks parted and resettled back together in his wake. The elderly Italians took a step to the side to let him pass untroubled, lifted as he was across the square, somehow riding a higher plane. A stranger in this new form of existence, he heard his own voice speak, and realised that those dark brown eyes, once so distant across the square, were now angled up towards his face, just inches away.

"Cosa stai facendo?" he asked, with the little pidgin Italian he had picked up on his daily patrols.

The girl answered in English. "What am I doing? What does it look like I'm doing?"

"Is it your shop?" he asked softly.

"My father's," she replied, in almost a whisper, their eyes never fully unlocking as they spoke.

From across the square, Ernest heard Patterson's voice rumble. "Come on lad, stop fraternising with the local totty. There's work to be done."

Ernest knew there was no work to be done, but raised his hand in acknowledgement. "Just coming Sarge."

He looked down into the gentle face.

"Dove andare domani?" he asked.

"Tomorrow?" she muttered and laughed quietly.

"Yes, tomorrow. I'll meet you here, tomorrow. Domani."

"Tomorrow," she said again, but more softly. The laugh had evaporated, and she whispered the word almost like an incantation beneath her breath.

"Tomorrow," he repeated. "We'll go somewhere."

She sighed – he felt her breath touch his cheeks. There was a sweetness to it, like the softest Mediterranean breeze carried through a lemon grove at dusk.

"But I can't go anywhere," she added, suddenly coming-to, and breaking the lock between their eyes, to cast her glance to the ground and brush some non-existent fluff from the front of her dress. She brushed away at the magic of the moment with a defeated shrug of her tiny shoulders. "My father," she added, by way of explanation, and her hands erupted palms-out, in that catch-all gesticulation of the city.

"Ok, sure," Ernest muttered, his out-of-body moment of confidence starting to wilt. "Well, maybe I'll just call by to say hello again. I'll let you laugh at my Italian."

She smiled shyly.

"I'm Ernest, by the way."

"Preghiera," she replied, but seeing Ernest did not fully comprehend, she quickly added: "My name – my name is Preghiera de Rosa."

"Preghiera?" Ernest repeated, trying the name on his lips. "Preghiera."

"Preghiera. It means … how you say in English, 'prayer'? My father, he is very religious." Her frown knotted together as she whispered confidingly.

"Suitably divine," Ernest said quietly. "So tomorrow then, Preghiera?"

"Yes, ok then, tomorrow," she nodded, and turned her attention back to the crowd, counting four customers into the shop, with a gentle tap on each shoulder. But the moment Ernest's back was turned, those dark eyes looked back up and followed him across the square. Ernest turned once more to catch a final sight of her over his shoulder, as Patterson swept a playful grappling arm around his back, and with his other hand tousled his hair with his cap.

"Dirty bugger," Patterson chuckled. "I didn't know you had it in you."

Mouse and Smudge exchanged their own grins. "Fair play Ernest," Mouse muttered. "I mean, you would, wouldn't you?"

"I would," Smudge added, grumpily. "Given half a chance."

The four soldiers ambled out of the square and continued their half-hearted patrol of this Neapolitan corner of purgatory.

1993

The wheels of the Boeing 737 bounced once, then a second time, as the aircraft came in to land on the dusty runway at Naples International Airport. Ernie's stomach did a fluttering little somersault. With a screeching of brakes, the aeroplane careered along the wide tarmac strip, cutting noisily through the heat haze. Ernie fiddled with the loose end of the seat belt that was fastened across his lap. Safely back on terra firma, he quietly exhaled, nervously patted his bony old corduroy knees and brought to a flourishing end the silent prayers for safe deliverance that always echoed around his mind at such moments.

The turbulence over the Alps had shaken him up a little and Ernie had found himself ordering a glass of Strega from the air hostess, when he had fully intended to ask for a coffee. The words, "actually, can I make it a Strega rather than a coffee?" had slipped out of his mouth apparently unbidden by his conscious mind. The air hostess had smiled, as if she understood. He had settled back into the big plush window seat, while the sticky liquor coursed through his body and sent him back to another time, long ago, and soothed his nerves in moments. It had always had that effect on him, he recalled. Back in the war, it was what they would have called "a stiffener". The rest of the flight had passed in a not entirely unpleasant blur, with long-extinguished memories flickering back into existence in Ernie's mind's eye; sparkling like a rack of votive candles.

Every time he closed his eyes he saw another alarming tableau from long ago – the lines of soldiers marching through the lanes of Salerno; blink – an ominous burly figure in a dimly-lit Naples alleyway; blink – the sight of bombs falling silently from a formation of B-25s against a pristine blue sky; blink – the gargantuan movement of a crackling, groaning lava flow, as it tore away the side of an old timber house; blink – a pair of smiling olive eyes, with a familiar beauty that made him catch his breath. Ernie had quickly realised he would get no rest on this flight.

There was a tangible sense of relief to feel the vibration of the aircraft taxiing across the ground. He turned to look out of the window at the huge concrete block of the terminal building, with the distinctive presence of Mount Vesuvius looming in the distance. An ancient cypress tree beyond the runway offered the only piece of greenery, and Ernie was struck by the arid dustiness of the landscape. It felt a world away from the last views he had seen from the same window of the English countryside as the plane had taken to the clouds just three hours before. The aircraft taxied and turned, casting in turn the bright sunshine and Ernie's own face in reflection on the insulated glass. The wrinkles around his eyes always took him by surprise whenever he saw himself in a mirror, but to be back in Italy and to be so visibly old sent a strange sinking feeling through Ernie's stomach. Where had the years gone?

A small dark-haired boy walked alone along the road that ran beside the terminal building. Ernie gazed at the child from his curiously removed vantage point behind the window frame of the aircraft. He shuddered and turned away from the window.

He closed his eyes for a moment, and flashing against the backs of his eyelids once again that series of vivid images took him back down the decades, the chaos of battle, the bare-foot children begging in the streets, shadowy figures in alleyways looming in the darkness, the terrifying elemental movement of lava cutting through the village, and finally that face; beautiful and benevolent in equal measure gazing down at him from a first floor window in the moonlight.

His eyelids lifted slowly. He turned his head to take in the interior of the aircraft, rubbing his shoulder a little as he readjusted his position in the seat. He took another deep breath. A few seats away he caught a movement, just out of the corner of his eyes; a dark-haired young boy shuffling in his seat, a few rows ahead of him. The dark-haired head turned and the boy's expressionless eyes held Ernie's gaze for a moment. Ernie turned swiftly away to look back out of the window. When he turned back, the boy's face was gone and had been replaced by the balding head of a middle-aged businessman. Ernie shuddered once more. He put his glasses up on to his scalp and with his thumb and index finger, rubbed at his eyes.

A gentle ping reverberated around the cabin as the seatbelt lights went out. The passengers had taken it as a cue to break into a frenzy of chatter and excitement. Tossing seatbelts aside, a mass tussle for the overhead lockers was set in motion. But travelling alone, Ernie remained patiently seated. He would let the rush die down before he attempted to move.

"You've got the right idea," the young woman sitting beside him said, removing her headphones, wrapping the cable around her Sony Discman, and flashing Ernie a gentle smile. "After all, none of us are going anywhere until they have opened the cabin doors."

Ernie returned her smile and tried to place the girl's accent. "What's the rush?" he laughed, with a shrug of his shoulders. "They'll all take just as long to get through passport control no matter how quickly they get their hand luggage."

The girl laughed and nodded. A silence descended between them for a few moments, as they stretched and looked around in different directions, watching the chaos and elbowing of their fellow passengers.

"Are you here for a holiday?" she eventually asked.

"Sort of," Ernie replied, wiggling his head from side to side in a universal gesture of non-commitment, before adding: "And how about you? Are you holidaying alone?"

"Sort of," the girl replied with a grin. "Gap year from my studies. I'm here to teach English as a foreign language."

"Oh fantastic," Ernie enthused – suddenly looking every bit like a proud grandfather. "What an opportunity."

He considered for a moment the girl's accent. "You are English then?"

"No, I'm Italian," she said with a smile. "But I've been studying in England for a few years now."

"Your English is really very good."

"Thank you," the girl nodded and gave another nervous smile. "I just hope my Italian is still up to it."

Ernie laughed. "So will you be teaching in Naples?"

"In one of the suburbs – a place called Torre Annunziata." She laughed and ran her fingers through her long hair. "Don't worry, nobody's ever heard of it."

"Oh, but I have actually," Ernie whispered. "I know Torre Annunziata very well. Or rather, I did once."

He glanced back to the window. The dark-haired boy was gone. A set of portable passenger steps was being pulled across the tarmac by a rusty little Fiat truck.

The girl held out a hand, pushing the knotted multi-coloured threads of a cluster of friendship bracelets further up her slender wrists as she offered her long fingers towards to the elderly man beside her.

"I'm Rachele by the way."

Ernie shook her hand and smiled. "I'm Ernie."

"Great name. Ernest?"

The old man laughed. "I've not been Ernest for a long time my dear. But yes, I was once. I certainly was once."

1943

Landing at Salerno had been remarkably uneventful for Ernest. He had never imagined that stepping into occupied Europe would be so straightforward. All those hours on the troop ship, the smell of vomit from the men who couldn't stand the swell, the nervous fluttering in the stomach when the moment came to be transferred to the landing craft. Then stepping ashore had been something of an anti-climax. No incoming shells. No firing from the hip. Just the slight discomfort of getting your boots wet in the warm waves of the Mediterranean.

There were certainly indications of fighting in the previous days, but by the time Ernest's unit scattered off the landing craft and waded up on to the beach, any German who might have provided opposition to their arrival had either been killed or had long since retreated. It left Ernest feeling an absurd sense of guilt – or was it more embarrassment? Surely it wasn't meant to be this easy?

For days the Allied forces had battled to achieve a beachhead at Salerno and push back the German forces, at the cost of many lives. But Ernest got lucky. He arrived after the struggle had taken place. The only sign of there having been any resistance to the landings in recent hours, was the arresting sight of 11 British soldiers' bodies neatly lined up at the edge of the beach. They had been placed in a row, as if even now, in death, they were on a horizontal parade ground. Flies were buzzing around their waxy faces.

Ernest kept his face up as he passed them, trying not to look at their blank staring eyes or to breathe in the putrid smell that hung in the air. He felt a curious emotion rising in him, a sickening combination of fear and disgust. The fluttering sensation came back to the pit of his stomach. Would he be next to fall into that deathly line? He glanced around him for signs of danger further up the beach, but saw nothing. No bullets, no blasts. He made a conscious attempt to ignore the great clogging mass of fear that was fermenting deep inside him, and focused instead on the more benign sense of puzzlement when he noticed that every one of the 11 fallen men was a sergeant. Did the Germans particularly have it in for sergeants? Or had they had sufficient time and inclination to sort the dead into rank order? Was there a heap of privates somewhere further up the beach? A pile of corporals? Ernest gave a cursory glance around, but could see no other dead soldiers of any rank. Just the sergeants then.

He looked at the three stripes on the arm of Sergeant Patterson, who was walking two or three paces in front of him, and wondered if Patterson felt uneasy to see this bouquet of sergeants cut down in their prime and displayed so neatly. He quietly hoped to himself that Patterson might not have noticed.

Ernest averted his gaze and turned his head into the faint breeze that drifted along the coastline. Italy looked every bit as he had imagined. A beach. A sweeping bay, mounted on all sides by jagged green hills dotted with villages. Even amid all the turmoil and cumbersome infrastructure of an invading army, the scene looked somehow classical. Ernest thought the landscape must have little changed since Roman centurions had marched these lanes to meet Hannibal sweeping down from the north. In his mind's eye he saw his old school book, with its etching of Hannibal's forces marching to battle. Ernest watched his own polished boots leaving their marks in the dirt, and wondered whose ancient footprints he was stepping in. The fact that he was stepping in the very real and recent footprints of the soldiers of the Wehrmacht, was also not lost on him.

Ernest felt uncannily as if he was marching through a novel. Somehow none of it felt like real life. The rising wisps of smoke in the distance betrayed the presence of German troops retreating methodically, with the Allied assault troops, who had landed many hours before, chasing them back towards Naples.

Long columns of trucks and Land Rovers, Jeeps and armoured vehicles rumbled through the lanes to the horizon.

Ernest watched an American armoured car pass by kicking up a cloud of dust as it rumbled along the track. A German coal-scuttle helmet had been strapped on to the grille that covered the radiator as a kind of smug trophy. Ernest imagined the Helmut that once wore the helmet and thought of a little German 'Mutter' back home waiting for news of her son.

The day passed swiftly in such reveries and Ernest's unit reached half-a-dozen miles inland before heavy mortar fire slowed their progress. Dull thuds at first, echoing like distant thunder, this wall of sound barraged gradually towards them across the landscape, until at last they could feel the shudder rattling geologically through their legs, as the mortars fell a field or two shy of their mark.

"Keep moving lads," Patterson shouted ahead of him. "We'll be eating spaghetti in Naples before the month is out."

But the promise of spaghetti proved fruitless. Ernest's unit would face weeks of scrappy, street to street fighting and the vicious counterattacks and alarmingly severe bombardments of an increasingly desperate retreating army.

Slapping at mosquitoes habitually every few seconds, Ernest primed his rifle time and time again, as his unit fanned out into a firing line at the sound of distant movement beyond another dusty street corner. The night's countersign challenge would be whispered into the darkness "Canadian", and the men tilted their ears to the night as they struggled to catch the agreed parole response: "wheat".

A couple of Americans walked through their lines in the darkness, one limping with a bloodied tourniquet around his thigh. The other with his arm wrapped around his back, offering structural support to every step. "Total shitstorm half a mile further on," the uninjured GI muttered to the British soldiers. The second man acknowledged their frowns. "Shrapnel wound. I'll be okay. There's a medic station at the other end of the village. There is a medic down here, isn't there guys?"

Patterson grunted a feeble response. None of the unit recalled seeing a medic. The British soldiers watched the Americans shuffle on through the shelled-out village and disappear into the darkness. They looked at each other, each of their faces suddenly a little ashen, as if they had just seen two ghosts ambling by. "Let's move on," Patterson muttered.

The unit travelled in this half-bewildered manner, never quite reaching the front lines of fighting, always on the backfoot, always left walking through stricken villages hours behind the battles. In every field a dead horse or mule, cow or goat, executed by the rifles of the retreating Germans. Barns had been torched, cars and buses destroyed, railway lines mangled with dynamite.

On the outskirts of the next deserted village, they came across the bodies of three Italian soldiers, horribly mutilated by a blast. It appeared the men had driven their vehicle straight through a series of mines placed by the Germans probably just hours earlier. In another village, they found the corpse of a German soldier, the back of his head in fragments, but the rest of him eerily intact, his finger still on the trigger.

They checked his pockets and pulled out a half-smoked packet of cigarettes, a silver pen and a half-written letter home. "Anyone speak German?" Patterson asked the men. One man raised his hand nervously. "My father was Swiss," Durrer said. "I can probably read it." Patterson handed over the letter. Durrer read it through in his head a couple of times, before he translated it for the group. He grinned a little. "Cocky bastard," he said beneath his breath. "Klaus here writes to his mother back in Hamburg." The men gathered closer to hear more clearly. "He says: 'The Tommies will have to chew their way through us, inch by inch. We will surely make hard chewing for them."

The gaggle of men turned to look at the corpse and a few gave out a little flurry of ironic laughter.

"Son of a bitch," Patterson muttered, and handed out the German's cigarettes to the men. They each pocketed them carefully, as if they represented a valuable currency. "Come on, let's move on. Give me the letter Durrer," he added, and folded it into his top pocket.

The following day the eagle-eyed Patterson spotted a rifle poking out of a niche at the very top of a church tower. He quickly indicated for the men to take cover behind a fragmented wall. "Sniper in the tower," the sergeant growled. "Who is the best shot?" The men looked at each other unconvincingly. Eventually Durrer volunteered himself once again. "I was a crack shot in training Sarge."

"Right then lad, you'll get one chance," Patterson said, doing little to reassure the youngster, who lifted his rifle sight carefully through a gap in the wall and trained it on the shadowy outline of a helmet behind the pencil-line of a rifle a few hundred yards away. Durrer took a deep breath and pulled the trigger. The helmet silhouette slumped backwards. "I think I got him Sarge."

Three men were sent to accompany Patterson up the church tower, primed with rifles at the ready, while Patterson clung on to a grenade, his fingers nervously playing with the silver detonator loop.

Ernest and the other men remained behind the wall, waiting quietly. They heard no shots, no sound of a grenade exploding, but a few minutes later Patterson and the three others wandered out of the church and over to the wall.

"You can all get back to your feet," the sergeant grumbled. "The bastard had been dead a while I reckon. Sorry Durrer."

The young soldier brushed down his knees and complained quietly. "So that doesn't count as a kill for me? How doesn't that count as a kill?"

"He was already dead," Patterson chuckled.

"I don't see how that matters," Durrer grumbled. "He could have been alive. I took out a sniper, whichever way you look at it."

The sergeant patted his shoulder. "If you like Georgie, if you like."

They moved gradually up through the country. The fighting ahead of them seemed to intensify as they reached the outskirts of Naples. The Germans were offering a dogged resistance, street by street, as they departed the city. But once again, Ernest and his unit were just too many miles behind to play a useful part in scourging the metropolis of the enemy.

When Ernest finally watched his own boots marching into Naples on October 1, the streets had been swept of Germans, and the locals were out in force to cheer them as they passed by. He kept his eyes lowered. He was grappling silently with the constant danger of being overwhelmed by the sights and sounds of a city so thoroughly ravaged by war. Even the most experienced squaddies, those who had been professional soldiers before the war, had never witnessed misery on this scale. The slums of Liverpool, London and Glasgow had prepared none of them for the unadulterated destitution that stretched gruesomely across this shell-shocked landscape.

For Private Ernest Green, at just 22 years old, it felt like another world. Green by name, green by nature, the other soldiers said, and it was true enough – until a few weeks before, the furthest Ernest had travelled from the quiet avenues of

Birkenhead and the university common rooms of Liverpool, was for his basic training in Chester. Nothing could have prepared him for the sights and sounds of the Neapolitan suburbs. Nothing could have readied him for the misery and bitter suffering of ordinary people – weary women and grimy children, sad-eyed elderly folk with their leathery faces set like frowning masks.

Like all the soldiers in his unit, Ernest looked young to be marching through a city, and some of the elderly Italian women had more than a touch of maternal tenderness when they reached out and kissed the incoming soldiers' cheeks. When he wore his reading glasses, Ernest looked much older than his years. But he hardly ever wore them, except when he was alone in his bunk reading letters from home or his well-thumbed leatherbound pocket edition of *David Copperfield* – a gift from his mother, which he had managed to retain, despite a few close calls during kit inspection. The book had once belonged to his father. Its red leather spine had been a familiar sight in his late father's bookcase. He carried it with him now as a connection to both of his parents.

Without the glasses on, he looked as if he could be 16 or 17 years old. Albeit, he looked more rugged than some of the other boys, with the smiling eyes and well-defined jawline of a matinee idol, but with an awkward, gangling gait that betrayed his film star good looks. They were looks that had seemed not to fit his civilian life as a trainee teacher, but here, in the midst of war, he looked every bit the heroic Tommy. Yet no matter how well-defined his jawline might be, Ernest was as scared as the next man. A perpetual humming of background fear haunted his every wakeful moment.

Stepping through the rubble-strewn streets, he kept his pack on his back and his sleeves rolled neatly above the elbows –

though this neatness did nothing to mask the smell of his own sweat, which was just distinguishable amid the rancid aroma that seemed to hover in an invisible cloud over and around every drain. Sometimes it took all of Ernest's focus to stop himself retching at the smells that ambushed his unit around every corner.

Ernest kept his helmet tilted down to shade his eyes, and to prevent the locals from seeing the fear in them. They watched on from the shadows. Elderly women mostly, standing in the doorways of the crumbling houses, or leaning precariously on the cast iron balcony rails that seemed to be held in place only by the grubby lines of washing that criss-crossed above the street. The occasional half-hearted V for Victory sign welcomed them, but the general attitude was of mild indifference as to which particular foreign soldiers were tramping through their street this week. Ernest watched the V-signs and acknowledged one from an elderly man with a quiet nod. It would have been a Nazi salute a few hours before, he thought to himself.

One elderly lady threw a few limp flowers in their path and Ernest watched as the tracks of an armoured vehicle crushed them to a pulp, leaving behind little more than a pile of muddy petals. The occasional gun shot could be heard far in the distance, like an isolated hand-clap. Partisans were hunting down fascist collaborators and carrying out summary executions in alleyways across the city. Occasionally, Ernest's unit would turn a corner to find a heap of bodies, hair freshly matted with blood and carrying a sickly smell of death.

Turning another corner, his unit edged along a narrow lane, made shadowy and dank by the blank walls of the high tenements raised up on both sides. He cast a glance at the crumbling remnants of a stencil of Mussolini that had survived on one of the pock-marked walls. The words "Il Duce" were just about still visible beneath the faded outline of his bull-headed silhouette.

Ernest's unit turned another corner. A group of middle-aged women were seated on wooden chairs in a neat line along one side of the road. Ernest could see some sort of price lists marked out roughly on bits of board beside each of them, but for the life of him couldn't see what they were actually selling. He asked Patterson.

"Christ, you're slow lad," Patterson chuckled. "They're selling themselves."

Ernest looked at the women's troubled faces, with black creases beneath their eyes. Not one looked under 45 and their drab floral dresses, and even in some cases, utilitarian pinafores, betrayed the fact that these had until very recently been respectable working-class housewives, rather than professional whores. Ernest blinked, as he attempted to understand the implications of Patterson's words.

"You kidding me Sarge?"

The women sat and waited patiently. Honour, it seemed, was cheap in times of war. The price lists revealed they sold their various services with little fuss and, Ernest noted, little profit.

"Welcome to the real world lad. But you know what, I reckon the one with the glass eye would give you a discount," Patterson laughed as he marched on. "She certainly seems to be giving you the eye, if you know what I mean."

A group of his fellow soldiers joined Patterson in a momentary cloud of laughter, but Ernest ignored them entirely. He studied the price lists as he passed by – more out of incredulity than personal interest.

"Is that one lira for a leg-over?" he asked the sergeant.

"No, you numbskull, it's one tin for a leg-over." It was only then that Ernest noticed the little pile of tins of Army-ration bully-beef beside each woman.

"They're doing it for food?" Ernest sounded more incredulous than ever.

"Of course," Patterson said. "The currency isn't really worth having, especially as there's nothing in the fucking shops anyway."

The two men marched on in silence.

The welcome from the Neapolitans had been generally half-hearted until the unit reached the Piazza del Plebiscito. Unknown to the British troops, the square had for centuries been the site of jubilation when conquering heroes were to be welcomed to the city. Here the crowds swarmed like ants, young and old. Italian boys carried kitchen knives and German Lugers, waving the weapons in the air triumphantly. Some had clusters of red Italian grenades hanging from their belts like grapes. Crowds of young women were shouting hysterically, swooning themselves into a frenzy of chanting – "Viva, viva!" and "Grazie! Viva!" Older women genuflected and held rosaries in two handed gestures of thanks up towards the heavens, while the old men just looked on, resting on their sticks and nodding sagely.

A woman in her 50s bustled her way through the crowd, grabbed Ernest by both shoulders and planted a heavy wet kiss on his lips. "Viva! Viva!" she screamed into his face, as he laughed with embarrassment, and wiping his mouth with the back of his hand, pulled himself away, skipping a few quick steps over the cobbles to get himself back in line with his unit.

An hour after this stage-managed triumphal march through the city centre, Ernest marched with his unit back out to the suburbs. They were to be stationed at Torre Annunziata, a grimy place on the outskirts of Naples, where the outline of Mount Vesuvius loomed large – a constant, brooding presence. Pompeii itself, that city-sized monument to mortality, was just a few miles away from their makeshift barracks. Ernest regularly saw signposts for it. As if he was here on holiday, the school teacher in him quietly thought that he must try to get to see the ruins if the opportunity arose – though he found it difficult to imagine how that opportunity might arise. He had read an article about it once – the way the volcanic ash had swept through the city in moments, freezing their world in a permanent deathly tableau. To be so close and yet unable to see it frustrated Ernest enormously. It was like being stationed in Cairo, but not allowed to visit the pyramids. Or being billeted in Agra, but not getting the chance to see the Taj Mahal. Every time he saw Pompeii on a sign he had the same thought – one day I must get there.

Despite its stretch of dismal seafront, Torre Annunziata wouldn't make much of a holiday destination, Ernest quickly realised. So many lives here had been devastated in the previous few years. They may not have lost their existence in the blink of an eye, like the folks in Pompeii. But somehow, the blank and world-weary expressions on the faces of many of the locals gave them something peculiarly in common with the ash-cast figures of Pompeii. They too seemed somehow frozen in time. Their lives had been paused for years. They were living a hand-to-mouth existence with little or no thought for what the future might hold for them.

Ernest, on the whole, did not fraternise with the locals. British soldiers didn't generally attempt to speak to the Italians. It was as though they were another species – spirits that moved around him and his fellow squaddies. The Yanks, on the other hand, were more likely to get chummy, or chatty – or when sufficient quantities of the local spirit Strega had been consumed – a little leery.

Ernest and his pals were not quite without sin when it came to Strega however – the distinctive kick of the spirit became the taste of their nights off. Bottles of the amber coloured liquid could be purchased for a few lire and a bag of sugar from the Strega factory itself, which had mysteriously avoided the bombardments of both Allies and Germans alike. Being pleasantly drunk on that sticky nectar in the heat of a Mediterranean evening was unlike anything Ernest had ever felt. Surrounded by the warmth and camaraderie of his fellow soldiers, the aromatic liquid slipped down easily beneath the rustling branches of the ancient stone pines. But far from making him loud or leery, he found it had a peculiarly quietening effect, often transporting him into a gentle reverie or a period of silent and serious contemplation.

Always a loner as a child, Ernest had never experienced the sort of fellowship he felt in the army. There were always the occasional bad eggs of course – the ones to look out for; the bullies or the oddities. But on the whole, they were a good bunch and he was quietly proud to number himself among the men of his unit.

The barracks, such as they were, occupied an anonymous-looking building. It might once have been a school or a hospital, an office building or a dental practice. Its original purpose was no longer clear. But there was a general clinical feel to its corridors, so Ernest imagined it had been medical. Army beds were far from clinical. They were hopelessly simple springy affairs. Four to a room, you quickly got to know your roommates pretty well. For Ernest, that was Sergeant Patterson, Lance Corporal Derek Tanner (known as Smudge, on account of a birth mark on his cheek) and Private Micky Lambert –

known to all as Mouse. They made for a curious group of pals – Patterson loud and boisterous, while Mouse lived up to his nickname and hardly ever said a word. Smudge on the other hand tended to speak in a constant flurry of gags and word plays. It seemed to be his one goal in life to keep things light-hearted.

The electricity had been off since the Germans left and torched half the substations as they departed. But Ernest quickly got used to passing the evenings by the flickering candlelight deep inside this old hulk of a building.

The days passed with regular, but generally uneventful patrols of the neighbourhood. Naples already had two police forces of its own – a fact that bemused Ernest – but nevertheless, it seemed the British Army's main role in the city was to act as a kind of further police force alongside the Carabinieri and the Polizia di Stato. The former of the native forces was more military than the latter, but both were reliably ineffectual and often corrupt, though the officers were always flamboyant in their pristine uniforms. The real power in the city lay with the camorra, the local mafias, who waged tribal wars within the shadows of the world war, and had every official, civil servant and police officer in their pockets. They held a constant unseen presence on the streets of the great sprawling metropolis.

The various incarnations of military police from the British and US armies, along with more specialist intelligence units, did much of the actual policing. Ernest's lot were there to make up the numbers and act as "a presence on the streets", until that is, such a time as they were needed to fight the Germans again and act as "a presence" on the battlefields. But from everything he had heard, the frontline battles had ground to a halt just 100km to the north – at the so-called Gustav Line. The Jerries had embedded themselves neatly in the Aurunci Mountains, as well as being anchored at Rapido-Gari, Liri and the Garigliano valley, and in the winter of 1943-44 the Allied advance had ground to a halt.

Ernest's life had become consumed by the blind-eyed patrols of the town. The battles that were happening, were taking place far from the back streets of Torre Annunziata. But the crippling sense of tedium lifted before him like a theatre curtain at the very moment he met Preghiera. As he was jostled by Patterson out of the corner of the square, he turned to catch one last glance over his shoulder at her tilted face with its fretful brow. A smile flickered involuntarily across his own lips.

Chapter two
1993

The old man and the young woman stood side by side as they watched the clanking luggage carousel make its way laboriously around the room. Ernie looked at his watch.

"How can it take them this long?" he muttered, more to himself than his new companion. But she laughed quietly.

"Don't worry," she said, leaning towards him for emphasis. "My bag is always the very last to come out. No matter when I checked it in, it'll always be the very last one to make it to the baggage reclaim belt. I think there's some sort of a conspiracy."

Ernie smiled. "I certainly wouldn't put it past the Italians my dear."

By the time both bags actually appeared, the unlikely pair were almost entirely alone at the carousel, with Ernie gallantly, though somewhat disastrously, attempting to lift the young woman's bag off the conveyor belt, only to be taken by surprise by the immense weight of the case and subsequently finding himself being dragged along the edge of the carousel in a series of trips and stumbles, before he finally managed to lift the bag clear.

"What have you got in there, rocks?" he laughed, dropping the case down on the floor.

"I'm here for six months – a girl has to have her clothes," she beamed with mock demureness. "But thank you Ernie. That was most gallant of you."

"That's quite okay," Ernie said with a shrug. He reached into his jacket pocket and took out his glasses. He gave them a quick rub on a cloth before placing them on his face and looking around carefully. "Now how the hell do you get out of this place?"

"This way I think," Rachele said, pulling her case behind her. Ernie picked up his rather more battered suitcase – a small and ancient looking thing, held together with a leather strap. He shuffled behind the young woman as they followed the "Nothing to Declare" sign. A bored Italian customs officer in an elaborate, tasselled uniform waved Ernie towards him.

"Here we go," Ernie whispered under his breath, turning on his heel to redirect himself towards the official.

"Good luck," Rachele smiled, and carried on walking towards the exit.

"Niente da dichiarare!" Ernie announced expansively to the official, holding the little old suitcase aloft, by way of demonstration.

"Place the bag down on the table please signore," the official said with a dourness that betrayed the tassels of his uniform.

"I'm going to miss my coach," Ernie grumbled.

"Place the bag down on the table please signore," the man repeated, with a resigned patience.

"Do I look like a drugs baron, or some sort of international Mr Big?" Ernie said, with growing frustration causing his cheeks to flush.

"Just place the bag down on the table please signore, and step back."

With a shrug, Ernie finally did as he was told.

1943

Ernest awoke to the sounds of panic – shouted orders, a collected groan of muttered blasphemies.

"Well, that's put the kibosh on your plans for a romance," Patterson said to Ernest as he dragged him by the scruff of the collar out of his bed.

"What the hell's happened Sarge?" Ernest asked, rubbing his head as if trying to kickstart his brain into life.

"Shit's hit the fan," Patterson gabbled, picking up the youngster's boots from beneath the bed and thrusting them into his hands. "All hell has broken loose. Intelligence boys picked up a Jerry hiding in a basement. Reckoned he'd been there hidden away since the Germans pulled out. Apparently, this Jerry, he told them the whole fucking city is wired up with delayed-action mines. The minute the electricity supply is switched back on the whole place will go up like a Roman Candle. Or a Neapolitan one, at least."

"Jesus," Ernest gasped.

"We're to get in there and get the people out."

"Which people?"

"All of them – the whole fucking city is being evacuated," Patterson stood breathless a moment as he struggled to comprehend his own orders. "Don't ask me how we're going to do it, but the electricity is set to be switched on at 2pm, which gives us exactly eight hours to clear the whole place."

Ernest's unit travelled so quickly, he was still barely awake when their lorry reached the outskirts of Naples. But already the exodus was in full flow – a great mass of humanity was streaming out of the city at a Biblical scale. He watched from between the flaps of canvas at the back of the lorry as a middle-aged Italian man carried an elderly woman on his back. A thin cigarette was hanging limply from the Italian's lips, the ash built up in a precarious droop, as he headed breathlessly up the steep hill away from the city centre, muttering under his breath as he went.

"This is going to be some fucking job," Patterson grumbled. The lorry rumbled on through the streets towards the centre. Ernest's unit was tasked with clearing the entire 92nd General

Hospital, which was packed with thousands of casualties of the recent battles. The lorry screeched to a halt outside the hospital and the men jumped out on to the gravel.

"Ward by ward," a calm, crisply spoken captain was saying to each unit as it arrived at the hospital's main gate. A stream of fellow soldiers was travelling in the opposite direction from Ernest, carrying every conceivable kind of makeshift stretcher, each fully laden with a casualty.

"Ward by ward, ward by ward," the captain continued. "Good chap. Ward by ward."

The men moved as one through the main entrance and headed for the big oak staircase, squeezing past their fellow soldiers who were on their way down carrying the wounded and sick. Within moments Ernest was grappling with the deadweight of a corporal with a gangrenous leg wound. The bemused corporal let flow a perpetual stream of swearwords beneath his breath, as his grip on Ernest's shoulder became tighter and tighter.

"Sorry pal, they were all out of stretchers," Ernest groaned beneath the weight. He led the corporal out of the hospital and painstakingly across the city, heading towards the relative safety of the heights of Vomero. A pair of American GIs were carrying an elderly Italian woman ahead of Ernest. They used a table top as a stretcher. But on the archaic stone steps that zigzagged their way up the hillside, the pair fumbled and dropped her to the ground. The table made a tremendous clatter, causing a momentary uproar of screaming from a nearby group of women who had mistaken the sound for an explosion. They erupted into a flurry of genuflections, sanctifications and Ave Marias, elbows out in their panic as they clung to the crucifixes around their necks.

Ernest was hit by a pungent smell of urine. "They're all literally pissing themselves," he said to the injured corporal under his breath. The corporal gave a little ironic laugh despite his pain and shook his head. Then, with a sigh and a heave beneath the corporal's arm, Ernest found a new reserve of energy. "Come on, let's get the bloody hell out of here," he said, quickening his pace up the steps, and dragging the corporal bodily up the hill.

From the top of the hillside the city stretched out before them like an antique landscape in oils. Ernest carefully lowered the corporal to rest beneath a tree, where an orderly from the hospital received him by handing the injured soldier a water flask.

The corporal hadn't yet got his breath back, but reached up to shake Ernest's hand as he panted in the heat.

"Good luck pal," Ernest smiled, before turning and heading back into the chaos of the city below.

For Ernest, it would be the first of many such journeys up and down the hillside that day – a marathon effort to support so many of his injured comrades to clear out of the city centre that he quickly lost count of how many he had helped. But with each trip up the hill, he would deposit a casualty in the same place, so that quickly he had made his own little crowd of new friends, sprawled out like a scene of the Death of Nelson in their various states of decrepitude.

The 2pm deadline was swiftly forgotten – nobody would be switching the electricity back on for some time – and the evacuation dragged on for hour after hour. The day passed in a blur of exhausting journeys up and down the hillside, some seeing Ernest holding one end of a stretcher, some in which he manhandled the casualties single-handedly up the steps, as he had with the corporal. By the time night fell, the gardens of

Vomero were covered in the bodies and blankets of the injured, the sick and the elderly. It was more like 2am before the Allied high command gave the nod for the electricity to be put back on. A strangely peaceful sort of silence descended on the hillside as everyone awaited the moment when somewhere in the city a switch would be flicked.

"They reckon they've found nothing," Patterson said to Ernest, wiping the sweat from his brow. "But if they're wrong, we're about to witness the most spectacular firework display we'll ever see."

Ernest smiled weakly. In the seconds leading up to the allotted time of 2am, the whole hillside seemed to hold its breath. Those who could stand peered over the shoulders of those in front of them, almost flinching at the expectation of a city-wide explosion. But the time came and went and nothing happened. The breeze blew gently on the crowd from the sea, and Ernest saw a meteor cast a momentary trail above the scene. But as quickly as he'd seen it, the flash of light was gone. With only the moon and the stars for light, the great mass of humanity around him began to exhale with relief almost as one entity. Lights began to flicker into life across the city.

Patterson leaned forward on to a low wall and shook his head in disbelief. He gave a bitter sort of laugh and then stopped again just as abruptly, his lips tightening against his front teeth as the anger seared through him and he tried to put his feelings in to words, but ended up stammering around an exotic collection of curses.

"Bastard Nazi son of a bitch," Patterson muttered under his breath, spitting out each word in turn. "Christ Almighty, you've got to hand it to the swine, he caused the maximum possible disruption with that little tale. That bastard has just been left behind to cause the maximum possible disruption with the least effort on the part of the Germans. They didn't even need to wire anything up. We all believed every god-damn word he said."

Ernest shrugged his shoulders quietly. "Well Sarge," he said. "I suppose we had to be certain. What else could we do?"

It was dawn by the time all the patients had been returned to the hospital wards. Ernest staggered back to barracks with Smudge and Patterson – all three too weary to speak. They dragged their bones across the cobbles in a tableau of misery and exhaustion, occasionally spitting absent-mindedly towards the gutter. The silence was broken by a clatter. It was coming from a dimly lit alleyway, where a British intelligence officer was interrogating an Italian by repeatedly hitting him about the head with a wooden chair. Ernest, Smudge and Patterson instinctively stepped back into the shadows unseen. They looked at each other in the darkness, their eyes silently asking what they should do. Eventually, Patterson gave a flick of his head to indicate that they should move on.

"What kind of fucking world are we living in?" Patterson whispered to his two fellow soldiers, before adding a swift, "come on, let's go." The intelligence officer hadn't even heard them pass – or at least, if he had, he hadn't cared sufficiently to pause from beating the Italian, whose face was now lost behind a mask of blood.

"What the hell was that about?" Ernest said to Patterson as they walked on through the darkness before the dawn.

"Christ knows," the sergeant muttered. "May be something to do with that Jerry they found, after all…" but his words were interrupted by the sound of a single gunshot.

The three young soldiers stopped and looked at each other again for another indication of what they should do next. After what seemed like an interminable hesitation, Patterson spoke first.

"Keep walking," he muttered quietly. "Just keep walking. Whatever is going on, it's none of our concern, do you hear?"

The three men looked to the ground, and didn't exchange another word all the way back to the barracks.

It was the next morning when Ernest opened his eyes with a start and the sudden realisation that in all the chaos of the previous day, he had failed to keep his promise to meet Preghiera.

"Damn it," he hissed to himself, taking an ill-advised sideswipe at the metal bed frame, as he rolled out of bed and reached for his wash kit.

"That's right," Smudge said comically from the other bed without opening his eyes. "Damn it all. What are we damning exactly?"

"Fate," Ernest whispered, more to himself than to Smudge. "That bitch with her fickle finger, which always seems turned against me somehow."

"Ain't that the truth," Smudge grumbled, turning back over and wrapping the sheets around himself.

Ernest dressed grumpily and began to form a plan. Would he have an opportunity on the usual patrol of the neighbourhood later in the morning to make his way to her father's shop? It might just be possible, if...

"Smudge," he muttered. "I don't suppose you fancy covering for me for a bit this afternoon?"

Smudge's face emerged out from beneath the sheets frowning thoughtfully. "What's it worth?"

Ernest reached into his pocket and held aloft a box of cigarettes, presenting them to the room like a boxing belt being held up from the ring before a big fight. Smudge grinned and turned back towards the warmth of the mattress, adding cheerfully in a singsong voice: "I do like your style Ernest, I do like your style."

***

Preghiera was standing in the doorway once again, counting customers into the shop when he arrived. Was this all she ever did? Ernest wondered. One, two, three, four. One, two, three, four. What kind of a life was she enduring?

"Sorry I stood you up," Ernest said sheepishly as he moved alongside her, kicking at the dusty streets. "You must have heard? You must have heard about the evacuation?"

"Are you wanting to buy meat?" she said curtly, her eyes refusing to connect with his. "Because my father won't serve soldiers – whatever uniform they're wearing."

"I didn't want to buy meat," Ernest said, a flicker of laughter in his voice. "And I certainly didn't want to cross your father."

"Perhaps you wanted to cross me?" Preghiera growled, with a playful frown.

"Nor you. I am sorry."

"I'll forgive you," the young woman whispered, and her face erupted into a smile. "Of course, I knew you wouldn't make it," she added, pushing at his shoulder playfully. "The whole city was in chaos. So why did they evacuate the entire city? What's going on? My father says you're all mad men."

"He's probably right," Ernest said. "But never mind about all of that. After all, who would notice any more mad men around here? So, tell me, when do I get to take you for a drink?"

"Who mentioned a drink?" Preghiera shrieked, apparently scandalised by the thought of accepting a drink from a soldier. "Do I look like that kind of girl?"

Ernest trod carefully before answering. "Well how about a coffee? All Italians like coffee don't they?"

"A coffee?" she danced her head from side to side as she considered it. "A coffee. Sure. A coffee maybe. If we can find somewhere in this city still serving coffee, I will take a coffee from you. After all," she examined him carefully with her big brown eyes. "I think you have a kind face. For a soldier."

"Really? You think so?" Ernest's eyebrows raised up as he considered his own face.

"Yes," she added, touching the stubble of his cheek with gentle fingers. "Yes, there is a kindness in those eyes."

"Well, well," Ernest stammered a little, before composing himself. "Truth is, I've not done much actual soldiering. I'm just a normal chap I suppose. Just like the chaps you grew up with. I just speak a different language, that's all."

"And you're still breathing," Preghiera snapped. "The boys I grew up with, they're all dead."

Ernest held her stare for a moment, and reached out for her hand. It felt tiny in his palm. Her fingers tapered elegantly, but were rounded off with short, chewed nails. A silence descended between them for a moment.

"It's been tough for you, hasn't it?" Ernest said softly. "This bloody war." Preghiera smiled a little and said nothing. He nodded slowly, and took a step closer to her face, before asking once again: "Dove andare domani?"

"Domani, domani, domani," Preghiera giggled. "How come it's always domani with you?"

They looked at each other intently for a moment before her face blossomed into a coy smile that seemed to give a silent nod to domani. Ernest nodded encouragingly.

"So, I can meet you again tomorrow?"

Preghiera reached up a hand and rested it idly on the top of the soldier's arm. She nodded. "Of course, you can. Of course, you can." A white-toothed smile beamed out from Ernest's face.

A familiar English voice bellowed across the square. "Break it up lad!" Patterson roared.

"Tomorrow then?" Ernest said swiftly, with a glance over his shoulder.

"Tomorrow then." Preghiera nodded, her eyes fixed on his. "Domani, domani, domani."

Chapter three
1993

The old man shuffled out of the airport, carrying his case. He stopped to study a tangled mess of signs, which were supposed to direct travellers to the correct bus stop. He put down his case and brushed absently at the stubble on his cheek as he attempted to make sense of it all. A voice called from a nearby bench.

"It's this one Ernie!"

Ernie looked across to find the smiling face that had been beside him on the aeroplane.

"It's Rachele again," he said with a grin. "You waited for me. How kind of you."

Rachele laughed. "Not exactly if I'm honest. Like you, I also just missed the bus for the centre."

Ernie picked up his case and ambled over to the bench.

"Bloody fooling customs officer emptied every last thing from my case," Ernie grumbled, as he took a seat beside her. "Right down to my spare pants."

Rachel raised her eyebrows. "So you're down to the pair you're wearing?" She resisted a laugh, before whispering conspiratorially: "But they didn't find the drugs?" There was a silence for a moment before she broke into an infectious laughter.

"How ludicrous. I said to him, do I look like a drugs' baron? I mean, really." Ernie turned and looked at his new companion, and his frown slowly evolved into a grin. "They had a jolly good look at the pot of beta-blockers for my angina though."

"I bet they did," Rachele laughed.

"I did get my spare pants back, thankfully," he added with a sigh. "You know, I don't remember anyone checking my bags or looking at my passport last time I was here. During the war you just waded up the beach and that was that. Though having the full might of the British and American armies helps cut down on that kind of red tape, I find."

"I'd imagine so," she smiled.

Silence calmly descended between them for a few moments. Ernie searched his inside pockets for a half-empty packet of cigarettes, and held it open towards Rachele. She declined with a smile and a shake of the head. Ernie shrugged and lit his own cigarette. "Good girl," he muttered. "Filthy habit." He watched the cloud emerge between himself and the sprawling city beyond the edge of the road.

"Where are you staying?" she asked after a while.

Ernie searched his pockets and produced a collection of dog-eared tickets and scribbled notes. "Hotel Il Convento," he read aloud. "It has three stars, views of an alleyway and I fear it might be a bit disappointing. But it's cheap. Very cheap."

"Sounds perfect," Rachele said. "Do you mind if I join you?"

Ernie looked momentarily alarmed.

"I don't mean to share your room, you understand," she quickly added. "I just mean, would it be okay if I come with you as far as the reception desk. I've got three days to kill before I can get my apartment. I was hoping to just get as near to the centre as possible, and find a hotel for myself. But I like the sound of the alleyway view."

"Be my guest," Ernie laughed. "I'll be glad of the company. The first time I entered this city, I was in rather less charming company, I can assure you."

"When were you last here?"

"I've not been here in nearly 50 years," he said. "It was the war – the place was in a state of carnage. We liberated it – though not all the Italians saw it quite that way."

Ernie paused a moment, catching the figure of a small dark-haired boy trotting along the pavement, just at the edge of his vision. He took a long drag from the cigarette, and gave a funny little combination of a single laugh and a clearing of his throat.

Rachele's eyes were transfixed to Ernie's face as he looked back through the wisps of tobacco smoke to the dark days of battle, with the rising tobacco smoke replaced in his mind's eye by the rising smoke of an explosion at the centre of the city back in 1943.

"Bloody Jerries booby trapped everything here before they left," he recalled. "There was one really big evacuation we carried out, which was a waste of time and effort, but it wasn't entirely an idle threat as it turned out. The bastards wired up so many door handles before they headed north, it got so that you would never dream of knocking on a door with anything other than the butt of your rifle.

"Of course, it was the locals that really suffered. The little kiddies were often the unsuspecting ones who opened a door, and had their lives ended before they'd barely begun." He shook his head at the memory of it. "Those utter bastards."

1943

The blast hit Ernest physically long before he heard any bang. It wasn't so much like a gust of wind, but more the opposite of wind – a suction, a vacuuming of the air in the cobbled alleyway he and Smudge had been making their way along. Up until that moment, it had been a very normal sort of patrol. The lane had buzzed with the singsong chatter of the children who danced and played nascondino – hide and seek – amid the dirt and grime.

It was the door handle of an old outhouse – a ramshackle little structure on the edge of the yard of a bombed-out tenement building. It was a little hand that reached up, working for the inquisitive little brain that bubbled and fizzed with mischievousness deep inside that dark haired little head. It was those little brown eyes that peered through the gap to see what was inside. It was that little cherubic mouth, smiling with its shards of baby teeth, that spoke his last words: "Sei qui Marco?"

The door handle clicked. Then the air of the whole city seemed to suck itself into the outhouse before the blast rocked the neighbourhood.

"Jesus fucking Christ," Ernest gasped as he stood up, disentangling himself from the legs of Smudge where the pair had landed awkwardly entwined on the floor.

"Booby trap," Smudge muttered as he brushed himself down and picked up his rifle.

"Yeah, do you reckon?" Ernest answered, with an instinctive sarcasm.

The soldiers pulled their helmet straps down firmly on to their chins and ran towards the blast site. The outbuilding was entirely destroyed. Only a pile of rubble remained, smoke and dust rising from it and children all around screaming, crying and running in all directions. But there was nothing left of the dark-haired boy – no evidence of his ever having existed. Ernest pulled back the rubble with his hands, but there was nothing – not even a patch of blood. He knelt in the debris a moment, his head bowed, and laid his hand on the rubble.

Ernest didn't sleep that night and the next day, a Sunday, he joined the morning parade as usual in the yard at the back of the barracks. With its pock-marked walls, where bullet and shrapnel holes told the story of a previous battle, it felt a long way from a church – no stained glass or flowers or embroidered altar frontal here to soften the devotion. Here, where death was ever-present, the devotion of the troops was visceral. He could see their lips moving along with the Lord's Prayer, clinging to the words in a way he never saw in church back home.

But while the men around him sang *Abide With Me* in their usual drone, Ernest's mind was focused on that dark-haired boy and how he could be here one moment and gone the next. Simply gone.

Padre Crawford Smythe was a benevolent little fellow with his clash of dog collar and battle dress, a small wooden cross tucked in his belt instead of a side arm. He led the soldiers with the *Prayer in Time of War* from his small leatherbound *Treasury of Devotion:* "Almighty and most merciful God, deliver us, we beseech Thee, from the tumult of war: for in bestowing peace of mind and body, Thou dost give us all good things; through Jesus Christ our Lord. Amen."

The men rumbled a deep "Amen" in response. Ernest twitched his head to the side as he caught the briefest sight from the corner of his eye of a little dark-haired figure skip across the back of the yard silently. Ernest's gaze returned to the Padre and then turned back to look again at the child, but nobody was there.

"Can you cover for me Smudge, in the down time?" Ernest whispered. "There's something I need to do."

Smudge turned to him with an "asking no questions" raise of the eyebrows. "Course I can pal," Smudge said. "If you can stand me a tab in the meantime."

Ernest grinned, reached into his breast pocket and produced a packet of cigarettes. He slipped one out and handed it to his fellow soldier. "Nice one Smudge," he whispered, as the Padre offered the ragtag congregation a closing benediction.

It was mid-afternoon before he was able to slip away from the barracks and the streets were deserted. Ernest made his way quietly through the alleyways, with their pungent aroma of human dereliction. A rat munching on a scrap paused for a moment to take in the figure of the soldier, before returning its focus entirely to its meal. On closer inspection as he passed the creature, Ernest realised the rodent's meal was the mortal remains of another sewer rat. He hurried on past the moment of casual cannibalism.

Ernest paused outside the butcher's shop. He looked around nervously, keen to not be seen. The shop was closed, and he waited until the square was fully deserted before he collected a small handful of stones and slung them towards the upstairs window on the righthand side of the building. Inside the family was snoring softly, in the depths of their siesta. But Preghiera was not asleep.

Her face emerged from the window, and her brown eyes frowned down at the figure of the young soldier.

"How did you know which was my room?" she asked, her frown turning gradually to a smile.

"I was guided by love," Ernest said, returning the smile nervously. "But if your father had appeared, I would have been on my heels sharpish."

Preghiera didn't follow the young soldier's every word of English, but she got the general idea. She nodded.

"You would need to run away very quickly I think," she said. "My father has his suspicions about you. He's seen you talking to me outside the shop. He asked me what you wanted."

"What did you say?"

"I said you were just a drunken soldier."

"Fair enough I suppose," he laughed, and started gingerly to climb a drainpipe to get closer to the girl.

"There are plenty of drunken soldiers," she said, pretending not to notice that the young soldier was now making his way towards her. "I knew he wouldn't be too worried about another one."

"Even if he was kissing you?" Ernest asked with a newfound twinkle in his eye, now leaning just yards from Preghiera's lips.

"If he saw you, he would murder you."

"Murder a soldier of the British Empire?" Ernest whispered, gazing into her eyes. He was close enough now that he could take in the faint scent of her soft skin – some unique combination of carbolic soap, garlic and just a hint of raw meat.

"Anyway, there's far more peril in your eyes, than in 20 Italian fathers," he added and reached in for the kiss. Her lips were as soft and sweet as the flesh of a freshly-sliced melon. Ernest was transported. He was no longer surrounded by war and deprivation. His own mortality became instantly irrelevant. The moment was imbued with a warm hue of the eternal. He and Preghiera were elevated in that moment to something higher, part of a greater celestial force, an entwining of souls.

"I would not for the world have him find you here," she whispered, with a glance over her shoulder. "Don't forget he's a butcher."

But Ernest was no longer listening to her words. He leaned in again for another, longer embrace.

"You do know Shakespeare I suppose?" he eventually asked. "I am afeard... all this is but a dream, Too flattering-sweet to be substantial."

"Does that make you my Romeo?" she grinned. But her thought was interrupted by a movement in the apartment behind her – what sounded like a wooden chair being drawn across a tiled floor.

"Preghiera?" her father's gruff voice croaked from a distant room. "Con chi stai parlando Preghiera?"

A look of horror swept across Preghiera's face. "You must go!" she hissed. Ernest stole one last cheeky peck on the lips, before sliding back down the downspout athletically.

"Nessuno Papà!" she called behind her.

"Domani?" Ernest whispered back up at the window.

"Si, domani, amore mio," she whispered back. "Domani, domani, domani."

Chapter four
1993

The flashing light above the door to the lift seemed to take forever to get down to number 1. It flashed on three for a bit, then headed down to two, then much to Ernie's irritation, headed back up to four. He stood there pulling faces at the little light as it frustrated him.

Rachele walked across from the reception desk and stood beside him watching the flashing light.

"They found you a room then?" he said. Rachele held up a key with an oversized cork fob.

"They found me a room," she nodded. "Now I too get to experience the wonders of Hotel Il Convento."

They both laughed and looked around at the faded charms of the place.

"It's going to be great," Ernie agreed. "It's everything I had hoped for, and more." He looked back at the tubby middle-aged man behind the reception desk with his two-day-old beard and his cigarette sitting on his bottom lip, hanging idly with a line of ash.

"We'll have a lovely time."

Finally, there was a ping, and the lift doors creaked open.

"After you my dear," Ernie said, stepping aside to allow Rachele to venture into the precarious old lift, pulling her luggage behind her. Ernie squeezed in alongside.

"Floor four for me," Rachele said chirpily.

"Me too," Ernie muttered, double checking the number on his key fob. "Floor four. Must be the penthouse suite."

It turned out to be more a series of loft rooms, with the apex of the roof perilously low on either side of the bed. Ernie walked to his window and looked out. He could hear Rachele moving around in the neighbouring room. The window offered

Ernie a high, but somewhat constrained view of a back alley, with the crumbling fabric of an old apartment block opposite seemingly within touching distance if he had been brave enough to lean out. He opened the window wide, and creaked his neck, first in one direction and then in the other, in search of a view. But there was none to be had. As he turned his head a second time, he was met with Rachele's face from the next window.

"It's everything you said it would be," she shouted across to him.

"Isn't it just!" he laughed, then more to himself, "isn't it just."

He turned back towards Rachele. "How's your back alley?" he asked with careful comic timing.

"My back alley is looking fine Ernie. How's your back alley doing?"

"Just the ticket my dear. Just the ticket." He reached out and gave the lead guttering of the downspout a little shake. "There'll be no climbing up that, if we get locked out after hours," he said with a smile.

"Well," Rachele seemed to be thinking aloud. "Maybe we had better go and find somewhere to have a drink nice and early then?"

"Yes, maybe we should," Ernie agreed. He looked at his wristwatch. "Do you suppose the sun is over the yardarm yet?"

"It's five o'clock somewhere!" Rachele beamed. "Meet you outside in five."

"It's a date!" the old man chuckled.

1943

Ernest woke with a start. It was early. The sun had not yet risen and the lamplight from the street was still casting a sulphurous glow on the dormitory. He stretched his legs down to the end of the springy bed and turned his feet at the ankles, being careful not to make a sound and wake the others. The sheer joy of it – not being dragged out of the bed by Sergeant Patterson. He looked up at the ceiling with its crumbling layers of paint and thought to himself, this is my day.

He had a much-anticipated day's leave stretching ahead of him. The next 24 hours would be entirely free of patrols and parades and the Army in general. He would wear his uniform, there was of course no alternative, but other than that one sartorial reminder of his responsibilities, he could pretend he was completely carefree. He was in Italy. He was in love. He was truly alive.

He washed, shaved and dressed swiftly and left the barracks at the first opportunity. He had plans and they all involved Preghiera. He skipped out of the dormitory and immediately met the chaplain on the stairs.

"Morning Ernest, you're looking full of the joys of spring."

"I have a day's leave Padre – couldn't be happier," Ernest said.

"Ah, good, good, very important," the Padre added. "And how do you plan to spend your day?"

"What the Italians call Preghiera Padre."

"Preghiera? Prayer?" the clergyman looked confused for a moment – a look that quickly turned to suspicion. "I never knew you were so devout."

"I'm particularly devout when it comes to Preghiera, Padre," Ernest grinned and carried on down the stairs.

"We shouldn't joke about prayer you know my boy," the chaplain called down after him, but Ernest was already out of earshot. "After all, you never know when you'll need it."

Ernest walked with a bounce in his step as he made his way across the city whistling contentedly under his breath. He strolled up to the butcher's shop and threw a handful of stones at the shutters that were still closed across Preghiera's bedroom window.

"It is tomorrow – domani, domani, domani," he whispered, grinning up at her when Preghiera eventually opened the shutters and looked out. He had half expected her to still be asleep, but it was clear from her immaculate presentation that she too had been awake for hours. Her hair was carefully brushed and he even thought he could see a touch of blusher on her high chiselled cheekbones.

"Wait there," she whispered, with a mischievous glance around the square to see if there was anybody else around. It was entirely deserted at that time of the morning. She slipped back into the shadows and emerged moments later from the side of the butcher's shop.

"We should go, in case my father wakes," she said in a hushed voice. She took Ernest's hand and they tripped nimbly across the square. For a while neither spoke. They walked hand-in-hand through the back streets. Preghiera led the way. To Ernest it seemed like a warren. It was a route he had never before taken and he was sure he would not remember it to take it again, winding in and out of alleys and cutting across tiny squares, each with their cluster of crumbling houses and always with a little water fountain in the middle.

"How do you find your way around this place?" Ernest laughed.

"I was born here, I grew up here, this is my place," the young woman smiled, pirouetting mid-step and opening out her arms enthusiastically. "This is home."

After what felt for Ernest like an age, the carefree young couple was eventually spat-out by the city on to the esplanade. The sea looked blue and tranquil and with its pure and perfect form, stretching untroubled by the war all the way to the horizon, it seemed to present a stark contrast with the broken city that stood behind them. Preghiera led Ernest down a flight of concrete steps on to a deserted beach.

The sun was still only a little way into its ascent in the east, and their shadows were long on the sands. Despite being November, it was not cold, but it was also no longer too warm. The breeze was comfortable and friendly as it met them from across the waves.

"Shall we sit down for a while here?" Preghiera asked. Ernest nodded and they chose a spot up against the sea wall, where they would be hidden from passers-by on the road, and where they could lean back against the old weather-worn stone and share this moment of peace.

Preghiera settled her head on Ernest's chest and her fingers played idly with the buttons of his shirt as they talked. Both were struck by the same unmissable feeling – a sense of being perfectly comfortable in the company of the other person. The conversation ebbed and flowed freely, as they each joyfully unfolded their lives for the other. Moments of silence had no sense of awkwardness, they took the opportunity of any break in the conversation to simply enjoy each other's presence and to feel the breeze and the warmth of the day rising up from the sand around them.

Ernest closed his eyes and thought to himself that he had never felt this happy. He had never felt this at ease in anybody's company. But Ernest was a man who tasted lemonade and saw lemons. A new cloud began to loom in his mind – how long could they be together like this? Was he being shown a paradise, only to have it cruelly taken away from him? It was difficult to shake a vague, background hum of uneasiness. As the morning turned towards the afternoon, Ernest took Preghiera to a little seaside café. It was rough around the edges, but a waiter served them huge bowls of minestrone, which they devoured hungrily, along with a jug of lemonade. Ernest gazed at it and thought of the lemons once again.

Looking out across the seafront, Ernest sat back and smiled at the young woman opposite him who was still working her way through the bowl of soup.

"You look as if you've not eaten in a week," he laughed. She smiled weakly and Ernest immediately wondered if perhaps she hadn't eaten in a week.

"My mother works wonders with what food we have," Preghiera said at last. "But – how you say – we don't have much in our cupboards. People think because my father is the butcher, we must have all the food we want. It doesn't work like that though. I think we eat less meat than anyone else in the whole of Torre Annunziata." She laughed softly and touched her lips with her napkin. "Everything my father can get his hands on is quickly snapped up by his customers. He keeps the best bits behind for his regulars, his favourites and of course," she paused.

"The camorra?" Ernest smiled.

Preghiera nodded, with a sadness in her expression. "This is Italy," she shrugged. "There are always local gangsters that you need to keep happy."

"And your father keeps them supplied with meat?"

"It's that sort of neighbourhood," Preghiera explained quietly. "You help each other, whether you want to or not. And my father's business does better than it would if he didn't give something back to the local families."

"Families?"

"For the camorra its always about families."

"Of course it is."

"Well," Preghiera snapped dismissively. "How do you think my father gets his meat? Do you see other butchers in the city with queues that reach all the way around the block?"

"Your father should be careful who he gets involved with," Ernest sipped at his lemonade. It suddenly tasted a little sour.

"He might say the same to you," Preghiera smiled. Ernest raised his eyebrows.

"Is that a threat?"

"It is a warning."

"It's worth the risk."

"Is it?"

"It is for me," Ernest whispered.

Preghiera studied his face carefully, putting down her soup spoon.

"Good," she said at last. "It is for me too." She reached out a hand across the table and Ernest's hand met it. Their hands rested there a moment, before Preghiera slipped her hand back towards her soup spoon with a smile.

Neither Preghiera nor Ernest noticed the bulbous-nosed man behind counter, idly listening in to their conversation, as he looked out to sea and polished glasses with a tea towel. But Ernest gave the man a nod as they stood up to leave. A small stack of coins weighing down the bill had been left in the middle of the table. "Grazie," the gruff man muttered, as the young couple walked away.

They ambled hand-in-hand along the seafront, occasionally stopping to look out to sea.

"What if your people see you here with me?" Ernest asked.

"They won't," Preghiera said with a flick of the wrist. "They don't come this far from home. People live small lives within their own neighbourhoods here. They don't venture across the city."

Ernest accepted the idea silently, but could do nothing to quieten the persistent background hum of unease.

"Where does your father think you are?"

"Not with you certainly," Preghiera laughed.

"Will they not be missing you at home by now?"

Preghiera's eyes looked down to the ground, as if a spark of shame cast them there.

"They think I'm helping out at church," she said. "The preparations for the feast of Saint Andrew Avellino. It's tomorrow, so there's lots to prepare."

"Will the priest not miss you?"

"He thinks I had to stay at home to help my father."

Ernest laughed. "You're playing a dangerous game."

"It's a risk worth taking. That's what you said."

Ernest nodded and turned to the sea. "So, who is Saint Andrew Avellino? He might not be too happy about you using his feast as cover." He grinned ironically.

Preghiera looked a little shocked that he didn't know who Saint Andrew Avellino was, but chose to ignore the second half of Ernest's question. "He was a priest here in the city 350 years ago. The archbishop gave him the task of cleaning up the local convent. Certain wicked men who were accustomed to have meetings with the nuns became angry at Andrew's interference, and one night he was attacked and badly hurt. He was brought to the monastery of the Theatines to get better. While he was there, he decided to devote himself entirely to God and he entered the Order of Theatines."

"So why is he a saint?"

"He had a gift for converting sinners," Preghiera grinned mischievously at the young soldier standing before her as she leaned in for a kiss.

"Maybe we could do with him here today," Ernest whispered.

"Maybe we could."

Chapter five
1930

The nine-year-old Ernest was almost too afraid to open the door. He stood in the hallway outside the sitting room and could hear his father's breathing on the other side. He would be sitting where he always sat, beside the fireplace, occasionally reaching down to grab the poker and trouble the coals for a little more heat. His reading pile would be sitting on the little table beside him, and on his blanketed knees would be resting whichever book he was currently reading.

His father's breathing had the rasp and hiss that was a remnant of his encounters with mustard gas in the war. But according to his mother, his father was the picture of health now compared to how he had been when he first came back from the Somme. The shaking had long since eased. He was less distant. The war was always there though with his father – it was the frame in which he lived his life. For a long time, he wouldn't speak of his experiences in the trenches, but in recent years that had changed. He occasionally opened up to Ernest about the hardships he had endured as a young man.

The biggest legacy of the war on his father, as Ernest was all too well aware, was not the rasping breath or the coughing or even the occasional shaky hand, it was the anger – the uncontrollable, flaring temper that could rise up and erupt like a volcano at any moment. It left Ernest and his elder brother Reginald in constant fear. This was why Ernest was hesitating in the darkness of the hallway, as he attempted to summon the courage to raise his hand to the doorknob and enter his father's presence. He took a step forward towards the door and paused for a moment in the shaft of sunlight, coloured by the stained glass in the fanlight at the other end of the hallway.

Ernest had long since learned, it all depended on which glass of gin he was on. If he was still on his first, his father was generally unresponsive and would huddle in his chair, his head buried in his book. By the second the anger turned vicious, with vitriol liable to be cast violently towards anyone unlucky enough to get in his way. This would ease a little during the third glass, and by the fourth he would become positively friendly. By the fifth or sixth the friendliness would turn to sentimentality and by the seventh and eighth, more than likely it would have turned to tears and a world-weary retreat to his bed. Such was the cycle of his father's day.

The family, once reasonably wealthy, had lost out badly during the previous year, when stock invested after the war crashed spectacularly and devastatingly. They were still surrounded by the relative grandeur of their middle-class home and the leather-bound books in the bookcase. But now the family could only afford to keep one fireplace lit and the books had all been read long since by his father, who could not afford to spend money on new ones.

So it was, that one of Ernest's jobs each week, was to visit the public library – a little over a mile away, to choose three new books for his father to read that week. It was a mission that was always charged with risk. What if he brought home a book his father had already read, or one he didn't want to read? What if he brought home a book by an author whom his father deplored, or on a theme that went against his own truculent view of the world? The result was often another eruption of anger aimed towards the young boy.

Ernest raised his hand, quivering a little, towards the doorknob. He took a deep breath and stepped inside the dimly-lit room.

His father was sitting beside the fire, just as Ernest had expected. He raised his head slowly towards the boy, revealing a face in the flickering shadows that looked 20 years older than his years. The three library books from the previous week were stacked on the little table beside him.

"Ah Ernest," the figure muttered. "You've come for the library books?"

Ernest nodded. His father picked the first book off the top of the pile and examined the spine. "G.W.M Reynolds' *Omar: A Tale of War,*" he muttered. "A strange choice Ernest."

The boy visibly tensed on the other side of the room.

"This is a book that glorifies war," his father said. Without warning the book was flung towards the boy, missing him by inches and fluttering to the ground like a butterfly killed in mid-flight.

He picked up the second book. "George Tomkyns Chesney," his father said, once again studying the name on the spine with disgust. "*The Battle of Dorking: Reminiscences of a Volunteer.* Do you know what this book is Ernest? This book is an insult to our nation. I do not want to imagine an invading German army, even in fiction." The book fluttered through the air towards Ernest.

"And finally," it was clear from his father's facial expression that he had kept the worst until last. "William Thackery's *Vanity Fair.* What on Earth were you thinking boy? Do I look like somebody who would read *Vanity Fair*? Do I? Well do I boy?"

Ernest's voiced quavered in the darkness. "No father. I didn't know what it was about, you see."

The book began its inevitable flight across the room, though unlike its companions this book seemed to have a more malicious intent. It didn't open its wings and flutter, it held its wings tightly by its side, so that with each tumble the weighty tome seemed to gather momentum, until finally and with pinpoint accuracy, the top corner of the book's spine connected violently against the temple on the righthand side of the little boy's head. Ernest cowered and yelped both at the same time, raising his hands to his face, and lifting them away to gaze at the scarlet liquid that now dripped from his fingers.

"Oh, my boy, my boy," his father exclaimed, the anger turning swiftly to horror at his own actions. "Come to me here Ernest. Your head – your head is bleeding."

"It's okay father, it's okay," Ernest whispered, keen not to approach. "It was my fault."

"Come here," his father's voice took on a sharper tone. "Here, here, into the light."

The boy approached cautiously, turning his body shoulder-on towards the man in the chair.

"Let me look at what we've done there," his father dabbed a little at his temple with his handkerchief. "It's fine, just a flesh wound."

Ernest nodded and quickly moved back across the room and started to pick up the library books from the floor.

"I'll try to find better books today father," he said.

"Good, good," his father nodded. "I do like Dickens. There are still a few I've not read. Look for Dickens. Even the ones I have read, I could happily read again. Dickens was our finest writer perhaps. Do you agree Ernest?"

"Yes father."

"And listen to me boy," he added quietly. "Any book that glorifies war or takes pleasure in imagining a war against our own nation is wrong, very wrong. Do you understand?"

Ernest nodded silently.

"My generation went through a war so that your generation won't need to," he went on. Ernest wondered if he should make some sort of gesture of gratitude, but his father continued, now wandering deeper into his own thoughts: "War is to be avoided at all costs. It generally brings out the very worst in humanity and only occasionally the very best."

The old man turned back towards the fire. His gaze seemed to fix on the flames as they danced and flickered at the back of the grate.

"But it must never be allowed to happen again," he whispered. "Such a waste. Such a waste. It was all such a waste, you see Ernest. I had so many friends who never came back from the front. Where are their children now? Never born. Never born, do you see Ernest? There are whole families that were cut down, not just individual soldiers. It was what might have been, it was the people who would come and now will never be."

The old man's face, twisted slowly in the flickering light into a mask of pain. He might have been weeping a little, Ernest couldn't quite tell from the far side of the room.

"To take a man's life is wrong, but to take the life of a child or one who has never even been given the chance to live, well that's the worst kind of sin. Do you see Ernest? Do you understand?" The old man reached for the bottle on the table beside him and poured out his next drink.

"Yes Father, I understand," Ernest said, holding the library books in a neat stack. "I will look for Dickens."

"Good boy, good boy."

Ernest retreated from the room into the darkness of the hallway. He paused to take a deep breath, and clutching the stack of books under one arm, he reached with his free hand to touch again his blood-stained temple. He dabbed at the wound, flinching to himself.

"Don't hover about boy," his father roared at him from behind the door. "Get yourself along to the library. I need a book to read. Get along now!"

"Yes Father, just going Father," Ernest called back towards the closed door in the darkness.

1943

Patterson gave Ernest a firm pat on the shoulder. "Now then lad. Do you want the good news, or the bad news?"

Ernest thought for a moment or two. "The bad news?"

"Right," the Sergeant grinned. "The powers-that-be are determined that there will be no more complete evacuations of the city – no more rogue, stay-behind Nazis springing up with idle threats causing chaos."

"Excellent. That sounds like the good news."

"Unfortunately – and here's the bad news – that requires us to check every last nook and cranny in this God-forsaken city," Patterson added wearily. "And believe me, this is a city of nooks and crannies. Have you heard of the catacombs?"

"I've heard of the catacombs in Rome."

"Similar idea I'm sure," Patterson nodded. "They have them here too – more than 60,000 square feet of tunnels and burial chambers, with I am told around 2,000 ancient burial recesses. Whatever a burial recess might be when it's at home. Well, whatever it is, our task is to slip down and check out every single one for hiding Germans."

"Sounds like a bit of a faff," Ernest groaned.

"It sounds like a bloody ball-ache if you ask me," Patterson grumbled in agreement, "but remember, ours is not to reason why."

"That's right Sarge. It's all about the doing and the dying for the likes of you and me I suppose."

The monks at the church of San Gennaro were equally unenthusiastic about the idea. A couple of young and sombre-faced monks outrightly blocked access to the entrance to the catacombs from the church, waving their arms wide like a farmer trying to redirect an errant cow away from a gate. It was as though they believed their waving arms could stop the pair of soldiers even being able to see the door.

"Your people have already searched our sacred burial place at length," a more senior-looking monk bellowed as he arrived at the scene of the disturbance. A line of perspiration had gathered on his upper lip and the beads of sweat on his forehead vibrated with each word he spat out at the two soldiers.

"Now look Father," Patterson stammered. "We're not looking for trouble. But we have a job to do, you see."

"The Americans had 50 men here just last week and they found nothing," the monk said angrily. "Nothing at all! Why do you need to go back down there?" The monk panted deeply and moved his face closer towards Patterson's face. "It is the final resting place of 2,000 souls. Why do you need to disturb these souls?"

"We need to make sure nobody is hiding down there," Ernest offered.

"Hiding down there, hiding down there," the monk scoffed dismissively. "If you two imbeciles go down alone, you'll be hiding down there too – you'll be lost for days. I don't think you understand what you're dealing with."

"It needs to be done Father," Patterson stood firm.

The monk paced up and down as if studying the cracks in the paving slabs for clues as to what he should do next. Eventually this pacing seemed to calm his mood a little.

"You can have a quick look, but only if I come with you," he conceded at last. The monk turned to one of his fresh-faced underlings and demanded a lamp. He turned back to the two soldiers. "I can assure you, if there were Germans down there, I would know about it."

"Yes," Patterson said, eyeing the monk with undisguised suspicion. "That's true enough."

Moments later a great oak door was unlocked and opened with a long creak. The older monk led the way down a long flight of steps cut into the bedrock, his cassock swirling behind him as he rushed on deeper into the ground. The soldiers followed the monk down into the darkness cautiously, clinging to their rifles. At first Ernest could see almost nothing, but after a while the ground levelled-off and he became increasingly aware of the scale of the place. Rows of niches carved into the rock formed a series of seemingly endless burial chambers. Many appeared entirely empty, others clearly housed skeletons in various states of completion. The monk led the way beneath a series of ancient frescos, and nodded towards an enormous pile of skulls. "Our plague victims," he muttered, by way of explanation.

Patterson paused to examine the stack of skulls in more detail, clearly revelling a little in the gruesome novelty of the sight. But as he stepped back, his left foot skidded off the path and into a black void. Ernest reached forward and pulled Patterson back away from the hole. The Sergeant turned and looked down at the yawning chasm that had gone unnoticed behind him.

"Jesus Christ," Patterson mumbled more to himself than to Ernest, causing the monk to crease his brow into a frown in the lamplight. "Sorry Father," he added, raising his hand to his lips by way of apology. "But I could have died."

"We will all die," the monk whispered philosophically. "Look around you. All the souls that we care for down here are testament to that one simple fact. From dust we came, and to dust we will return."

The monk left the grim thought hanging in the air between them for a moment longer than was necessary, before turning his lamplight back towards the passageway.

"Please keep to the main path," he grunted officiously. "We don't want to lose anybody now do we?"

"Quite right Father," Patterson nodded, and followed behind, keeping to the older man's footsteps with extreme caution.

The three men walked on through the darkness, the monk occasionally stopping impatiently to allow the soldiers to check the deeper recesses of the burial chambers for any signs of life.

"We're looking for a needle in a haystack," Ernest whispered to Patterson. "Anyway, if this bugger was hiding a Jerry down here, we'd be none the wiser. He could be walking us round in circles for all we know."

Patterson shrugged his shoulders and broke into a little run to catch up with the monk who had moved on a long way down the dark passage. In his haste to follow, Ernest felt his boot make contact with something round and hard. It rolled like a football along the passageway and came to a stop at the foot of the monk. He turned his gaze down at the floor and his torch lit the distinctive shape of a centuries-old human skull.

"Will you please be careful!" the monk hissed. "You come here and start desecrating our dead." He reached down and picked up the skull, giving it a gentle dusting before placing it protectively into the nearest niche."

"I don't think that's his body," Patterson said, in an attempt to be helpful. The monk slapped the Sergeant around the arms testily. "You have seen enough. There are no living souls down here I can assure you."

Patterson turned to Ernest. "It's a hopeless case anyway," he said, looking around at the multiple black chasms dotted in the walls around him. "There are entire galleries up there that we can't get anywhere near. If somebody really wanted to hide themselves away down here, we wouldn't stand a chance. I mean, they could be anywhere."

Ernest nodded. "We've done what we can Sarge."

Patterson approached the monk. "Fair enough Father," he said, trying to establish some semblance of authority. "We've seen everything we need to see."

The monk tutted at him impatiently. "Follow me. I don't want to lose you two imbeciles down here," he added with a scowl as he led the way back through the maze of darkness.

1993

Ernie walked through the backstreets with Rachele in search of a suitable bar. He was struck by the musty smell that seemed to permeate the darker corners of the neighbourhood. His senses shuddered back to fifty years before as if he had been here just yesterday. The sights and sounds were new. More than anything, it was the smells of the city that seemed to connect in Ernie's brain, undiminished by the passing of time.

"Of course, you know that Dickens visited Naples, in 1844," he said to the young woman, suddenly slipping back into full school teacher mode.

"Did he really?" Rachele smiled.

"Not that I've ever been a fan of Dickens myself, apart from *David Copperfield*, of course," he added with a frown. "Although my father thought he was the greatest writer that ever lived."

"You didn't agree?"

"My father adoring him, was enough to give me a lifelong distaste for the man."

"And what did Mr Dickens think of Naples?"

"He called it 'all that is wretched and beggarly', if I recall correctly," Ernie laughed.

Rachele looked at Ernie with mock offence. "I think perhaps I'm not a fan of Dickens either."

"Oh, that's nothing my dear, wait until you hear what he called the people."

"What did he call them?"

"He called them a 'hollow-cheeked and scowling' people."

"Hollow-cheeked and scowling?" Rachele scowled theatrically at Ernie, battling the flicker of a smile on her lips.

"Well, perhaps on second thought, Dickens knew what he was talking about," Ernie grinned, causing his companion to playfully slap at his upper arm as they strolled.

"A terrible thing to say," she growled.

"If I remember correctly, he said that everything is done in pantomime in this city, the movements, the gestures, everything is theatrical and larger than life."

Rachele stopped and placed her hands on her hips. She frowned at the old man beside her. "What nonsense," she said, flicking at the inside of her upper front teeth with her thumb.

Ernie chuckled. "I do remember that gesture from when I was last here. And this one." Ernie held together his thumb and forefinger, and made a twisting gesture beside his temple.

"That means you love me," Rachele said, "but be careful, because the same gesture twisting the other way means you hate me."

Ernie tried both.

"At least, that's what they meant where I grew up. Italians have hundreds of hand gestures. But nothing quite as common as this one." She grouped together all the fingers and thumb of her upturned right hand and made a flicking movement at the wrist.

"Oh yes," Ernie laughed. "That's a classic Italian."

"It's known as the pinecone," Rachele enthused. "If you want to look less English and a bit more Italian, start throwing a few pinecones into conversation. She demonstrated, "Ma cosa stai dicendo?"

"But what does it actually mean?"

"It normally means you're not taking something seriously – you're questioning something sarcastically." Rachele reached across and helped the old man to get his fingers into the right place. "Perfect," she said, and demonstrated once again, "Ma cosa stai dicendo? What are you talking about?"

"Ma cosa stai dicendo?" Ernie aped the gesture a couple of times, before smiling in a self-satisfied sort of way. "Well, I shall certainly need to remember that one."

1943

Patterson, Smudge and Mouse were seated with Ernest at a rickety old round metal table, flaking with rust at the edges. A half empty bottle of Strega was being handed around, each man pouring the sticky liquid freely into his own tiny little glass tumbler.

"So, what were you doing before you were called up then Smudge?" Patterson asked. Oddly, nobody had ever asked Smudge anything about his life before the army, and he looked slightly taken aback by the question.

"I was apprenticed as a fitter's mate," he said.

Patterson nodded, and deciding that needed no further explanation, he turned to his left: "Mouse? What did you do?"

"Brickie."

"What about you lad?" Patterson asked, turning to Ernest.

"Grammar school boy I'm afraid, Sarge," he said, receiving a chorus of whoops and jeers from his pals. "Then a few years of university education."

"Oxford or Cambridge?" Patterson asked, without a flicker of humour.

"Neither Sarge," Ernest laughed. "The University of Liverpool was as far as I got. Though I did join the rowing team. Not that we ever made it to the Thames. I graduated, then I was training to be a teacher when I was called up. But that feels like a long time ago now. I wanted to teach boys history, but they ended up out there in the world making history. The battles were always the best bits when they were in a text book. Not in reality of course. Turned out the reality was all a bit more grim and less glamorous than we were all taught in our history lessons."

There was a general low-level chatter of agreement around the table and all the men spent a moment looking down into their drinks. Nobody asked Patterson what he did before the war – it was too hard to imagine him out of uniform, without the three stripes on his arm. Ernest quietly wondered to himself if he had been born with his sergeant stripes.

"Anyway, I'm not sure I'll ever get back to all that now," Ernest added. "Even if the war ended tomorrow – how could we all just go back to doing what we were doing before? It could never be that simple. It couldn't be the same. Everything's changed. We've all changed too much. It's a different world we're living in and we're all different things living in it."

"Nonsense," Patterson laughed. "You'll get back to your teacher training. Your books will still be waiting for you when you get back from all of this, just as there'll be plenty of bricks waiting for Mouse and, erm, fitting for Smudge."

"Aye," Mouse said. "But all the bricks will be smashed up in piles on the ground eh Sarge?"

"Somebody will have to rebuild it all Mouse," Patterson said. "Your skills will be in high demand."

"I suppose so," Mouse shrugged.

"And who will I be teaching?" Ernest asked. "Half the young lads will be forever resting in some corner of a foreign field."

"All the more reason that the other half should get a decent education I say," chipped in Smudge. "Patterson's right. We'll have to get back to some kind of normality, otherwise, what are we doing any of it for?"

Ernest smiled and took another sip of his drink. "Maybe you're right. But, I don't know, I just don't think things will ever go back to normal somehow. All of this, it's just the start. The world's changed, and when the world changes, it tends not to change back."

"Is that what it says in those school books?" Patterson grinned and reached once again for the bottle of Strega.

"If you read between the lines, yes I suppose it does," Ernest mused. "Total War the Nazis call it, you know. That's what I reckon this is now – just one long perpetual state of war."

"Come on lad, we'll beat the Jerries sooner or later."

"No doubt," Ernest said thoughtfully. "We'll beat them or they'll beat us, but who will be next? Somebody will come along and try to fill the power vacuum that all of this shit storm leaves behind."

"That'll be the Yanks no doubt," Patterson grumbled.

"The Yanks, the Soviets, the British and our Empire," Ernest mused. "But whoever it is, they'll only get their brief time at the top, then something will come along to upset the apple cart and there'll be another ungodly scramble to be top dog. Like I said – Total War. That's how the world is set up now." Ernest put his glass down on the table with a thud and took a deep breath that seemed to say he was about to get into his stride. "If you think about it," he went on, "this war is just a continuation of the last one. We were just about still civilised enough to have a half time break to pass around the oranges. My father and his brothers went to war and some of them never came home. Those that did probably wished they hadn't. Now it's our turn."

"Well, there's a bloody cheery prospect," Patterson said. "I think you're wrong. The Jerries are on the run. It won't be long before we finish them off and we can all get back to Civvy Street."

"I hope you're right Sarge," Ernest said. "Certainly, when we do finish the Jerries off, as soon as I can get demobbed, I'm going to live a bit."

"More than this?" Smudge laughed, rocking back on his metal chair and raising his glass of Strega before downing it in one.

"Maybe Smudge," Ernest smiled sadly. "Or maybe this is it. I know Naples is a shit hole, but I quite like Italy. I can see myself coming back here, settling down, family life."

Ernest lifted his glass: "Here's to happy endings!"

"Oh aye," Patterson bellowed. "This is what it's all about – that lass in the butcher's shop."

"I could do a lot worse."

"She could do a lot better," Patterson sniggered.

"Wouldn't you rather settle down with a nice English wife?" Mouse said. "Get your cushy job teaching kids to read books, come home each night to your meat and two veg waiting for you on the kitchen table?"

"That's true," Patterson interceded. "Think of all that pasta and garlic you'd have to eat if you married a Wop."

"I like pasta actually. And garlic."

"You bloody would," Patterson added, before burping theatrically. "Good luck to you, I say. You and your Wop Mrs, and your two little kiddies Minestrone and Macaroni, or whatever you'd call 'em."

Ernest rubbed his eyes wearily and muttered inaudibly to himself, while the other three rolled around in laughter.

"Anyway sunshine," Patterson added, when he had finally composed himself. "I do hope you managed to get your leg over with Wendy Wop, because we'll be getting our marching orders soon enough."

"What are you talking about Sarge?" Ernest looked up, suddenly sobered.

"Yeah, they're not going to leave us here, policing a load of octogenarian dagos for the entirety of the war," he slurred. "Unfortunately enough. They're going to expect us to fight the occasional Jerry while we're here. You mark my words."

"Bollocks are they."

"They are too," Patterson said, squaring up to Ernest.

"With all due respect, you know fuck all about the British Army's battle plans Sarge," Ernest laughed.

"That's where you're wrong, grammar school boy," he growled. "I've got a pal who has a pal who is the mechanic to General Alexander himself you see, and he said that come the new year, there'll be a big push on the Gustav Line and they'll need every shit-arsed private to make up the cannon fodder. So, stick that in your history books."

Ernest raised his eyebrows.

"Nice," Smudge muttered.

"Anyway," Patterson waved him away drunkenly. "The point is, if you think we're going to be able to settle down here and serve out the war clipping the ears of the occasional 10-year-old pick-pocket and screwing around with the Italian housewives while their pasta is on the boil, I'm afraid you need bringing down a peg or two." Patterson paused, to look around at the three ashen faces looking back at him in the moonlight. "There'll be plenty of opportunities for us to experience a battle yet," he added, a comment that delivered little in the way of reassurance.

The four men studied each other across the table as if considering their next move in a game of chess.

"Sod this for a lark, I'm going to bed," Smudge said, finishing his drink and kicking back his chair.

"Me too," Mouse added, following Smudge into the darkness.

Ernest was left watching Patterson pouring out another drink and struggling to get the cork back into the bottle afterwards. Patterson took one more sip, then settled back into his chair. "It's all change soon, you mark my words lad." He closed his eyes, and within minutes he was asleep, his head slumped down to one side, so he dribbled on to the three stripes on his sleeve. Ernest took one more sip of the liquor, and quietly walked away.

Chapter six
1930

Ernest had left the library books on the little table that stood beside the chair in which his father was asleep. He looked at the embers of the fire glowing in the grate. He hoped he had chosen wisely. The boy crept out of the room and made his way upstairs.

The following morning was a Sunday, and he opened his eyes and thought immediately about the library books once again. He washed and dressed, shivering in the half light, before making his way downstairs for breakfast. He met his mother in the hall. Her face was lit with patterns of colour, as the sunlight shone through the stained glass of the fanlight above the front door.

"You'll need your tie Ernest," she said. "We'll be setting off for church very shortly."

There was a grunting noise from behind the closed door. "Ernest!" his father called. Ernest's stomach twisted with a sinking sensation as he made his way through the dark doorway. His father's face was illuminated only by the flickering of the fire, which had just been lit in the grate.

"Thank you for the books," his father said quietly. "I couldn't have chosen better myself."

A smile erupted across the boy's face. "Thank you, Father. I'm glad."

An hour later Ernest was sitting in a shadowy pew alongside his mother, listening to the rumbling of the organ. One of the great stone columns of the church rose up beside him as if it was holding up the heavens. The dark wooden pew itself had been cut to accommodate the shape of the column, which reminded Ernest of a tree that had grown up through the fabric, regardless of the structure around it. The sun, still low in the sky, was cutting a swathe through the ornate east window behind the high altar. The light caught the dust that hung in the air above the altar itself. Ernest wondered how it got dusty all the way up there.

It was the sort of question he might have asked his mother. But he could tell his mother was praying – her eyes were closed and her head was tipped devoutly. He thought better of interrupting her conversation with her maker. Ernest looked up again at the enormous stained-glass window that dominated the east end of the church. He gazed quietly at the benevolent face of Jesus, slumped in His agony on the cross.

"I chose the right library books this time Lord," he prayed silently in his own head. "Thank you for small mercies."

The church was filling up swiftly, and the people were settling into their regular pews. The organ music came to an abrupt ending and from high up in the outer fabric of the old building, Ernest could hear the clock tower chiming eleven. The ancient vicar walked down the aisle with a frail gait, stopping halfway to cough, as he did every Sunday. The venerable clergyman opened the service with a suitably wrathful prayer, as he also did every Sunday. Ernest's mind began to wander. He decided impishly to himself that the dust must all come from the old vicar, who looked like he might crumble back to dust at any moment. From dust we came, and to dust we will return. Perhaps he was disappearing before the eyes of the congregation, week by week?

At the end of the service his mother took Ernest's hand and hurried him towards the door, slipping past the elderly vicar with a flurry of polite, but meaningless conversation.

"Your father will be wondering where we are," his mother whispered as they left the sanctuary of the church. "That was a very long sermon this week. A very long sermon indeed. We shouldn't keep your father waiting at home like this. I do wish he would come with us occasionally."

Ernest trotted alongside his mother as she rushed all the way home along the rain-soaked streets.

"Mother?" the boy looked up through the rain. "Are you afraid of father?"

"Of course not," his mother snapped. "Afraid? Ernest you do say the strangest things. But we must respect him. He has not been well for a long time, but he is still the head of our house."

"You don't hate father then?"

"Ernest! Of course I don't hate your father. I'm his wife, he is my beloved husband. I love him dearly. Of course I don't hate him."

The boy pondered the comment for a few moments as they walked on through the rain.

"Do you suppose you love him just because you are his wife?"

His mother stopped abruptly and turned to look down into Ernest's face. "Ernest, your father's favourite author, Charles Dickens, had the answer to your question."

"Did he mother?"

"Yes, he said 'a loving heart is the truest wisdom'." She reached down and gave Ernest's cold hand a tender little squeeze, before hurrying on towards home.

1993

The bar was tiny, with the walls mirrored, presumably in a vain attempt to give the place a sense of space. For Ernie it meant he had to endure the ominous presence of his own reflection staring back at him from over Rachele's shoulder whenever he looked across the table. In that way that only happens in Italian bars, the majority of the space seemed to be taken up by hulking stainless steel espresso machines and a glass case of day-old pastries, which seemed curiously out of place among the line of smoking middle-aged men who propped up the bar.

"Looks like we could pick up breakfast here in the morning," Ernie said without much enthusiasm for his own idea.

"Good idea," Rachele nodded. "I'm so glad I'm not trying to work all this out alone."

"Everyone needs a friendly face. Anyway, you're the native, not me. I'm sure you'd cope well enough without me. How's your beer?"

"It's certainly cold," she said, running a finger down the condensation that misted the outside of the glass. "What's that you're drinking again?"

"It's called Strega," Ernie said, picking up his little shot glass and examining its luminescence in the light. "We used to drink it during the war. I'm amazed you can still get it."

"My grandfather used to drink it."

"Did he? Would you like to try one?"

"Maybe later."

"Yes, it is a little early I suppose."

"Shall we find somewhere to eat after this?" the young woman asked, the edges of her eyes creasing into a smile.

"Absolutely," Ernie said taking another sip of his drink. "If you're sure I'm not cramping your style – it can't do your street cred much good to have an old fella like me hanging on your arm."

"I'm delighted to have your company," Rachele gave a mock formal bow of the head. "Anyway, I don't have any street cred. I'm far too geeky for that."

"I was always a bit geeky myself, I suppose," Ernie laughed. "I never heard the end of it after I'd told the other lads that I was training to be a history teacher."

"The other soldiers?"

"Yeah, the lads in my unit had all left behind a trade back on Civvy Street. They thought I was a right toff because I was going to become a teacher. Some of them took to calling me Sir – sarcastic bastards."

"What was it like here during the war Ernie?"

"What was it like?" Ernie put down his glass, and turned his eyes out of the window into the street. "It was a total shit hole, to be honest with you. You have to remember that apart from being ravaged by war, brought to its knees by the retreating Germans, by the time I was here, Naples was also the largest resting camp for Allied servicemen in all of liberated Europe. It was a cesspit of vice and black market activity. Rotten to the core. They used to say that Naples was the worst-governed city in the Western world, a place that lived only on scheming, cunning and back biting. As I say – this place was rotten to the very core. The city was like some terrible psychological experiment – what would society be like if all effective government was removed. I can tell you what it would be like – it would be rotten to the core.

"Then there was the hunger," Ernie added, shaking his head at the memory. "The starving kids, crying pitifully in the streets because their bellies were so empty. To have a bawling child thrust towards you by a desperate-eyed mother in the street became a regular occurrence. I'm ashamed to say it, but you hardened to it after a while. You get used to anything in a few weeks." Ernie paused a moment. "And there was food about in fact," he added. "If you knew where to look, there were black market restaurants where you could get steak and eggs and spaghetti and a big salad, all for just a few US dollars. The Italians didn't like to deal in their own lire – the real value was in getting their hands on dollars or on food or cigarettes for that matter."

"It sounds so awful," Rachele whispered.

"It was my dear. It certainly was. Although we had our fun too, occasionally," he added, his mood visibly lightening before her. "It was such a melting pot of nationalities – British, Indians, Americans, Poles, Gurkhas, New Zealanders, to name but a few. There were lads from all over the world rubbing each other up the wrong way. There was this one time I recall when I heard an old British General taking on one of the New Zealanders – a divisional commander I suppose. The old General marched up to him and demanded he did something about his men." Ernie adopted the voice of an elderly General: "'I have just followed a lorry load of your men – they were obviously drunk – and were hanging out of the back of the lorry offering me bottles of wine.'" Rachele laughed.

Ernie turned his head a little and adopted a New Zealand accent: "'Is that right General? That's nothing. You should have seen them yesterday. They filled one of our water tankers with Chianti and ruined the bloody thing.' The old boy didn't know what to say, and stormed away. Christ, we laughed."

Rachele laughed again and took a sip of her drink. Ernie laughed for a moment, but his eyes were distant, as if he was back there once again, seeing the misery of it all as well as the moments to smile about. He gave a little cough and sat up in his chair.

"But it wasn't all fun and games of course," he muttered. "More often than not, it was all a bit gloomy to be honest with you my dear. There was a sort of End of Days feel about the whole place," he added sombrely. "You saw the very worst and the very best of humanity every day. Lives were played out before you like tragedies." Ernie shuddered a little. "No my dear, being here then, well it was like life had ended. Or perhaps that it was going to end soon enough. Which it could have done when you turned any corner in the city to be honest. Though in those first few months you were in more danger from the local mob than you were the Jerries."

"The mafia?"

"Oh yes, they were the real power in the city then," he looked back to the empty street outside. "They probably still are."

1943

The gas lamps were mostly smashed, hanging off the walls, or had been removed altogether from their stands. The few that remained in the back streets of Naples didn't seem to work anyway. The result was a labyrinth of darkness to navigate at night. After a few drinks, even the relatively simple stagger back from the bar the soldiers frequented to the safety of the barracks was fraught with menace. Eyes watched their every step – some were real and some imagined and normally a glance over a shoulder revealed no obvious presence. Though that was no guarantee that they were not being watched from a distance.

Ernest sensed this pervading menace as he walked alone through the darkness. The smells seemed more vibrant by night – the rich tapestry of sewer stench intertwining with the earthy aromas of cooking that wafted from the half-shuttered kitchen windows – the herbs and spices that were unfamiliar to Ernest's nose, and yes, the garlic that hovered as a subtle base note in this warren of ramshackle homes.

He began to feel a hint of remorse. Perhaps he shouldn't have left Patterson asleep there in the square. He should have made an effort to carry the drunk bugger back to the barracks. Perhaps he should go back and get him, he thought. He went to turn on his heel. But at that moment, the silence of the alleyway was broken by the sound of a bottle rolling on a pavement. Ernest looked around again, and this time he saw a definite figure – shadowy against the brick wall. It was a tall man, surprisingly well built, jowly, with broad shoulders and thickset arms like a docker. A match was struck, and as the figure raised the flame to the cigarette hanging from his lips, the face was briefly revealed in the flickering light. A bulbous broken nose, and a mop of heavily greased wavy black hair was slicked across the head.

"Buona sera Ernest," the figure spoke in a gruff voice that seemed to carry effortlessly through the alleyway even at little more than a whisper.

"Who are you?" Ernest demanded, attempting to imbue his voice with authority, but hearing the nervous quavering of his own words in the night. The figure approached him, dragging a foot in its wake. "Who are you and how do you know my name?"

"Now that's not too friendly Ernest," the voice said quietly. "I thought we were all friends now? Allies?" A big fleshy hand patted Ernest's shoulder as the man came close. "Are we not all friends now Ernest?"

From behind him, in the shadows, Ernest heard the sound of more feet scuffing against the cobbles. He turned quickly, and saw three more burly figures shrouded in the darkness.

"What are you after?" Ernest muttered quietly. "What is it you want?" He patted his pocket to find any cash he might have left on him after a night of drinking.

"Do we look like thieves in the night to you Ernest?" the gruff voice said, aping a tone of disappointment. "No, no, no.

We are your friends Ernest. It's like I keep telling you. We are your friends."

A stubby finger ran across Ernest's cheek. It made Ernest shudder.

"But we help our friends in Naples," the man added, the voice turning sharper, somehow more pointed. "Especially when we think they are making a mistake. Are you making a mistake Ernest?"

"What are you talking about?" Ernest said. "Who are you?" The man's face was now so close to his own that he could smell his breath, musty and damp in the night air.

"Are you a good boy then Ernest?" the voice asked. "A good Christian boy? Do you pray Ernest? Do you pray?"

"What's it to you?" Ernest felt a lump in his throat. The adrenaline seemed to be pumping down to his toes and impelling him to turn and run. But there was no escape from these men. He was cornered, like a rabbit in a trap.

"I pray Ernest. I pray for those I love," the man went on, his voice once again little more than a whisper. "I pray for Preghiera. I pray Preghiera isn't making the wrong decisions in her life. It's so hard for a young girl these days to stick to, how you say in English, the right path. It can be so *hard*." With no warning, the word hard was emphasised with a vicious upper cut to Ernest's stomach.

The young soldier felt his body fold in two like a hymn sheet.

"We must pray for Preghiera," the voice went on. "Will you pray with me Ernest? You must pray *hard*." Once again, the word hard was married to another crippling punch to the stomach. As he crumpled again, he felt hands reaching from behind and dragging him backwards to the floor. His body was peppered with kicks and stamps, as he rolled one way, then the other way, in a hopeless attempt to deflect the attack.

Then the whole thing stopped as swiftly as it started. Suddenly the alleyway was quiet once again, and he was only aware of the burly figure walking away into the darkness, dragging a foot behind him.

Ernest spat and coughed out blood on to the cobbles. He reached for the bayonet that he knew was in his pocket, but before he had even unfastened the button, he gave up and flopped back on the ground panting for breath. The night evaporated around him.

It was hard to say how long he was out. It might have been a minute, it might have been an hour, but when he opened his eyes it was still night, and he was aware of another burly figure approaching him through the darkness.

"Fuck me lad, what in God's name happened to you?"

He looked up as Patterson's grimace emerged from the shadows.

"Italians," Ernest managed to cough out. "Fucking Italians."

Patterson put an arm around Ernest's back, and grappled his fingers under his arm, dragging him up to his feet in one swift, unsentimental movement.

"Come on you poor bastard, let's get you back to barracks. Didn't they teach you to box at grammar school?"

"They're trying to warn me off Sarge," Ernest said, before retching out another mouthful of blood on to the cobbles. "The bastards are trying to warn me off."

"You don't say?" Patterson laughed sarcastically. "I think you might have something there, you numbskull."

He grappled awkwardly to get a stable purchase on Ernest's torso, before the pair began to hobble through the backstreets.

"You'd better steer clear of that Italian totty, you dozy fucker," Patterson muttered.

"Not happening Sarge," Ernest groaned, but his sentence was broken by a sharp pain from his ribs that caught his breath. He stopped and leant against a wall as he calmed his breathing. He wiped his forehead with the edge of the sleeve of his jacket and spat into the darkness. "It's just not fucking happening."

"Come on lad," Patterson grappled him once again, taking the bulk of his weight, and helped him hobble a little further.

"I'll kill the bastards," Ernest said.

"Yeah? You and whose army?" Patterson said. The pair stopped and looked at each other for a split second, before both erupted in a burst of laughter, which was almost immediately cut short by another shooting pain from Ernest's ribs.

"Come on then Sarge," he conceded. "Let's get the bloody hell out of here."

1948

Ernest frowned at his brother across the table, then turned his head to take in the gaudy colours of the dance hall. It was decorated, somewhat inexplicably, with an ancient Egyptian theme – all pyramids and Cleopatras wherever you looked. Why had his brother brought him here if he was going to spend the whole evening whispering sweet nothings into Angela's ear? And why had Angela brought her best friend along anyway? Ernest felt uncomfortably as if he had been set up. He gave the young girl beside him a polite smile and a nod. She took a sip of her drink and looked around at the dancers, her shawl wrapped around her shoulders. The dance hall music was so loud, Ernest was unsure he would be able to hold a conversation with the girl if he tried. He pretended to take an idle interest in a nearby

Sphinx that had been sloppily painted on the wall, as he attempted to avoid getting caught up in a conversation.

"Angela and I are going for a dance," his brother shouted across the table. "We'll leave you and Marjorie to get to know each other better." Ernest's brother flashed a knowing smile before taking to the dance floor.

"But Reg..." Ernest called after him, but he was already out of earshot. He smiled again politely at Marjorie and turned back momentarily to re-examine the Sphinx.

"So, what do you do, for a job, I mean?" Marjorie asked, leaning across the table so she could be heard above the music.

"I teach," Ernest said, finally turning his eyes from the paintings on the wall to address his companion.

Marjorie nodded. "How wonderful. You must be ever so clever."

"Oh no," Ernest demurred with a little laugh. "Not at all. Not that clever at all. You only have to know your own subject, you see? It's memory more than anything else."

"What is your subject?"

"History. I've always been interested in the past – the idea that people came before us, and lived full lives, just like you and me and then left again almost without a trace."

Marjorie nodded and took a sip of her drink. "Yes, I saw you looking at all the Egyptian stuff." Her eyes, glinting in the half-light, were fixed on the young man before her. But Ernest didn't notice her beauty.

"I've always had an interest in history I suppose. I went to Pompeii once, during the war," he said. "Do you know, there are casts of the bodies of those who weren't quick enough to escape when Vesuvius erupted almost two thousand years ago."

"How awful."

"Oh yes, it was awful – in the truest sense of the word," Ernest agreed. "Truly awful. That was the feeling you got when she erupted – sheer awe."

"You were in Italy when Vesuvius erupted?"

"Yes," Ernest shrugged and took a drink of his beer. "It erupted during the war – 1944. It was the last thing the poor Neapolitans needed at that moment to be honest. All hell breaking loose – almost literally."

"You must have been so scared," Marjorie's eyebrows seemed to have stuck in a freeze frame of alarm.

"It was the least of our worries, if I'm honest," he said. "There was so much going on at the time. It was just one more thing to deal with I suppose. Evacuating villages, that sort of thing."

Marjorie's eyebrows finally settled. She smiled again and went to ask a question, but stopped herself. She sensed the young man didn't want to speak about it. This momentary conversational stumble created a little pocket of awkward silence on both sides of the table. Both Ernest and Marjorie tried to fill the void by taking another sip of their drinks, smiling at each other a little, and looking around the room as if they had taken a sudden interest in all the dancers.

It was Ernest who broke the silence after a while. "When you see those casts of their bodies, caught in the moment of their death like a three-dimensional photograph, well it puts everything into perspective, if you know what I mean?"

Marjorie nodded. Her eyes returned to the man sitting across the table from her. There was a world-weariness to his face when he talked about the war, she noticed. "You must have been glad to get home," she said.

"Must I?" Ernest mused. "Sorry, I'm just considering that. I'm not sure really. I'm not sure I was that glad to get home. I was leaving a lot behind out there." He paused a moment. "And a lot had changed when I got back."

"Yes, I was sorry about your mum," Marjorie added, casting her eyes to the floor. Ernest looked up and took in the young girl's face properly for the first time.

"You knew my mother?"

"Yes, well, a little," she flustered. "I had a little Saturday job as a kid in the box office at the cinema. Selling the tickets, you know. It was easy work. Funnily enough, it seemed somehow glamorous at that age. The silver screen and all that."

Ernest smiled.

"Anyway," Marjorie went on. "You got to know people – the regulars, you know? Your mum was a regular. After your dad died, she would come to the cinema every Saturday morning without fail. You got to know the regulars like your mum a little bit. There would be a little conversation each week through the box office window. You know how it is. Anyway. I liked your mum. She was such a nice lady. She was always talking about you and Reg. How proud she was of the pair of you out there, fighting the Germans."

"My father wouldn't have allowed her to go – he didn't see the point in the cinema. It was all about books with him," Ernest explained. "If it didn't have a leather-bound cover and a spine with gold lettering on it, well it just didn't exist. He was always buried in a book. When he went, she had that little bit of freedom. She could do the things she enjoyed – a walk around the shops, a couple of hours of pure escapism in the picture house. It's nice to know she took the opportunity to enjoy herself, while she still could."

"I was there, the day she died," Marjorie blurted out nervously, keeping her eyes on her drink. "I just wanted to mention it, in case you wondered."

Ernest nodded.

"It was quick. Peaceful, you know," she added. "She couldn't have known anything about it. There was no pain – no suffering. She was there one moment and gone the next." Marjorie paused and slowly shook her head from side to side at the memory of that day. "She'd been so excited about the film, because it was a Cary Grant and he was her favourite. He was my favourite too," she confided, leaning forward towards Ernest. She reached out and placed her hand on his, where it rested on the table. "I sat with her until the doctor came. But she was already gone. It was ever so peaceful. It was just the way she would have wanted it, I reckon."

Marjorie gave Ernest's hand a little squeeze and then withdrew it once again, to lift her glass and take another sip of her drink. Her mind was momentarily back at the Savoy, kneeling beside Mrs Green's lifeless body at the top of the staircase.

"Yes, well, that was another thing the war took from me," Ernest muttered. "Those last few months with my mother."

"Yes, I suppose so," she agreed sadly. She looked across the room, as if casting her eyes around in search of a lighter topic of conversation that might be plucked from the air around them. After a moment she found just the thing and her eyes sparkled a little in the light from the mirror ball as she beamed a smile across the table. "But you must make such friendships in the Army? All the boys together, and all that?"

"Oh yes, there was that too," Ernest nodded and gave a little laugh. "Mind you, we made for quite a ragtag lot in my unit. Some real characters. You can imagine." He looked more closely at the girl as she smiled at him and then took another sip of her drink. "Do you work?"

"Oh yes," she said. "I work in Littlewoods."

"The Pools?"

"That's right," Marjorie smiled proudly. "I'm the checker girl. There are thousands of us actually. But I'm one of the checker girls."

Ernest smiled. "Is that what you call a chequered career?"

It took a moment of processing behind Marjorie's eyes for the joke to land. Her whole face erupted into a grin. "I said you were clever."

"It's a lovely job – it's a bit like you were saying about the Army. It's all girls together, if you know what I mean," she laughed. "We have a wail of a time. Some of the girls are a scream, they really are. There's nothing like the feeling when you're the one who checks a winning coupon. It's only happened to me a couple of times, but honestly, you feel like you've won the Pools yourself when you find one."

The girl's eyes were on fire with a sort of unbridled joy at the very thought of finding somebody else's winning Pools coupon. Once again, Ernest found himself smiling at her across the table.

"Did she like you, my mother?" Ernest asked, suddenly changing the course of the conversation once again. "You said you knew her a bit and that you liked her. Did she like you do you think?"

Marjorie smiled nervously, as if she was slightly taken aback by the question. "I think she did," she said. "She was always very friendly to me. I suppose she must have liked me. Why do you ask?"

"I don't know." Ernest shrugged, took another mouthful of beer and placed his pint glass down on the table. "I suppose I should be asking you to dance?"

"I suppose you should. I thought you'd never ask."

Ernest held out a hand. "Come on then checker girl."

On the dancefloor Marjorie felt stiff in Ernest's arms. It was like dancing with a mannequin. But she was nice enough, he thought to himself.

"We're going to powder our noses," Angela announced in her shrill voice, as she took Marjorie's hand and swept her away from Ernest. He wandered with his brother across to the bar. "I'll get them in," Ernest said.

"So, what do you think of Marjorie?"

Ernest shrugged. "She's nice enough."

"Nice enough?" Reg laughed. "Jesus, Our Kid, you do realise that in three years' time you'll be 30. You'll be an old fella. You need to think about settling down with some nice girl."

"I know, I know," Ernest growled. "Like I said, she's nice enough."

"Nice enough? What, nice enough to settle down with?"

"Jesus Reg, I've only just met the girl."

"She likes you – Angela says she can tell."

"I suppose I'm not expecting lightning bolts anymore."

"How do you mean?"

Ernest shrugged again. "I just mean that nice enough might be, well, enough." He turned to the bald man behind the bar. "Two pints of best bitter and two halves of Mackesons."

Chapter seven
1993

The shabby little backstreet restaurant Ernie and Rachele had settled on had flimsy pine tables with red and white chequered table cloths, which were clipped on to the tables with stainless steel grips, as if even they were being held there against their will.

Ernie ordered a bottle of Chianti, and they both swiftly opted for the spaghetti all puttanesca starter, followed by pizza marinara. Both dishes were striking for their plainness at first sight, but both tasted like the very essence of Italy.

"This is incredible," Rachele enthused through a mouthful of pizza.

"What's that? It's inedible?" Ernie fretted. "We can send it back."

Rachele swallowed and tried not to laugh. She gave the elderly man a playful slap on the wrist across the table. "Incredible Ernie! Not inedible."

"Sorry," Ernie smiled, shaking his head in desperation at his own infirmity. "My hearing is not what it once was." He reached for the Chianti. "Here, have a top up."

Before Rachele could refuse, the rich, luxuriant wine was bleeding profusely out of the neck of the bottle and filling her glass.

"My God Ernie," she smiled. "You're going to get me totally off my face."

"Well, if you can't do it in Naples, where can you drink?" he shrugged.

"I guess so," Rachele laughed. "After all, you've already promised me a decent breakfast. That'll get rid of any hangover."

"Ha, I'm not so sure the pastries in that bar tomorrow morning will be any better than the ones in there tonight," Ernie said. "In fact, I'm certain they'll be exactly the same pastries."

"Well, I'm sure the coffee will be good," Rachele added, reaching for her glass of wine. "A decent coffee is the only thing I really need in the morning."

Ernie laughed a little, and lifted the paper napkin from his lap. He wiped at the edges of his mouth, and his ancient, watery eyes beamed across the candlelit table.

"You know, I've not had a meal out like this for years," he mused. "Not since my wife died."

"You were married?"

"Oh yes. Marjorie and I were married for 41 years." Ernie replaced the napkin on his lap and took another sip of wine. "Sorry, had I not mentioned her?"

"Do you miss her?"

"I do," he said without hesitation. "Oh, we had a cat and dog sort of relationship most of the time – she would hiss at me and I would bark back. But we were happy in our own way. It's all about familiarity at the end of the day."

"Kids?"

Ernie shook his head. "No, that never happened for us."

"Oh, I'm sorry."

"Don't be," he smiled. "You get to see more than your fair share of children as a school teacher. It's more than enough to put you off the idea of having your own off-spring."

"Still, it must be lonely for you, with your wife gone?" Rachele wondered if she'd gone too far. "You don't have to answer that Ernie, sorry."

"It's been..." Ernie looked around the restaurant for the right word, as if it might be hanging from the shabby old light fittings. "It's been quiet," he said. "It's been a quiet few years."

"So sad," Rachele whispered, stretching out a comforting hand across the table. Ernie allowed her young fingers to cling to his ancient hand. He could immediately feel the warmth in them.

"Sad?" Ernie thought about the word. "Yes, it was sad to lose her. It was terribly sad. We'd been together a long time."

"I envy you that Ernie – finding your soul mate."

"Soul mate?" Ernie gave a look of surprise. "I'm not sure Marjorie and I were what you might call soul mates."

"No?"

"No – nothing so soppy. It was the Forties. People were more practical in those days about this sort of thing. We had a tough time. We tried for a family you know. But people didn't focus on being gloomy then. Nobody would admit to depression. We all had to be completely..." he searched for the word.

"Practical?" Rachele offered.

"Yes, practical," Ernie nodded. "We were all terribly practical. Especially when it came to marriage. We weren't all riding around waiting to fall head over heels in love with the next person. But we had been together for a long time. Such a long time."

A mousy-haired little waitress appeared at their side.

"How is your meal?"

"Fine thank you," Ernie smiled.

"Wonderful," Rachele added. "This pizza is incredible." The waitress nodded and returned their smiles, pausing a moment longer than might be natural, to look at this curious couple so distant in age. A light then seemed to be switched on behind her dark brown eyes as she realised what she thought to be the situation. "It is so nice," the waitress beamed. "So nice for you to bring your grandfather here on a holiday."

Rachele and Ernest shot an embarrassed glance at each other across the table. Rachele turned to the waitress and delivered a pitch perfect smile. "I know," she beamed. "Well, we have to appreciate the older generation while they're still around, don't we?" She gave Ernie a comical pat on his upper arm.

"I'm her great grandfather actually," Ernie said. "Could you pass me another napkin dear, when you get to my age drooling becomes an occupational hazard."

The waitress' expression changed a little once again, she frowned briefly with an undisguised puzzlement. She handed Ernie another napkin, then with a little nod of the head she swiftly departed. "Enjoy your meal."

"Thank you dear," Ernie said, erupting into laugher, before whipping Rachele playfully with his napkin across the table the moment the waitress' back was turned.

"So, it wasn't love at first sight then?" Rachele asked.

Ernie turned to look again at the waitress – now halfway across the restaurant.

"Not with her," Rachele giggled. "With your wife."

"Oh," Ernie said, the smile slipping from his face. "I don't suppose it was." He took another sip of the wine. "Though I have known that feeling once, and frankly, love at first sight isn't everything it's cracked up to be."

"No?" Rachele sounded surprised.

"No. It's," Ernie stopped to consider the word. "It's disorienting and painful."

"Painful?"

"Yes, in a way it is painful," Ernie paused again to think and took a deep breath before continuing. "When you know it can't be. When you know it absolutely should be – it absolutely must be, but it just can't be. Then it gets you right where it hurts."

Ernie lifted his hand and patted his podgy, wrinkled old fingers against the middle of his chest. "It hurts like hell."

1943

The moon cast an oblique glow across the square. The shuttered butcher's shop looked more ominous now to Ernest, even in the dead of night. He wondered if he was being watched from one of the shabby sets of shutters, even now as the whole city seemed to sleep around him. He cast a few small stones towards Preghiera's window. But this time, when she appeared, it was clear she had been asleep. She looked dishevelled and confused.

"Preghiera!" Ernest whispered from the shadows. "I need to speak to you."

Preghiera scanned the darkness, and rubbing her eyes, she gradually made out Ernest's form in the square below.

"It is the middle of the night!" she whispered. "You couldn't wait to see me?" She smiled. Then as Ernest stepped forward a few steps into the moonlight, the smile swiftly turned to a grimace.

"Mia dea! What has happened to your face! You are hurt!"

"Don't worry, I'm okay," Ernest said with a shrug of his shoulders.

"What happened?"

But before Ernest could begin to explain, she raised a hand into the air.

"No wait," she hissed down into the darkness. "I'm coming down to you."

"No, you mustn't!" Ernest said, but it was too late – Preghiera's silhouette had already disappeared from the window. A moment later a side door opened, and Preghiera slipped out to join Ernest in the shadows.

She stood before him, her nightgown billowing a little in the warm moonlight. Her face was a picture of concern as she raised a hand to touch the young soldier's bloodied features.

"They hurt you?" she said. Ernest nodded. "My father kept saying I shouldn't talk to you – that bad things would happen. I didn't think he meant bad things would happen to you."

"They were fairly persuasive."

"Oh amore mio, how could they do this to you?" Preghiera was gently stroking Ernest's cheek and her lips were moving almost imperceptibly slowly towards his.

"They don't want me to see you anymore."

"No," Preghiera said, her brown eyes dampening in the dim light. "We must not see each other anymore. It is too dangerous for you."

Their lips continued their magnetic pull towards each other as they spoke in whispers.

"I don't care," Ernest said. "I'd rather die than lose you."

"No, no..." Preghiera mouthed almost silently as the soldier's lips reached hers with a kiss that was as soft and gentle as winter's first flakes of falling snow. Their faces moved apart for a moment, as each set of eyes took in the other's face, then the two sets of lips were drawn together once more, but this time fervently, with a visceral impact, like tectonic plates colliding. Ernest took in every inch of her face in such detail that deep inside his brain the image of that face was burnt on to his memory like a photograph that could never be lost. Ernest's hands caressed the peaks of her shoulder blades, and moved down to feel the smooth trembling valley of her spine through the flimsy night gown.

Preghiera turned first one way, then the other, and contenting herself that the square was empty, she smiled, took Ernest's hand and pulled him into the darkness of the alleyway that ran alongside the butcher's shop. She guided him through the darkness, where the shadows became darker still beneath the thick-set branches of an old plane tree. The leaves rustled above their heads, as they flickered in the breeze, revealing the stars of the Milky Way gazing down at the young couple from far above in the cosmos.

Preghiera's hands fumbled to unfasten Ernest's leather belt, and the young soldier flinched at the pain in his ribs.

"Oh, my love," Preghiera whispered, caressing his body gently, tenderly. But the pain drained away as something electrical stirred deep within him. Preghiera leaned back against the trunk of the old tree, and grasping the front of her night gown, submitted to the warmth of the young soldier's body in the darkness.

1948

Ernest and Marjorie walked out of the registry office to be met by a feeble showering of confetti.

"Congratulations Our Kid," Reg beamed, shaking Ernest's hand firmly. Angela shrieked at Marjorie, dabbing at her mascara to suggest she was about to be overcome with emotion.

"Well, that's the formalities over," Ernest said. "When do we get to the pub?"

"Not yet," Reg said. "I booked this chap to take your photograph. It's the least I could do as Best Man."

An apologetic middle-aged man ambled towards them holding a camera strapped around his neck.

"He's a mate of mine, works at the Echo, but does the odd wedding on the side," Reg whispered to his brother. Ernest nodded.

"Okay then, where do you want us?"

"Just here's perfect," the photographer dabbed at the perspiration on his brow as he spoke. "Do you folks have any of that confetti stuff left? When I count down from three, I want you to throw it as high as you can over the happy couple."

The photographer shuffled backwards, fiddling with the dials on his camera, and fitting on a new flash bulb. "Everybody ready then? If the happy couple can look right this way. And three, two, one..."

Inside the camera the shutter mechanism cranked open and light flooded in for less than a second. But with it, time stood still, burning itself on to the roll of negative film that was locked inside. The image of Ernest and Marjorie, with her looking straight down the lens and him looking up at the confetti fluttering down from above, was captured forever in an image that would grace the couple's mantelpiece for decades.

Chapter eight
1993

The waiter was stacking chairs on to tables all around them, and Ernie and Rachele had the distinct impression they had overstayed their welcome. Ernie called for the bill.

"I'll get this," he said, reaching for his wallet.

"You will not, let's split it."

"No really, I insist," Ernie smiled. "I'm of a generation where I wouldn't dream of letting you pay for your own meal my dear. It would embarrass me enormously."

"Well thank you Ernie," Rachele conceded. "Maybe that does make this a bona fide date then?"

"Like I said, you'd better worry about your street cred," Ernie laughed.

"Okay, okay I'll let you pay old man. On one condition."

"That is?"

"You let me buy the ice creams."

"Ice creams?"

"There must be somewhere still open selling ice creams," Rachele enthused.

"I suppose so," Ernie smiled. "This is Italy, after all. Fair enough – you can buy the ice creams."

Ernie fumbled with a pocketful of Lire notes, which he handed to the waiter in something of a flap.

"Let's get the bloody hell out of here," he said to the young girl, who looped her arm through his as they walked out into the fluorescent glow of the street lamps. A Vespa skidded past them and the neon of a nearby pharmacy crackled in the night. In the distance an ice cream parlour glowed like the Blackpool Illuminations.

"It seems you're going to get your ice cream fix after all," Ernie said. Rachele smiled, and pulled herself closer to the warmth of Ernie. She could smell his cologne in the Italian night.

"So, tell me more about the war Ernie," Rachele said, huddling into his jacket as they walked along.

"What do you want to know?" he asked, sounding genuinely puzzled. "I was in the Sixth Battalion of the Cheshire Regiment. We served under the 44th Infantry Division, before being transferred to 56th Infantry Division, just before Monte Cassino."

"No, no, no," Rachele admonished him with a playful slap on the wrist. "I don't mean all of that sort of waffle you boring old fart."

"Well what sort of waffle are you after my dear?"

"The real stuff," Rachele smiled in the darkness. She stopped and turned to look at the old man's face. "What was it *really* like?"

"It was a shit hole, the whole place was a shit hole."

Rachele giggled. "But you fell in *love*."

"Love, love, love," Ernie tutted. "Yes dear, if you want to call it that. I suppose I did fall in love. I was a very young man. I was young and impressionable."

"So, what happened?"

"With what?"

Rachele's eyes swelled with exasperation. "What happened? Why did you spend your life with Marjorie and not Preghiera?"

"Oh, lots of things happened," Ernie shrugged. "Things do happen in life. What was it John Lennon said? *'Life is what happens to you while you're busy making other plans'*. He was spot on there. Lots of things happened. Her people didn't like the idea – that much was certain. But also, the war got in the way."

"The war?"

"That's right – the day after we had made love for the first time, that's when we got the shout."

"The shout?"

"Yes, the shout. Our services would be required on the front line once again. We were sent north to the Gustav Line – to a place called Monte Cassino."

"Another shit hole?" Rachele smiled mischievously.

"Now, now my dear – you won't find me referring to a monastery as a shit hole," Ernie looked along the line of street lamps, and his eyes scanned the ornate marble frontage of a street-side church. "For me it was a kind of hell, that's for sure. But Monte Cassino is a whole other story."

1944

The truck in which Ernest, Smudge, Patterson and Mouse had been cramped together with the rest of their unit for hours grumbled its way along the pock-marked road. Naples now felt a long way away, and the landscape had morphed into menacing clusters of mountains, separated by wide river valleys.

Ernest looked out from between the gaps in the canvas of the truck, and watched the River Liri feeding smoothly, like silk into the Rapido beyond. The sun beat down and the air in the truck was soupy with the aroma of sweat. Men groaned and moaned at intervals. But on the whole, there was a nervous sort of silence. You could hear it somehow, even above the growling and grinding of the engine.

From out of the oil painting landscape that stretched beyond, a giant emerged – great, high and wide, its sheer surface glinting in the midday sun, and sitting atop of this mountain a square white shape clinging to its upper reaches, which soon focused into the outline of a large, wide building.

"That's Monte Cassino," Patterson said to Ernest, as the pair gazed up at the scene. "The Jerries have taken over the monastery on the top of the mountain to take their stand. It's bloody perfect for them – they have sightlines in every direction for miles and miles."

"Tell me you're not serious," Ernest muttered. "They don't seriously expect us to be able to launch an attack on that mountain."

Patterson rubbed wearily at his eyes with the thumb and forefinger of his right hand and turned away from the view.

"I'm afraid that'll be the general gist of it, lad," he said. "They've got us stitched up this time."

Ernest turned back and looked through the flap in the canvas. There ahead, standing placidly at the edge of the river was the dark-haired boy, a smile on his face, his little hand waving at the passing truck. Ernest recoiled back and pulled the canvas shut. Something deep within his fabric told him not to look. A shudder rippled through his body.

Sitting across from him, on the opposite bench, the Padre was holding his little black leatherbound Bible in his hands, his thumb caressing the well-worn pages. Ernest studied him for a moment. He's praying, Ernest thought to himself, without feeling at all reassured by the Padre's silent intervention. Perhaps he's praying for all the lost souls uprooted from their lives by this war, he thought. Or maybe he's praying for us? Perhaps he's just praying that he's able to save his own skin? Who can possibly know the innermost thoughts of the Padre?

The truck crossed a little bridge and tracked along the edge of the Rapido itself. The town of Cassino was now clearly in sight. Compared to the suburbs of Naples, these villages on the outskirts of Cassino looked remarkably intact to Ernest's eyes. But there were few people around – the occasional country peasant walked along the roadway towards the town, but mostly the streets seemed deserted.

"Casinum," the Padre shouted above the rumble of the engine.

"What's that Padre?" Patterson asked.

"Casinum - it's what the Romans called Cassino."

"Is that right?"

"Yes, Cicero writes about this place. Mark Anthony had a villa here, where he devoted himself to his countless orgies."

"Crikey Moses," Patterson muttered, raising his eyes comically towards Ernest.

"Well, I'm not sure we can hope for those Padre," Patterson shouted above the noise of the engine.

"Dear me Sergeant no," the Padre seemed mildly scandalised by the giggling of the soldiers around him. "I'm sure the Benedictines have sorted all that sort of thing out long since."

Ernest smiled and looked back out at the mountain that loomed over the town, with the ancient monastery now appearing larger than before. It dominated the peak, rearing its venerable walls against the sky. It was the rectangular solidity of the structure that made it seem so unlikely, perched as it was so close to the heavens. It stood out as being hopelessly unnatural in this stunningly natural landscape. Part fortress, part palace. Could this really be where Benedict came to found his order so many centuries ago, Ernest thought to himself. Could the Germans really have chosen this holy of holies as the place to draw up their battle lines?

"They think we won't bomb them I suppose," Ernest shouted across to the Padre. "They think we will respect holy ground and all that."

"It's just a building," the Padre said. "It's seen wars before – it's been sacked four times in the heat of battle and it's always been rebuilt mightier yet. Remember Romans 12 my boy, 'Do not be overcome by evil, but overcome evil with good.'"

"Fight the good fight and all that," Patterson offered.

The Padre leaned forward, still clutching his Bible. "Put on the whole armour of God, that you may be able to stand against the schemes of the devil," he said.

Ernest frowned at the old man. "Did not Jesus himself say, 'all who take the sword will perish by the sword' Padre?"

The Padre nodded. "He did my boy, He did indeed." The clergyman thought for the briefest moment, before adding: "But remember, the Bible also says there is a time to love, and a time to hate; a time for war, and a time for peace."

"Like I said," Patterson added with simple-minded certainty. "Fight the good fight and all that."

Ernest rolled his eyes silently. He looked back towards the scene outside. Beneath the walls of the monastic pinnacle, the great mountain was robed in olive, fir and acacia, and peppered with occasional oak branches that flexed their muscles against the January air. Barking at its ankles, a smaller hill, mounted with its own little castle formation, stood like a loyal rocky watchdog. With a squint, Ernest could just make out the dusty line of a switchback roadway working its way up the slope with a series of hairpin bends.

He took a long, deep breath to steady his nerves and tried not to imagine the kind of horrors that the coming battle would subject him to in just a few short hours.

"Well, let's hope we have God on our side," Ernest said sardonically. "Because that's one fucking hell of a slope to attack."

1953

It was a death sentence. Nothing more, nothing less. The words hit Marjorie in the chest like a hammer strike.

"I am terribly sorry," the doctor said, washing his hands thoroughly in the sink in the corner. "It's the hardest news we have to deliver as doctors, you know?"

"Yes," she said, staring ahead blankly. "I suppose it must be awful for you."

Before a voice of logic in her mind could cut in and stop herself, she even added an automatic apology. "I'm sorry to cause so much trouble."

The doctor waved it away magnanimously. He smiled, which felt so very odd under the circumstances.

"So, what happens now?" she asked. The doctor gave a funny little shrug. Hadn't he just told her what would happen?

"Is there really nothing you can do, nothing at all?"

"If there was, I can assure you we would be doing it," the doctor said, straightening himself in the chair. "We can give you medication for the pain, of course. When the time comes. But I'm afraid in this case, it really is a matter of letting nature take her course."

He reached for a handkerchief from his top pocket. It appeared to have already been half extracted in readiness for grief. He handed it across the desk.

"Listen," the doctor said, barely disguising a glance at his wristwatch. "You'll want some time alone. It's a lot to take in. Someone will come and have a chat to you."

He was already on his feet and heading out of the door. She was left alone in the consulting room. The clock ticked on the wall. She looked at it, and couldn't help but think it was now almost a taunt; a countdown to the inevitable.

She looked to her fingers as they played with the edges of the appointment card she had been holding since she arrived. She reached into her handbag and took out her little address book. She flicked through it quietly. The names flashed before her eyes. All the people she would need to tell. Her breath caught in her throat. She couldn't yet imagine telling anybody.

Footsteps approached the door. A click of heels. Marjorie quickly put the address book back into her handbag. But without even pausing, the heels continued past, leaving her feeling even more alone. Through the window she watched the movement of vehicles in the car park. Coming and going, bringing in their worries and their ailments, taking home their good news and their bad news.

Marjorie sighed deeply and sat primly in the chair, carefully examining her finger nails, unsure what to do or what to think.

More footsteps padded beyond the door. This time, they were so swift, she didn't for a moment think the door would open. Within a few seconds they were gone, and she was alone once more with the ticking of the clock. She looked up at the minute hand slotting rhythmically into its next position on the dial. What was she waiting for? To be handed a dusty leaflet offering advice on managing emotions at "this most difficult of times"? What was the point of waiting?

She walked back along the hospital corridor with its freshly-wiped skirting-boards and gleaming floor tiles. She walked past the reception desk, where the same lady who had greeted her half an hour before, now averted her eyes. Another patient in the waiting room also seemed to turn away. Did they somehow know? Was death's stain already marked upon her? Were people reeling to disassociate themselves with the shadows.

She sat behind the steering wheel of her Morris Minor, and slammed the door shut. It was only then that something emerged from within her – a half scream, half sob. More panic than anything. A shudder from deep within her. Then it was gone. She started the engine and drove away from the hospital. At first, she didn't know where to drive and found herself negotiating the suburban streets without purpose or direction. Then something primeval told her to drive toward the coast road.

Leaving the car a few streets away from the promenade, she walked busily towards the gust of sea air and the sound of the gulls. It was off-season and grey. A few families walked along the seafront, their coats buttoned up against the chill. She took her place on a bench facing the sea and looked out towards the expanse of it, with its granite waves breaking in a froth against the ironwork of the pier.

How strangely we behave at such times, she thought to herself. How curious it is the way our brain abandons us at the bleakest of moments, pausing all feelings, turning us blank and unable to compute the real implications.

She crossed the road and stepped into a telephone box. She dialled her own home number. "Ernest," she whispered. "I'm at New Brighton Pier, please come." She replaced the receiver and stepped back out into the wind.

Marjorie walked slowly along the promenade and heard her footsteps resounding on the wooden boarding as she turned on to the pier itself. A gull circled overhead, checking her out with a beady eye for signs of food. Having contented itself that she wasn't carrying a newspaper-wrapped portion of chips or an ice cream cone, the bird gave an ungainly flap of its wings and changed direction in mid-flight, heading off in search of better opportunities.

The pier was almost entirely devoid of life – apart from an elderly couple, who walked with sticks trying to keep up with a grandchild. The child skipped around their ankles giggling with a singsong sort of voice, although his words were lost on the wind.

She gave an envious glance towards the family and walked on by, lifting her collar against the cold as she hurried past the flashing gaudiness of the empty amusement arcade, where a mechanical Laughing Policeman figure seemed to mock her with its cackle.

Beyond the weather-worn glitz of the empty ballroom, she made her way around the shabbiness at the end of the pier, beyond the putrid collection of bins, where in the ley of the helterskelter, she finally settled on another cast iron bench and gazed out at the storm clouds gathering over the sea.

He arrived quicker than she had expected. Gentle footsteps, then the smell of his aftershave and his tweed jacket nestling in beside her. She leaned into the warmth of his shoulder and tears came for the first time. Big proper tears, leaving their mark on the tweed. "It was bad news then?" he said at last.

She nodded, at first unable to speak. Then with a sharp intake of breath, she steadied her nerve. "It was a death sentence," she said at last. "I'm so sorry."

He nodded silently, his eyes glistening down at her face. She smiled up at Ernest, a cold and broken smile. Her hand moved down to rest gently on her belly.

"We're losing the baby."

Chapter nine
1993

The ice cream sundaes were magnificent, served in great crystalline glasses, and presented with long-handled spoons that allowed Ernie and Rachele to quietly mine for the chocolate sauce that had run down to the very bottom.

"Tell me about Marjorie," Rachele said, releasing her spoon into the now empty glass and wiping her hands with a paper napkin. "What was she like?"

"She was a lovely lady," Ernie nodded. "A very lovely lady – and she certainly looked after me. She looked after me for years and years, until one day, I found that I needed to look after her. Well, it was the very least I could do for her."

"Cancer?"

"No, no," Ernie said. He stopped and thought for a moment, looking down as if all the answers were embedded in his ice cream. "She left me gradually – ever so gradually. Dementia is a strange condition. It takes your loved ones from the inside, and one day you wake up and find you're left with the husk that once contained your wife. She's not there anymore. At some point when you weren't looking, she slipped away."

Tears welled suddenly and uncontrollably in Rachele's eyes and rolled down her soft cheeks.

"Oh, my dear," Ernie looked at her with alarm. "I'm so sorry – I didn't mean to upset you."

"It's okay," Rachele sniffed. "It's always so sad I think when people lose their loved ones that way. We've had a similar experience in my own family."

"I'm sorry to hear that," Ernie nodded sombrely. "It's a terrible experience. It was so wearing; so exhausting to care for someone like that for so long – although those final few weeks were peaceful. Mercifully, she slipped away serenely in the end. I thank God for that peace at the last."

Rachele nodded, drying the last of her tears with the napkin.

"It must have been so tough for you Ernie."

"You know the worst thing about it," he mused quietly. "The worst thing of all is the guilt that it leaves you with, because at the end there's part of you that welcomes their departure and the peace it brings at last. And that seems so wrong somehow."

"Not at all."

"She was a lovely woman. She deserved so much more than she ever got and the manner of her passing was just the final sadness."

Ernie put down his own long handled spoon and rested his hand on the table beside the glass. Rachele reached out and gave the frail old hand a tender squeeze. Ernie shrugged a little.

"I'm not sure I'm going to be able finish mine," he said, pushing the ice cream sundae away from him towards the centre of the table, before adding, "You know, you never quite get the ending that you want."

Rachele nodded silently, unsure whether Ernie was now referring to his ice cream sundae or his wife of 41 years.

"But," Rachele began, then she allowed the sentence tail off. She was unsure how to ask her question tactfully.

Ernie gave her an encouraging nod. "Go on my dear, you can ask me what you like."

"But she wasn't the love of your life?"

"Oh, what does that even mean?" Ernie grumbled. "It's just an expression they use in trashy novels. We are what we are my dear. We get the hands that are dealt to us in life."

Rachele cast her eyes to the floor.

"But as I told you, there was another, long before Marjorie came along," he went on. "It's a different sort of love when you're young and green to the world. Love can take you by surprise at that age. It can knock you off your feet and send you off your head a little bit."

Ernie laughed softly to himself at the memories. "When you get older and wiser, you toughen yourself up against those knocks. It's not the love that changes, it's ourselves that change."

Ernie turned his eyes to the street outside, and the Vespas that passed like wasps in the night.

"Do they never sleep?" he laughed, shaking his head. "Buzz, buzz, buzz. You wonder where they're all going." After a brief silence, he continued: "You know, I've always longed to make it back here, but I never imagined it would be like this."

"What did you imagine it would be like?"

"I suppose I always dreamed that one day I would come back to Preghiera. We all expect the happily ever after ending eventually, don't we?"

Rachele smiled. "I suppose we do Ernie. So, is that your plan? Have you come to look for Preghiera?"

"I rather think I have," Ernie tutted at himself. "Silly old fool, I know."

"Not at all," Rachele beamed. "But how do you know she's still here. How do you know she would want to see you?" Rachele faltered a moment, before adding: "How do you know she's still alive?"

"Ah well, that is one thing I do know my dear," Ernie announced, reaching into his pocket and producing a dog-eared postcard. On one side it showed a scenic panorama of the Bay of Naples, with Vesuvius looming in the background and the word NAPOLI etched across the perfect blue sky. He handed it across the table.

Rachele turned it over. In black, shaky writing were the words "Domani è adesso, amore mio. Preghiera x"

"Domani è adesso?" Rachele read aloud. "Tomorrow is now?"

Ernie nodded. "That's right. Tomorrow is now."

"So, she is still alive?"

"Seems that way."

"That's incredible."

"Easy there, I'm not that ancient, you know," Ernie laughed a little. "The week after I received the postcard, I received an envelope containing a plane ticket."

"Wow, amazing."

"Yes, a plane ticket to Naples," Ernie shook his head. "Well what else could I do? I got on the flight. Oh, and there was a note with the ticket. It simply gave tomorrow's date, the time of 7pm, and the words "Al nostro solito posto".

Rachele thought for a moment. "Our usual place."

Ernie nodded. "At our usual place."

She frowned a moment. "How did she find you after all these years? Where did she get hold of your address Ernie?"

"I'd given her my home address during the war," he explained. "I've always lived in the same house. My mother died when I was away in Italy, and when I came back my brother and I lived there for a few years. Then he married and I lived in the house alone.

"Then when I married, we decided to stay there. We've stayed there ever since. Preghiera must have kept that scrap of paper with my address on it. I suppose she just took a chance that the postcard would find me."

Rachele examined the postcard once again. "And you're going to go?"

"Yes, I mean, I think so. After all, what else could I do?"

Rachele's eyes beamed up into Ernie's face. They glistened once more with emotion.

"One last chance," she whispered.

"Yes, that's it my dear," he said. "One last chance."

With that, he reached back into the centre of the table and drew the ice cream sundae back towards him. He picked the spoon back up and began picking away again at the contents.

"One last chance."

1944

Ernest's unit was attached to a division of the Fifth Army that had been battling to reach the base of Monte Cassino for months. While Ernest and Patterson had been patrolling the streets of Naples turning a blind eye to pickpockets, these lads had been fighting for every mile of every road, mountain by mountain, river crossing by river crossing. To see them looking battle weary and brutalised, left Ernest feeling that same sense of guilt he had suffered when he first arrived on the landing beaches days after the initial assault wave.

"Do you ever get the impression that we might have had it all remarkably easy up to this point," he whispered to Patterson from between clenched teeth as he surveyed the miserable scene of exhausted young soldiers, waiting forlornly at the side of the road.

"Long may that continue if you ask me lad," Patterson muttered conspiratorially. "At least we're facing the battle fresh. Look at these poor bastards – they're all exhausted. What chance do they have?" He reached into his pocket and offered a young lance corporal a cigarette. He took it gratefully and Patterson reached for his lighter.

"Tough few months son?" the Sergeant asked.

"You could say that Sarge," the youngster admitted. "If I see another mountain or another river, I'm likely to turn the gun on myself."

The Sergeant looked momentarily alarmed by the sentiment.

"Only kidding of course Sarge," the youngster added.

"If you're sick of mountains, God help you," Ernest said. "Because that one over there is going to be an absolute bastard." He gestured towards Monte Cassino itself.

"Well, that's what it's all been about pal," the youngster said, drawing deeply on the cigarette. "If we take that, we've effectively taken Rome. The Jerries have put everything into holding Cassino. When that goes, we'll have them on the run good and proper."

"You seem remarkably confident," Ernest said.

"Of course he is lad," Patterson interjected. "We'll get those Jerries running with their tails between their legs before you know it."

Ernest looked up again at the great behemoth that overshadowed them. "I bloody hope you're right Sarge," he muttered. "For all our sakes."

"It's not just the mountain," the young soldier said. "The minute we're over the Rapido, it's going to be a shit-storm. The Jerries have got gun positions buried in the banks of the river. There will be mines and trip wires all the way through those woods. They're not going to wait at the top hoping to defend the monastery from up there. They'll start at the bottom and defend every inch of that slope. They won't retreat into the monastery until they really need to."

"Are you here just to cheer everybody up?" Ernest grinned. But the soldier didn't return the smile.

"I'm just warning you, that's all. We've been here long enough to know what we're facing. You poor bastards are straight off the last lorry. You're green as green can be. What chance can you have?"

"Well, you're not wrong there," Ernest admitted wryly.

That evening, as Ernest and Patterson chatted to the young soldier at the side of the road, their commanding officers, Captain Mark Wright (secretly known by the soldiers' as 'Every Girl's Mr Right') and Lieutenant George Stephenson (more obliquely dubbed "Choo Choo" by the unit), were among a large group of officers being briefed on the battle plan in the nave of an old church.

When they emerged, Captain Wright gestured towards them. "Patterson, Green, step into my office."

The captain led the way into a tumbledown yard, where he had found a wooden bench, which he had efficiently requisitioned for the evening. Choo Choo followed them in silence.

"So boys," the captain began. "The good news is, we are finally going to see a battle."

"Excellent news Sir," Patterson bristled.

"The Yanks will force their way across the Rapido tonight. The British will cross the Garigliano. Now I needn't tell either of you that an opposed river crossing is never pretty. Potentially we face two simultaneously."

The captain drew a rudimentary map on a sheet of paper.

"The 36th Texas Division will cross here," he drew a line on the map. "It's just sixty feet wide. But it is nine feet deep and has a current of eight miles per hour. But by crossing here, to the north and south of this village,"

He paused a moment, before the lieutenant interjected. "San Angelo, Captain."

"That's it, San Angelo. Well, if they achieve this, they bypass Cassino and break into the Liri Valley in conjunction with the boys from the Anzio landing. But the thing is, we don't want them to bugger it up."

The captain paused and carefully weighed up the two soldiers that stood before him.

"Now listen up you two," he spoke purposefully. "What you're being asked to do tonight won't go down on record. Whatever happens there will be no medals for you, no mentions in despatches – not a word of this in the history books. After all, we don't do this kind of thing in the British Army – checking up on our Allied friends' strategies. We trust them implicitly you see." The captain paused. "Do you see?"

"Yes sir," the two men spoke in unison.

Ernest watched the captain's pencil-thin moustache moving up and down slightly comically as he spoke, and focused on one thing alone – why the hell was the captain briefing Patterson and himself on this manoeuvre? He felt an instinctive flight-drive to leap to his feet and get as far away from the yard as he could. Patterson meanwhile, appeared to be having the time of his life, his chest positively bursting at the experience of being let into the captain's confidence in this way.

"So, here's where you two boys come in," the officer continued.

Here we go, Ernest thought, the pit of his stomach sinking.

"I've volunteered you boys to quietly slip on ahead and check the bastard Jerries haven't hidden any defensive positions at that point in the river. We particularly want you to keep your eyes peeled for nebelwerfers."

Patterson nodded.

"Know what a nebelwerfer is Patterson?" the captain asked.

"Erm, no not really Sir," the sergeant was forced to concede.

"Thought not. They're small cannon-like weapons. They dig the blighters deep into hillsides and these six-barrelled mortars fire six bombs simultaneously."

"Crikey," Patterson muttered.

"Crikey indeed," the captain snapped. "Keep your eyes peeled for the nebelwerfers."

"Yes Sir," Patterson nodded.

"And if they do have defensive positions hidden there Sir?" Ernest asked.

"You radio back with a thumbs up or thumbs down, then quietly slip back across the river."

"You don't think they might just shoot us before we can get to the radio Captain? Either with nebelwerfers or otherwise perhaps just with a rifle. I've heard that just the one bullet is enough to silence a chap."

"You know what Napoleon said Green? He said 'It requires more courage to suffer than to die'."

"That so Sir?"

"Yes, it bloody is so Green," the captain bristled. "Trust me, if you fuck this up Private, I'll make sure you bloody well suffer."

"What about the Americans Sir? Is there not a risk that they might shoot us themselves?"

"My dear boy," the captain said. "That is always a risk. Some risks we have to take in time of war."

"One further question Sir," Ernest muttered. "Why us?"

"I heard you can row a boat, Green."

It took everything in his power for Ernest not to scream.

Patterson smiled weakly and whispered, "I might have mentioned something about your time in the rowing club at university to the captain a few weeks ago."

"Mustn't hide your light under a bushel Green," the lieutenant chipped in.

"Quite right, quite right," the captain concurred.

The rest of the briefing was passed in a cold sweat of utter panic. Green didn't hear another thing from the captain – as far as he was concerned, the son of a bitch had just signed his death warrant.

"We're utterly fucked," Ernest whispered to Patterson, as they left the yard moments later.

"Nonsense lad, this is where you earn your medals," Patterson enthused.

"Posthumously? Anyway, the captain specifically said there'll be no medals."

"Now then my boy, we'll have none of that," the Sergeant smiled. "We have an important job to do. Anyway, it's not as if we'll be alone."

"We're completely alone," Ernest hissed beneath his breath.

"Were you not listening to the captain, there are lads from the 36th doing exactly the same thing a little further up the river. With the nod from us, they'll launch the assault at 20:00 hours, the Engineers will be over at 21:00 hours, and we'll have a jolly gang of lads around us."

"If you say so Sarge," Ernest muttered, crestfallen. "If you say so."

Later that evening, after they had eaten something that passed for a warm meal from their metal mess tins at the side of the road, the captain re-emerged and handed Ernest and Patterson both a blank form on which to record their "last will and testament". Ernest looked at it blankly. He was 22. He didn't have much to leave in a will, but he was more intrigued by the notion of leaving behind a "last testament". He examined the form. He noticed there wasn't actually a box for a "last testament".

"Just a turn of phrase," the captain grumbled, when Ernest posed the question.

He looked again at the form. It was very MoD. Army Form B243, it read. Touching, Ernest thought. "To be used by a solider desirous of leaving the whole of his estate and effects to one person". A place for his name and army number, a place for the name of his beneficiary, and a place to put the name of an executor. On the back, a box for a witness to sign.

Patterson lit a cigarette and wandered away along the road, folding his form into his pocket and muttering: "Going to stretch my legs." Ernest sat on a wall and looked at the form. "I suppose I would leave my 'entire estate' to my mother," he thought. Though, it consisted of little more than a few pounds, the pocket watch left to him by his father, and his best suit. The bulk of his army pay for these past two years had already been diverted to his mother to run the household alone, since the death of his father.

Ernest lit a cigarette and folding the form, placed it in his top pocket. The sky was edging towards that still moment of twilight as day passes into night. He looked out through his own cloud of smoke at the shape of Monte Cassino silhouetted against last rays of sunlight. The stars were already emerging directly above him and the Moon watched on unmoved by the scene.

Ernest was under no illusion. The hour was coming when he and Patterson would find themselves in enemy territory with nothing but a couple of rifles and a wooden oar with which to defend themselves. Would they reach the other side of the river and step ashore unopposed, as they had been promised? Or would they climb into that boat and attract a hail of bullets? They could be gone in moments – two corpses sprawled across each other, floating down stream in a silly little boat. Ernest tried hard to shake the image from his mind.

He looked up at the first of the stars glimmering overhead. It would only be a few hours before the sun started to re-emerge in the east and bring with it what could well be the last day of his life. The last day of life, he repeated to himself abstractly. He suddenly felt like a butterfly, crawling from its chrysalis, its time in the world measured by hours, not years.

His gaze followed the flight of an owl in the sky above his head, a black silhouette, coasting effortlessly towards the mountain that stood on the other side of the river. It struck him with a jolt that he might already have seen his last sunset. By tomorrow evening, he could be that corpse laying in the boat or a body hanging on a roll of German barbed wire halfway up that mountainside, he thought, before adding aloud: "Goodbye sunset."

Then he looked up at the rustling branches of the old spreading elm tree that stood alone on his side of the river. "Goodbye tree. Goodbye all trees." He took a final deep drag on the cigarette, and omitted a wisp of smoke into the air.

Preghiera's face suddenly glowed before him, as it had when they had been together beneath the plane tree beside her father's shop, charged with the electricity of their youth, fingers interlocking in each other's hands. Ernest put the thumb and index finger of his right hand to his face and rubbed wearily at his eyes. He took another long drag from the cigarette.

His mind went back to the dark-haired boy – no mortal remains to commit to a grave. He existed now only in his own head, Ernest told himself. And tomorrow, he may be vaporised from there too. He felt for the will document once again in his top pocket. The paper felt rough and a little ragged already. He pulled it out, and reached for his pen.

Driving his cigarette into the soil beneath his boot, he began to write. His name and army number. His mother's name as his beneficiary.

Ernest looked around and saw a young soldier smoking nervously nearby. "Hey Mac, do me a favour and witness my signature?"

"Sure," the soldier muttered, finishing his cigarette as he wandered over to Ernest.

With the form completed, Ernest folded it in half, and headed back to the yard where the captain had based himself. The officer was seated in the corner staring at the steam rising from his mug of tea. Ernest handed him the sheet of paper.

"My will, Captain," he added quietly. "My last testament, I suppose, will have to go unheard." The captain smiled, shark-like, and gave a funny little laugh as he took the form.

As he went to leave the yard, Ernest paused and turned back to add: "By the way Captain, I've left you a little something."

The officer's face went through a period of blankness, before his eyebrows raised in a kind of theatrical performance of shock. "Well, that's rather kind of you Green. But I'm not sure that's necessary."

"Yes, it is, I've left you the job of being the executor," Ernest laughed. "I believe it involves filling in a few forms yourself."

With a smile on his lips, Ernest stepped out towards the gathering darkness.

1963

The school was grey and drab – a grim breeze block construction, with grey tiles on the floor and grey paint around the door frames. Ernest sat at his desk, almost buried behind a stack of pupils' exercise books. He wrote 6/10 at the bottom of an essay, shook his head with genuine disappointment, closed the book and reached for the next.

He turned to the most recent page to find a note where the essay should have been: "Sorry Sir, I've not done the essay – the muse was not with me."

"Cheeky arsewipe," Ernest grumbled, drawing a large cross over the page with his Biro. "Detention Friday" he wrote tersely at the bottom and tossed the book on to the pile to his right, before reaching out to the pile on his left to take another exercise book in his hands.

Before he opened the book, his gaze turned out of the window at the muddy football match taking place outside. "I'm not sure I have the will to look at another half-done piece of homework," he thought to himself.

He lit a cigarette, drew deeply on it, and looked absent-mindedly into the cloud of blue smoke he had exhaled. He steeled himself and reached for the next book.

"*The Destruction of Pompeii*" the essay was entitled "by Lilian Grimshaw, Class 4C." This certainly sounded more promising.

"*The good folk of Ancient Pompeii had their lives hollowed out by the disappointment of it all,*" the essay began. "*In the same way that we look forward to Guy Fawkes' Night, they had been looking forward to the eruption of Mount Vesuvius for years. But as is so often the case with firework displays, the reality didn't meet expectations. The lava was limp. The ash was trash. The smoke was a joke.*"

Ernest took another long draw on the cigarette, and rubbed at his eyes with his thumb and forefinger. He continued to read:

"Disappointment can leave that awful hollow feeling in your stomach. You know the one Sir? But imagine the disappointment of being there for the big event of AD79 and being generally let down by the whole thing. So disappointed were they by the display, their very souls were left hollow and grey."

Ernest picked up his Biro and wrote on the bottom of the page. "This is not a history essay, but I think you may be a complete genius nevertheless Lilian. A philosopher and a poet. I am giving you 10/10 to avoid disappointment."

In the blink of an eye his mind was back in Torre Annunziata, with those olive eyes meeting his across the crumbling old square. He could hear her singsong voice ringing through his mind: *"Domani, domani, domani. How come it's always domani with you?"* He saw Preghiera's lips in an extreme close-up in his daydream, the edges swelling and sweeping into that softest of smiles.

He looked up at the clock on the wall. It was 5pm. He supposed it was time he should shuffle back home to his suburban existence. Marjorie will have cooked me something healthy, he thought, taking another lungful of cigarette smoke.

Ernest gazed back through the smoke, out at the dreary scene beyond the window. Disappointment can leave that awful hollow feeling, Lilian had written, and how right she was, Ernest mused. But a lifetime of disappointments, well that leaves us just like the victims of Pompeii – all hollow and grey.

Chapter ten
1944

Ernest's mother had the idea that she was a little bit psychic. But there was no sensation of unease, no hint in the back of her mind at the danger that her son was in so many miles from home as he had been writing his last will and testament, naming her as his single beneficiary.

This thought that she might be psychic was one of many little obsessions that had gathered force in her mind since the death of her husband. It had started with visits to a series of psychic mediums, in a desperate attempt to have one final conversation with the man she loved, despite his many failings. He hadn't spoken to her through any of these alleged mystics. That didn't come as much of a surprise, given that he had hardly spoken more than a few words to her in the last 15 years of their marriage. If he couldn't be bothered to lift his head from a book to pass the time of day with her while he was here on Earth with a pulse, it seemed a bit much to expect him to make the effort to engage with her from the afterlife.

But after careful consideration, she ended up blaming the mediums – a "bunch of charlatans" she eventually determined. She had more psychic powers than they did, she told herself – an assertion which swiftly evolved into a passionate belief. Each evening she would "psychically" convene with her two sons far from home – one in the army and one in the navy, neither even vaguely aware of the messages being beamed psychically to them across the oceans.

Church every Sunday was less a spiritual observance and more of a habit. But her Saturdays had fallen into such a regular pattern as to be bordering on the compulsive. She would always make her way to town, take a slow walk around the market, picking up a few bits and pieces, before visiting Boots' lending library to change her books. Then finally, the pinnacle of her weekend, she would head to the Savoy Cinema in Argyle Street.

Her husband had never agreed with picture houses as a rule, and particularly after the bombing of The Ritz in 1940, he had deemed them a danger to life and limb and she had been forbidden from attending in the last couple of years of his life. But once he was buried, she took the risk to her life and limbs on her own head, and headed straight to the Savoy. She had a romantic love for the grand, sweeping entrance lobby of the Savoy – though she did miss the organ that The Ritz had boasted. For some reason, they had never installed an organ at the Savoy.

She was such a regular on a Saturday morning – whatever the show – that the girls in the box office had got to know her by name.

"Morning Mrs Green, usual balcony ticket is it?"

"Oh yes my dear, thank you so much," she would bustle as she handed the coins beneath the little hole in the bottom of the box office window and the little stub of a ticket would be handed through to her.

"Any news on your boys Mrs G?" the box office girl would always ask.

"No news is good news my dear," would be the regular reply, as she grasped her ticket and headed for the carpeted staircase.

Then she would take her seat in the balcony, gathering her shopping basket close to her ankles in the darkness, and settling back to be transported away to the vasty fields of France, with Laurence Olivier cutting a swathe through the enemy at Agincourt, or swooning over a French pirate alongside Joan Fontaine in a 17th century Cornish creek. The films could take her away from her troubles in a moment. But first, there was always the Pathe news reel to get through – always keeping a careful look-out for a sight of Reginald's ship or Ernest's unit liberating Naples, her eyes rapidly sweeping the crowd of soldiers hunched around Montgomery as he perched atop an armoured car in some faraway Italian street.

More often than not, these newsreels gave her reassurance. With their chirpy commentary and smiles to the camera, she couldn't help but feel that things must be all right for her boys out there fighting the Nazis. They would be having quite the adventure, she would tell herself. While the adverts were on, she would close her eyes and send them each one of her special messages through the ether, wherever they might be.

1993

Ernie and Rachele left the glow of the ice cream parlour and made their way along the dimly lit back streets of the city. Rachele took his arm warmly, but Ernie's mind was elsewhere. The sights and smells of these crumbling streets took him straight back half a century. It was as if nothing had changed.

"So, you went off to battle and left poor Preghiera behind?" Rachele asked.

"You make it sound as if I had a choice."

"No, of course you didn't," she added. "I just mean, it must have been tough for Preghiera. It must have been tough for you both."

"Everything was tough in those days," Ernie shrugged. "The world was tough, you just had to get on with it."

"Did you miss her?"

Ernie paused in the glow of a streetlamp and turned to his companion.

"Are you serious? Of course I missed her," he laughed. "Morning, noon and night, she was all I ever thought about. I longed to be with her."

"But there must have been times when you just had to focus on surviving? In the battle I mean."

"There were," Ernie paused a moment to consider the question. "But even then – especially then – that's when you have to ask yourself what you're surviving for, you see? None of us were surviving to fight a miserable war. We were surviving so that we might live to see the peace. We were surviving to be once again with those we loved."

Rachele stopped walking for a moment. "But you didn't?" she said, turning to face the old man.

"Didn't what my dear?"

"You didn't get to see her again?"

"Oh, I did actually," Ernie nodded, leading Rachele to start walking forward again at a stroll. "But you're rather getting ahead of my story. There was a lot of water under the bridge by the time I next got to see Preghiera. And anyway, things became different."

"Different?" Rachele turned her head swiftly. "Different in what way?"

"Oh, my dear, different in all sorts of ways," Ernie said. "But listen, I don't want to stand here in the street talking about it. What time is it now? How about finding somewhere to get a nightcap?"

Rachele smiled. "You can certainly take your drink old man."

"Well, I would certainly hope so," Ernie chuckled. "I have had plenty of practice. Come on, I'll get you drinking Strega if it's the last thing I do."

Rachele laughed. "It's more likely to be the last thing I do! But come on, there's a nightclub down here."

"A nightclub?" Ernie sounded a little perturbed.

"Come on, you're never too old for a boogie Ernie." Rachele giggled as she led the way.

"Well, maybe just for that nightcap."

"Just for the nightcap," Rachele agreed.

1944

Ernest and Patterson were both fully kitted out, and were skulking at the side of a small boat, waiting for the moment to slip across the river.

"We appear to have been given a plywood boat Sarge," Ernest muttered, anger bubbling in his every word.

"It's not a plywood boat," Patterson said. "It is an FBE Mark III."

"Which is what?"

"Folding Boat Equipment," the sergeant said formally. "Folding Boat Equipment, Mark III."

"What's it made from?"

"Well, it is actually made from plywood, I'll grant you that," Patterson conceded. "But don't let that put you off. They're bloody brilliant things. Ingenious if you ask me. They completely fold up."

"I imagined they would somehow."

"Come on lad," Patterson enthused. "Don't have a downer on the boat before we've even got into it."

"I'm doing my best, thanks Sarge. You're not the one who has to row the blasted thing across. How the hell did you get caught up in this mess anyway?" Ernest whispered. "They chose me because I'd once done a bit of rowing, but what's your special skill?"

"I'd done a radio course back in Blighty," Patterson said, patting the rucksack that contained the radio. "I'm here to carry the Bergen with the radio and to cover you while you're rowing." He lifted up his rifle to emphasise this last point.

"I see Sarge." Silence descended upon the pair for a few moments. It was eventually broken by Patterson, with a little embarrassed cough.

"Also, I volunteered to do it because you're a good pal Green, and I knew I stitched you up a bit back there, cracking on to the captain about the rowing. I didn't think," Patterson added a little reluctantly.

"Apology accepted Sarge," Ernest added, patting Patterson on the top of his arm, as if his three stripes had been falling loose and needed reaffirming. "But you didn't need to get yourself killed just to say sorry."

"We'll be alright lad. We won't be killed. You're being melodramatic."

"I'm not sure," Ernest said. "The river looks pretty bloody wide here."

"That would be a good thing, wouldn't it?"

"How so?"

"It would mean we're less vulnerable when we're getting into the boat," Patterson reasoned. "That's the bit where we're most likely to get blown out of the water, if it's going to happen."

"Thanks for that Sarge," Ernest laughed. "You're nothing if not reassuring."

"That's what I'm here for lad," Patterson nodded, missing entirely the tone of sarcasm in Ernest's voice. "Anyway, it's not as wide as it looks."

"Do you reckon?"

"Yes, 60ft – that's what the captain said," Patterson nodded. "We'll be over there in no time. It's actually not very wide at all."

"But you just said it was wide?"

"No, I didn't lad," Patterson bristled. "I said it would be a good thing if it was wide, because that would lessen the chance of us being blown out of the water the moment we enter the boat."

"So, let me get this straight," Ernest hissed. "What you're actually saying Sarge is that the river isn't very wide at all, and there's a decent chance that we'll be blown out of the water as soon as we get into the boat."

"Well, I wouldn't phrase it quite like that, but yes I think that was the point I was making."

"Bloody hell Sarge, and that's you being reassuring?"

"We'll be fine lad," Patterson added, with another glance at his watch. "Come on, it's time to go and row, row, row your boat." He patted the young soldier on the shoulder. "Don't worry lad – I have every faith in you – what with all that time in the university rowing club and everything."

"Alright," Ernest nodded. "It's now or never, let's get this over with."

He slipped the boat into the water. It made the lightest splash in the night. Ernest deftly stepped inside, keeping his head lowered at all times. Patterson scanned the far bank through the sights of his rife.

"Come on Sarge, jump in will you?"

The older man's step was more precarious and the boat rocked alarmingly as he stepped inside.

"Watch out Sarge, you'll have us drowned before the Germans have a chance to shoot us."

"Don't worry, I'm in, I'm in lad – let's go!" The boat gradually eased its rocking. "Let's do this," Patterson added with whispered gusto.

With that, Ernest picked up the oars and began to row into the darkness, keeping the motion of the wooden oars gliding through the water as silently as he could manage. Ernest looked up to see the outline of a small dark-haired child standing on the pebbles at the side of the river from which they had just left. For a moment his heart seemed to skip a beat at the sight of the figure. But the boy just appeared to watch them closely as they glided out into the river. Ernest looked across to the opposite riverbank. It was still shrouded in darkness. By the time he glanced back in the direction from which they were moving, the boy had gone. There was no sign of anyone having been there. Ernest shook his head with a firm shudder, as if he was trying to shake his darkest emotions from his mind. Patterson glanced back at his companion for a moment, with a whispered "Easy lad," before training his rifle back towards the darkness of the opposite riverbank.

Just as the Captain had warned them, the darkness of the water betrayed a swift current, which immediately set the boat careering downriver far more dramatically than Ernest had anticipated. Patterson lay low in the bow, calmly focusing one eye through the sights of his weapon.

"No sign of any trouble," he whispered to Ernest. "Keep going lad. You're doing a grand job."

Ernest began to put more effort into each stroke, so keen was he to get swiftly across and on to dry land – even if that dry land was occupied by the Germans. The mountain loomed so powerfully over the scene, it was difficult not to think of it as a sentient being, quietly menacing the boat-bound soldiers from above. Ernest felt a cold sweat gathering across his brow. Just a few more strokes and they would be there.

In fact, the current had taken the boat so swiftly, they reached the opposite bank hundreds of yards from where Ernest had expected to moor. But he found a low-hanging tree branch, perfectly placed to give them some cover and provide a structure upon which to tether the makeshift vessel. Ernest held the boat steady while Patterson climbed off. He then turned around and offered a hand to Ernest, who shouldered his own rifle and clambered off the boat. With the slightest flick of his eyebrows, Patterson indicated a direction through the darkness before them. The two men slipped into the undergrowth unseen.

Ernest hadn't accounted for the sheer level of darkness that would greet them on this side of the river, and he slipped and tripped time after time, as he tried to follow Patterson through the dense thicket. A few times Patterson stopped abruptly in front of him, raising his right palm flat into the air as a signal for Ernest to stand still while he listened to the sounds of the undergrowth. Each time the sergeant reassured himself that there were no other footsteps patrolling the night and they moved on.

Every twig that snapped beneath Ernest's foot put the fear of God into him. He could feel his heart beating rapidly in his chest, but he followed Patterson as he gradually made his way up the heavily wooded slope. For the first 20 minutes, the two men saw no sign of occupation of any kind. But then, Patterson signalled a sudden stop, more abrupt than previous halts.

"Trip wire," he whispered, indicating an almost invisible line running between the trees in front of them. Patterson's hand flicked first one way along the wire, and then in the opposite direction. He caught Ernest's eyes glistening in the night. "Those bastard Jerries," the sergeant spat. "Watch yourself lad. You need to keep your eyes wide open."

The two men stepped gingerly over the wire, and moved on, more cautious than ever. Above them the stars were out, shining through the spaces between the branches. Ernest saw Preghiera's face appear so suddenly and so vividly in his mind's eye, he was almost startled. He felt a dull ache in his stomach, a sense that he would now never see her again.

He looked back at Patterson, who had stopped once again. He pointed down at the riverbank upstream from where they had left the boat. He could just make out the pepperpot outline of a concrete roof, covered over with broken branches. "Gun emplacement," Patterson said. "Do you suppose it's one of those nebelwerfer thingies? Looks like our boys aren't going to have it all their own way after all."

He turned back towards the darkness, as if to move on, but before he could take another step the night burst open with shots. Patterson crumpled like a wooden puppet with its strings cut. The great bulk of a man landed in a heap at Ernest's feet and the gun shots stopped as swiftly as they had begun. Ernest ducked down, wedging his own body between the mud and leaves of the slope and the warmth of Patterson's back. His rifle rested beside him where it had fallen unused.

Ernest lay still for a moment, but heard no further movement in the woods. He could hear his own breath panting and he tried to concentrate on stopping his own body betraying him. He took a long, deep breath, which he released slowly. After a while, he found the courage to lift himself up off the ground. Carefully scanning the slope ahead of him, he could see nobody. Had they fired from a distance? He turned Patterson over. A bullet had pierced his forehead leaving a perfectly circular black void where once there had been only wrinkles. Ernest fumbled momentarily with the body, before realising the Sergeant's helmet was holding what remained of the back of his skull in place. Patterson's body slipped through Ernest's bloodied hands and slumped back to the floor.

"You stupid bugger," Ernest muttered emotionally. "You should never have been here, you stupid, stupid, stupid …"

Ernest hit at the shoulders of the body with every repeat of the word stupid, before finally the breath caught in his throat and he could say no more. Ernest reached down to pick up his own rifle from the dirt, but as he did so a sharp click brought him to a standstill.

"Bewege dich nicht, du kleiner Scheißer," a hoarse voice hissed at him from the undergrowth.

Ernest slowly raised his head, lifting his hands into the air, palms out, as he did so. A middle-aged German officer was standing before him just a yard or two up the slope, the sleek black outline of a Walter P38 sidearm pointed down at him.

"Komm schon mein Freund, du kommst mit mir," the German said quietly, with a flicking motion of his pistol. Ernest couldn't understand a word he was saying, but he got the general gist. He took a step away from his own rifle.

Two other German soldiers of a lower rank appeared out of the woodland behind him, and began to pat him down. They found only his bayonet, which they removed and pocketed before pushing him forcefully up the slope towards their superior officer.

Ernest took one last look at the crumpled heap that had been Patterson, then was swiftly dragged away up the slope towards the great towering walls of the abbey.

1983

Ernie picked up the empty mug from his desk and closed the exercise book he had been marking. He put the book on to a pile and walked slowly from his classroom. Pupils skidded, tripped and swung around him like monkeys in a cage at the zoo. "No running in the corridor Peters." Ernie said this kind of thing on autopilot these days. It wasn't even a conscious remonstration any more. These words just emerged from him, although his brain had isolated itself away from these kinds of irritations. "Beanacre, the playground is the place to bounce your ball, not the corridor of the history department." Ernie rounded another corner and cut his way through the crowds of bubble-gum popping children.

A dark-haired boy was squatted against the wall, silently watching Ernie pass. Ernie refused to look down at the brown eyes he could feel watching him. He knew too well who it was and these days he chose to ignore him. He turned instead to a scruffy pig-tailed girl who was hovering around with her hands in her pockets on the other side of the corridor.

"Are those shoes school uniform Mandy Briggs?"

"I've got a verruca Sir," she called after him.

"I've got an in-growing toe nail, but it doesn't mean I wear sports training shoes to school Mandy," he shouted back without turning his head. "Regulation shoes tomorrow please my dear."

The staff room had its usual fetid air, with tobacco smoke hovering around eye level, creating an atmospheric mist in the room. The walls were yellowed with the decades of nicotine that had been breathed out by generations of despairing teachers before him. He reached into his pocket, and pulled out a packet of cigarettes. He lit one and sat down on a beige old sofa placing his empty mug on the coffee table. He watched the smoke glide up before his eyes as he exhaled.

Unexpectedly, Preghiera flashed into his mind. That smooth olive skin of her thighs. His hand running along it as she leaned against the old plane tree. Her breath on his ear as he kissed at her neck that arched supplely beneath her fine-cut jaw line. He heard the groan she made. The staff room door clicked open, and Ernie sat up swiftly and stubbed out his cigarette in the ash tray as if he had been caught doing something he shouldn't.

Pete Palmer, the gum-chewing, perpetually sweaty sports master ambled into the room swinging a whistle on a cord around his finger.

"Afternoon Ernie, hadn't you given up?"

"I give up every time I get to the end of a cigarette," Ernie said, reaching forward to pick up his mug before getting to his feet. "But then I wonder what I'm living for, if not for my nicotine kick."

Ernie gave the mug a cursory rinse in the sink and put the kettle on to boil.

"So, you've not given up the will to live just yet then?"

Ernie feigned a little laugh and put a teabag into his mug. "Funny you should say that, Pete. I was just wondering what I'm still doing here at my age."

"Come on Ernie, don't be daft, think of what all those kids would do if we sent them out into the world without an in-depth knowledge of Roman hypocausts," his colleague chuckled, tucking his flabby belly into the elasticated waist of his track suit as he spoke.

"Truth is, I'm getting on a bit," Ernie said as he poured the boiling water over his tea bag. "I'm only three years away from retirement as it is, and well to be honest, Marjorie is not too well these days."

"No?"

"Oh, it's nothing major," Ernie quickly added. "But she struggles by herself all day. We are neither of us getting any younger."

"Maybe you need to trade her in for a younger model, eh Ernie?"

Ernie pretended to smile as he reached around in the fridge for the bottle of milk. He lifted the little silver cap and gave the bottle a careful sniff before adding it to his tea.

"I'm thinking of bringing my retirement forward a little and finishing at the end of next term," he went on. "It'll give a younger teacher a chance to lead the department. There's a certain point where the history master has to confine himself to the history books, as it were."

"Well, I envy you Ernie," Palmer added. "If I could afford to retire, I'd pack it all in tomorrow. Or rather, I would have packed it all in yesterday. I'm sick of the little shits. Not one of them could kick a ball straight if their lives depended on it."

"It's a funny thing," Ernie went on as he stirred his tea. "I thought I would be excited by the prospect of retirement, but when you get to it, well it's just a bit gloomy. There's so much more behind you than there is in front of you."

"Nonsense," Palmer slapped him too firmly on the back. "There's plenty of life in the old dog yet."

Ernie shrugged and lifted his tea mug in a bittersweet toast: "Well, here's to happy endings Pete."

Chapter eleven
1993

The nightclub was remarkably empty, with just a few young men standing around the bar drinking beer straight from the bottle. A group of excitable young women sat around a table in the corner, somehow gossiping in spite of the music playing at decibels that prevented Ernie from hearing anything. The gaudy dancefloor itself stood empty and strangely hypnotic with its multitude of flashing lights.

"I'll get the drinks in," Rachele shouted into Ernie's ear.

"Oh, no my dear, please allow me!" Ernie bellowed back, but Rachele dismissed him with a double-handed wave.

"Go and grab a table as far from the speakers as you can get!" Rachele laughed, as she headed to the bar.

Ernie moved across the dancefloor towards the table in the far corner, self-consciously trying not to walk to the rhythm of the music, lest anybody think he was attempting to dance.

"What kind of a bloody old fool must I look like to these youngsters," Ernie said to himself out loud. He reached the table and settled into the chair with a groan. "I'm not used to late nights," he added to nobody in particular, removing his glasses a moment to give his eyes a rub. By the time he had replaced them, Rachele was seated across from him. She had placed a bottle of Strega and two shot glasses in the middle of the table.

"You've got an entire bottle?" Ernie shouted, incredulously.

"They've drawn a line on it," Rachele turned the bottle to show him. "We pay for what we drink."

"Bloody hell," Ernie mused to himself. "That would never work back home."

"What's that Ernie?" Rachele asked, struggling to make herself heard above the music.

"I say, they must trust us," Ernie laughed. "At the end of the night, I'll piss in the bottle and we'll get it for a song."

Rachele let out a loud bellow of laughter. "Is that what you would call double fermented?" she asked.

"That's right," Ernie beamed. "Something like that, my dear."

Ernie reached across and took the cork from the bottle. He lifted it to his nose and gave a long and theatrical sniff of the liquor.

"It sends me straight back," he said. "It's the queerest thing you know. Just one quick smell of that drink, and I'm straight back there or rather, back here, but back then."

"Yes, I know what you're trying to say," Rachele smiled.

"The years just go, you see. A lifetime seems like such a long time when you're young like you are my dear. But time speeds up the more you go on, so that one day you turn around and you're this ridiculous old man. You look silly whatever you do. I still feel the same – I still want to get up and dance on the dance floor, but it would be ludicrous, do you see? It's so cruel." He took another sniff of the bottle. "You get to realise that, I don't know, I suppose it's that all the happiness is behind you. All the big landmark moments of your life are suddenly behind you, long behind you. They exist now only in old Polaroids and when you get them out to look at them, you're shocked by how the fashions have changed. Did we really wear those flares? How did we put up with those sideburns? But what you should be shocked by is not the changing fashions – they come and go and come and go forever – no, what should shock you to the core is just how much you've changed yourself. Only you don't really see that in the pictures. You kid yourself you haven't changed. No, you only see that when you look in the mirror. That's when it's really shocking."

Rachele nodded sympathetically.

"It's a dreadful bugger my dear," Ernie's damp eyes smiled across the table, reflecting the flashing lights of the dance floor. "It's an absolute bugger getting old. It's like all your liberties are taken from you one by one."

Rachele smiled again and leaned forward to lay a hand on Ernie's hand. "That's all very well Ernie," she shouted over the music to make herself heard. "But when are you going to pour the drinks?"

Ernie laughed, and reached for Rachele's glass.

1944

Ernest sat on the stone floor of a small storeroom that stood off the monastery's main refectory. A great heavy oak door had been locked behind him. He was alone, surrounded by sacks of flour and a few barrels, which he imagined might be filled with wine. There was no window in the small space, and the only light was that coming from the gap beneath the door.

The silence was almost immediately broken by the sound of a heavy artillery bombardment coming from the direction of San Angelo. So, the Americans were going ahead with the attack, Ernest realised, despite Patterson's radio set laying unused in the Bergen still strapped to his corpse.

His thoughts were interrupted by the sound of a large key being turned in the wooden door. It creaked open and the same German who had taken him prisoner at pistol-point was standing in the doorway. He entered casually, followed by a monk who was carrying a bowl of soup and a servant who was dressed in the garb of a rural peasant rather than a monastic habit.

"I'm so sorry about the conditions in which we have had to house you," the German officer said, his accent surprisingly light. "Particularly the toilet situation," he added, with a nod towards an ancient chamber pot that had been placed in the far corner of the room. "As you will understand, we take our responsibilities to prisoners of war extremely seriously, and Brother Luca and his helper here will bring you food and water as you need it."

The monk nodded silently and put the soup down beside Ernest before leaving the room. The officer ran his fingers through his heavily greased hair, taking great care to ensure every strand was laying flat against his head.

"As soon as possible you will be moved to more suitable accommodation," he added with the flicker of a smile. "What was it Napoleon said? 'The first quality of a solider is fortitude in enduring fatigue and hardship: bravery but the second'.

Ernest nodded, slightly taken aback by the polish of the German's pristine politeness as well as his exacting knowledge of European history.

"That's right, I've heard that before," Ernest said. "Poverty, hardship, misery are the school of the good soldier. It's funny how officers always quote Napoleon. Some sort of complex I presume."

"You are a psychoanalyst, perhaps?" the officer flashed a smile.

"I just think all officers would secretly like to be an emperor deep down," Ernest grinned.

The German nodded with a sudden stiff movement, and turned to leave, but paused and turned back.

"You British and your American and French friends are ambitious too, yes?"

Ernest gazed at him in the darkness.

"You honestly believe taking Monte Cassino will be possible? Let me tell you, it will not be possible. That is why we are here. Your friends will be cut down and pushed back. They can send as many as they want to try to take the mountain, but from up here we can just keeping knocking them back like, how you say, skittles?" The German gave an abrupt little shake of the head, unleashing a few more strands of hair, which had to be quickly slicked back down with his palm. "But come now," he added, "that is no longer your concern my friend."

Without another word, he left the room and the darkness closed in on Ernest once more. The hours passed slowly at first and then after a while, time seemed to speed up for him in that place. The days began to merge together. It became increasingly difficult to tell night from day. The only way of keeping any kind of track of the passing of time, was the occasional arrival of Brother Luca with another bowl of soup and jug of water. He would place the food down silently, and then replace the porcelain privy with a clean one before leaving. He hardly ever spoke.

"You do the Germans' work?" Ernest asked the young monk and the peasant servant one day.

The monk stopped in his chores and turned to Ernest with a sombre frown. The servant seemed to completely ignore his intervention and continued with his work.

"We do the Lord's work," the monk said, before turning back to what he was doing.

"Your friend doesn't say much," Ernest muttered by way of response. The monk glanced over at the peasant. "He is deaf and mute. The abbot took him in a long time ago. The world outside was a cruel place for one so afflicted."

"The world is a cruel place for all of us, if you ask me," Ernest grumbled.

The monk smiled. "We all have our cross to bear my friend," he whispered.

"Some of us more than others I reckon."

The days passed slowly in this strange excuse for a prison. A few times a day Ernest would pass half a dozen words with the brother delivering his food, and carrying away whatever slops Ernest's tangled digestive system had managed.

After what Ernest judged to be about 10 days, he was moved to a space deep beneath the abbey. The officers called it the monks' refuge, but it struck Ernest that this was not an entirely manmade basement, but a natural structure, a cave-like room, carved into the bedrock itself. It was crowded with German soldiers and a few remaining monks, including a benevolent-looking old man whom Ernest took to be the abbot.

He overhead snippets of conversation between the German officer and the abbot in broken Italian. He picked up just enough to understand that the officer was telling the abbot that he was to sign a document stating that the German soldiers were no longer present. It was, it seemed an attempt to forge a truce with the allies to allow the monks and civilians at the monastery safe passage away from the battle. The abbot seemed uncertain about the path he should take – not least, presumably given the clear fact that the place was still peppered with German troops. Ernest was an almost forgotten onlooker to the drama as it unfolded.

The sound of the bombardment grew louder and louder by the day. By the middle of February, the more visceral sounds of battle on the slopes below echoed around the caves. From his makeshift prison cell in the far corner of the room, Ernest became gradually aware of a rising tension among the Germans. A stout little officer appeared to vent his frustration on a telephone set when it became clear that its wires had been cut. A young German soldier – a sergeant, Ernest noticed – was sent outside to investigate. Even to Ernest, it was clear that the young German had immediately been met by the barrel of an American gun. Ernest listened carefully, and could make out a broad Texan drawl echoing down into the cavern.

"Tell 'em all to get out of the cave with their hands up, or these grenades will be going in after 'em," the voice said confidently. "And the grenades are more persuasive in their argument than I could ever be. Got that soldier?"

The young sergeant returned into the cave and sheepishly relayed the gist of the message to an officer. There was an extended discussion in quick, staccato German among the officers, which Ernest couldn't follow at all. But then, remarkably suddenly, the officer who had initially captured Ernest, gave the order to surrender. Carefully running his palms over his head to flatten down his hair before placing his cap on his head as he gave out his orders. The monks left the cave first, accompanied by the deaf-mute servant, followed by two dozen German soldiers and officers, all with their hands in the air.

With the cave almost empty, the German officer approached Ernest and unshackled him.

"Congratulations my friend," he muttered in his crisp English, as he removed his side arm and placed it on the floor. "It looks as though you will get to fight another day after all."

He looked at Ernest with an almost embarrassed grimace.

"Look I really am terribly sorry that you've been kept in these conditions for so very long," he said. "It's really not 'the form' as you British might say. Not the form at all." He eyed Ernest for one final time. "And this my friend, is how quickly the tables turn in times of war."

He kicked the pistol across the floor to Ernest. He nodded formally and turned away. The German stepped out towards the light of the entrance, raising his hands in the air as he went.

Ernest paused a moment, and got to his feet. He gingerly picked up the pistol, casting a glance across the space to ensure nobody was watching him. He brushed himself down, and was just about to start moving towards the exit himself, when he heard the distinctive clinking sound of metal rolling across stone. A grenade had been lobbed into the cave. Ernest threw himself down on the ground and rolled as far into the corner as he could manage, dropping the pistol to the floor and forcing his body behind a rocky crevice just at the moment of the blast.

Of the blast itself, he knew nothing. There was no way of knowing how long he lay unconscious deep in the recesses of the cave, but the dust was still heavy on the air when he opened his eyes. He could still see the light from the entrance, though now the entrance appeared to be a fragment of its former size – there had clearly been a significant collapse of rubble around the mouth of the cave. Ernest's hearing had not yet returned, and he was haunted by a high-pitched buzzing in his ears as his auditory nerve gradually crackled back to life.

Ernest lay back against the rock and breathed deeply. At the sight of movement from the corner of his eye, he felt his whole body jump into life. Turning his head, he could just make out the figure of a small, dark-haired child walking towards him through the darkness. The child held out his tiny hand, and pointed frantically towards the light of the exit.

"I'm going, I'm going," Ernest said as he got to his feet and began to half run, half stumble through the remains of the space. When he reached the exit, he turned instinctively to help the child to clamber over the rocks. But the child had gone and Ernest was left gazing into the yawning mouth of the deserted cave. There, close to where he was standing, a body was splayed out, its arm outstretched, and its face twisted as if still in the throes of death. It looked to Ernest just like the ancient ashen plaster casts he had seen down at Pompeii. But this man was freshly dead, the blood still wet around the splinter wounds in his neck where the shards of rock had erupted from the hillside in the blast of the grenade.

Ernest walked towards the body and as he drew closer realised it was the deaf-mute servant. So busy and bustling in life, he appeared frozen now in a theatrical tableau, caught in the moment of horror at his own demise, just like his forefathers on the slopes of Vesuvius millennia before. Ernest kneeled a moment and gently closed the lids of the man's vacant eyes. "The world is a cruel place for one so afflicted," he repeated the young monk's words back to the servant, in the hope that now he might finally hear them.

Ernest wiped his hands together and turned back to the outside world, expecting to see the Americans, but the whole hillside had cleared. How long had he been out cold? He slipped down from the rubble and cast his gaze around him. He held his hands to his temples as he tried to get his thoughts straight. Then it came, the distinctive deep groan of B-25 bombers – a formation rumbled across the azure sky high above. He had time to count a dozen aircraft, with the outlines of B-17s and B-26s among the formation, before the bombs started to fall with all the streamlined grace of diving seabirds. They impacted in a hellish chaos of explosions across the whole of the mountain.

Ernest scrambled back into the cave, just in time to see a cluster of bombs find their target up on the peak, and the walls of the abbey itself appeared to crumble. He rolled back behind the rocks and took cover in the deepest recesses of the cave. The noise above was elemental – a cacophony that surpassed all comprehension. Surely there could be no mountain left? He felt his body shivering uncontrollably, as he curled up, foetus-like, deep in the heart of the mountain, while wave after wave of bomber released their deadly roars overhead.

After what felt to Ernest like an eternity, the blasts and rumbles died to a dusty silence. He waited a few more minutes in the darkness, uncertain when to emerge – or indeed if he would be able to emerge. But when he found the entrance, some light still shone through from outside. Stepping out, it became immediately clear that there was still a mountain to walk on, though now it was crowned not with the mighty sheer walls of the ancient abbey, but a pile of smouldering rubble.

He ran instinctively up towards the damage, when everything in his brain cried out to run away, down the hill, back towards the river. But his legs argued otherwise and he found himself drawn up and up towards the awesome pinnacle of the destruction. What had been the cathedral at the centre of the site was now a shell. Ernest clambered over piles of debris, until he found himself amid the remains of what must have been a series of cloisters. A statue that Ernest presumed to represent Saint Benedict stood now without arms, like a classical Roman artefact, peeking-out from the wreckage, torso-deep in dust and rubble. And there, to Ernest's utter amazement, rising out of the ashes, was one of the secondary chapels used by the monks for their devotions, apparently untouched by the bombs, unlike the nearby cathedral itself. The crumbling edifice rose in a series of archways out of the devastation like an architectural parable that Ernest couldn't quite understand.

He understood nothing of the world around him anymore, except this sense of being drawn to walk forward, to walk on towards these remnants of beauty amid the destruction. Ernest moved through the still noticeably ornate archway, and peered inside as if he was seeing a sacred place for the first time in his life.

The altar was still perceivable amid the rising plumes of smoke and ash, and a wooden crucifix hung precariously from the wall, the benevolent eyes of Christ unflinching amid the devastation gazed down at him. There, amid the crumbling ruins, two monks were on their knees side by side, heads bowed in prayer, arms clasped around each other as if in a rugby scrum. Their bodies were shaking violently beneath the dark swathes of their Benedictine habits, but from the synchronised movement of their lips, Ernest could tell that the prayers had continued throughout.

Ernest slumped to the floor. He could hardly believe his eyes. For the first time through these weeks of trauma piled upon trauma, he felt tears flow down his cheeks. "My God," he whispered, casting his eyes up towards the wooden Christ. "Oh My God, how can we still be here? How can this be possible?"

But the God of the crumbling chapel provided no answer to his questions. After a moment, Ernest allowed his eyes to close. He knew then that the silence would be enough for him.

1986

Marjorie stood on the path through the woodland and looked up. Trees stretched above her with all the perpendicular glory of a cathedral. A green canopy that enveloped and calmed her with its gently glowing tranquillity. She was alone with the oak and ash, the sycamore and the horse chestnut. The hawthorn, the hazel and the holly filled out the lower levels, and occasionally stretches of woodland were spliced with the sparse white trunks of silver birch, which formed up on their own parade grounds deep within the woods.

This was her place to unwind, to loosen her anxieties and bring herself back to a sense of calm. The anxieties had grown in recent years. The persistent, aching background uneasiness was now back at the sort of levels she reached after losing the baby all those years before. Other pregnancies had come and gone within weeks. More disappointments. More grief. She felt her inability to hold on to a child had brought a growing sense of weariness to her husband. The disillusionment had built up on him like layers of paint. It covered his face so thickly now, it was as though he wore a mask.

As her anxieties grew, so too did the desire to withdraw from the world. The logical side of her brain told her that friendships would help her cope. But the darker side reminded her that she would be safer alone. Her social nervousness had even grown to avoiding her husband as much as she could.

Ernest often looked unhappy. She would catch a sight of him reading his newspaper, when he didn't know she was lurking beside the open door. But he wasn't reading his newspaper. She could see that his eyes were gazing straight through it – working through his memories.

Ernest's wartime experiences were something he simply didn't talk about. By the time Marjorie met him, he had been keen to "put all that behind him". But sometimes she wondered what he had lived through – what it was he didn't talk about.

But they had been happy, Marjorie told herself, looking up again at the trees, following the skittish path of a grey squirrel moving precariously from branch to branch. They had been happy for the most part. Hadn't they?

Age had wearied them. It had certainly troubled Marjorie in recent months. The aches and pains had become so various, she no longer bothered visiting the doctor. She had discovered that GPs didn't like it if you listed your ailments. They worked only in isolation – one complaint per visit. Or else the complaint they labelled you with was hypochondria.

But it wasn't so much the physical ailments that troubled her these days. It was the forgetfulness. The absences. Her mind wandered terribly. Right now, for instance, she had been looking at these trees far longer than she had intended, standing gazing upwards for 40 minutes or more. The time was lost on her. It was as if she could become confused by the passing of time itself, with minutes sometimes feeling like hours, while whole hours could pass her by in what to her had only seemed a moment or two.

It would be the same old story when she got home. "Where the hell have you been?" Ernest would grumble. "I thought you were going for a 'stroll through the woods'? How long can it take to walk half a mile?" But she never had the answer. She had no sense of having been away so long. It was as if time was playing tricks on her.

The sound of distant footsteps crunching on leaves brought Marjorie back to her senses. She looked ahead and behind her along the path. In the far distance, where the path turned, a black Labrador came bounding along, before turning its a head a moment, its tongue lolling out to one side, and excitedly retracing its own steps in a fruitless attempt to hurry its owner along. Eventually a lady in a Barbour wax jacket followed around the corner swinging a leather dog lead in her hand.

What was it about dog walkers that made you feel as if you shouldn't be there as a solitary walker, without a dog? Marjorie felt self-conscious. It was as if they had cornered the market for country walks and frowned at you suspiciously if you should be out walking without a dog dancing around your ankles.

Marjorie turned and walked on, in the opposite direction from the dog and its owner. She had always been more of a cat person. She liked their spirit of independence, their disdain for humankind. We were clearly there only to service their demands for food. There was no real love lost. The mock affection at feeding time, the rubbing of the little furry head against your ankles, didn't fool anybody. They were their own boss. The moment they evolved the ability to use a can opener, the relationship would be over. It's not you, it's me, they would purr. None of the emotional neediness of a dog.

She heard the Labrador behind her woof mindlessly with an instinctive joy at being out and about in the woods. She wished she could raise her voice like that and express the joy of being in this place.

Ernest had bought her a cat, back in the Sixties, when it was clear that there would be no children. Perhaps he thought it would fill a gap, soothe a redundant maternal instinct. But it was run over by the number 49 bus. The conductress, Annie Barker, whom Marjorie knew from the Women's Institute meetings, came and knocked on her door ashen-faced and apologetic. "It's Jessie," she said. "He ran straight out."

Marjorie had dashed around the corner to the street to find a flattened Jessie, suddenly two-dimensional on the asphalt, with a few unidentifiable organs and innards emptied alongside. The driver gave her a sympathetic shrug. "Sorry love. He ran straight out."

Annie said she would stop and help if she could, but passengers were waiting and "well, you know how it is Marj." She pinged the bell from the back step, and called back: "I'm so sorry Marj. I'm sorry about the cat."

Marjorie had rushed back to the garden shed to fetch a spade with which to peel Jessie back up off the road. It had been irrational – this sudden desire to recover the body, or what was left of it, back to her own garden. It was partly that she didn't want another car to run over it. Partly, it was a kind of a shame – hiding this little personal catastrophe away from the prying eyes of the neighbours, which would no doubt be peeking through the net curtains from all sides.

She used the spade to scrape at the tarmac and prise the corpse up from it as best she could manage. It was a little like lifting a piece of frozen fish from a baking tray with a spatula halfway through cooking, and being unable to prevent strips of the batter from sticking to the tray and remaining welded on and immovable. Bits of the cat seemed to be permanently stuck to the surface of the road. She scraped and scratched as much as she could manage with the spade, before lifting the remains into a cardboard box. She didn't want another cat after that.

It was funny how she could recall these things from years ago, but could walk to the corner shop and not remember what she had gone there for by the time she had arrived. She would often pass the spot on the road, still slightly discoloured, where the cat had met its match in the shape of that double decker bus all those years ago and she would pause to remember Jessie. It felt like just a moment ago that Annie had stopped to bang on her door, all angst-ridden and flushed in the face. Funny thing, growing old, Marjorie mused to herself, and hurried on along the path towards the gate at the end.

Chapter twelve
1993

Ernie's brain was swaying a little and coupled with the thumping music and the flashing lights, it felt more like an epileptic fit than a night out. He reached for the bottle of Strega and removed the cork once more.

"Can I offer you another my dear?"

"Well, it would be rude to say no, I think, wouldn't it?" Rachele slurred.

"It would indeed," Ernie enthused, as he poured the liquor into the shot glasses. He put the bottle back down and returned the cork, before licking his forefinger and covertly wiping away the line on the side of the bottle.

He reached into his jacket pocket and pulled out a Sharpie. He then drew a new line, roughly where the measure now stood, halfway down the bottle.

"You see, my dear," Ernie grinned. "It's not necessary to take the piss with these things. There are cleverer ways in which you can get a free drink."

Both old man and young woman giggled like naughty schoolchildren, casting glances over their shoulders in opposite directions, to check that they were not being watched. Far from it, they now appeared to have the entire nightclub to themselves. A solitary barman was polishing glasses behind the bar, but his attention was elsewhere.

"It's been a genuine, how you say, a revelation," Rachele announced. "Is that the right word Ernie?"

"I would say so my dear," he muttered, taking another shot of Strega down in one. "Here's to old times."

"Old times!" Rachele concurred, slipping her glass back deftly.

"To old times and lost loves."

"Lost loves," Rachele lifted her now empty glass in melancholy solidarity. Ernie reached over with the bottle to refill it.

"To old times and lost loves and happy endings."

"Happy endings." Rachele echoed and she downed another glassful of the liquor.

There was a moment of stillness between them, as the dewy-eyed old man gazed at the half-empty bottle of Strega, with the hint of a fond smile playing on his lips. His thoughts were far away, or rather long ago.

"Ernie?" Rachele whispered gently.

"Yes, my dear?"

"Could I possibly have the honour of the next dance?" the young woman's smile emerged across the table in a pristine flash of white teeth.

"My dear, shouldn't that be my line?"

"Oh," Rachele demurred. "But I rather think the honour would be all mine."

Ernie held out a wrinkled old hand across the table.

"Well, that is where you are wrong my dear," the elderly man smiled. "For the honour is mine entirely."

1944

Ernest walked slowly out of the chapel and gingerly climbed over the rubble that now stretched across the peak of the mountain, where until moments before a great abbey had stood. The crumbled fragments of rock and scree that now surrounded the chapel slipped and skidded beneath his feet. He fell into the dust, and got himself upright, before slipping and falling again within moments.

This time though he heard a crack from his ankle as it twisted over and immediately a pain like electricity shocked through his leg.

"Jesus Christ," Ernest spat. "I've survived the biggest shitshow that a squadron of B-25s can throw at me, and then I break my fucking ankle crossing the god-damn fucking rubble." He slapped the ground beside him and made a series of pained groans.

He pulled himself up, and felt the pain shoot up from his ankle with every movement. He cursed gloriously across the ruins of the medieval rubble.

"Fuck it, fuck it, fuck it," he chirruped, while hopping down across the wreckage, his afflicted foot poised back precariously, as he fell and stumbled down the side of the scree. At last, with a cold sweat mounting on his forehead, he found himself at the other side of what was the abbey, and saw for the first time the view to the north. He kept moving towards a path, which seemed to be leading down away from the battle, albeit in the opposite direction from his own army, which was now fighting its way up the hill behind him.

At that moment he became aware of a figure ambling around the path before him carrying a large net on a stick. Though in the uniform of a German officer, the individual seemed to be without his jacket, and was walking around in a sort of stunned state. Ernest watched him in bewilderment – he hadn't imagined for a moment that any Germans might have survived the bombings of the previous hour.

A moment later the individual turned and looked straight at him. With a funny little wave, as if he recognised Ernest, he walked up the slope towards him. Ernest thought about running, but then remembered his beleaguered ankle.

The German held up his net, and by way of explanation said in perfect English: "Forgive me, I am a professor of entomology in civilian life. I was looking for butterflies when the bombers arrived."

Ernest nodded. "You're lucky to have survived."

"I hid down there in the copse," the German indicated towards a cluster of trees nearby. "It was quite something to see." He looked Ernest up and down. "Are you somewhat ahead of your compatriots or were you a Prisoner of War until the bombs fell?"

He reached into his pocket and produced a silver cigarette case. Opening the clasp, he offered it to Ernest, who picked one out nervously."

"The latter," Ernest said, also accepting the offer of a light.

"Yes, yes, I think I have seen you around," the officer nodded. "And now, I suppose it is for me to become the prisoner. If you could, perhaps, put a word in for me when your compatriots arrive?"

Ernest nodded. "I'll do what I can."

"Thank you, that is very kind." The German looked over at the gargantuan pile of rubble that stood between them and the battle that raged below. "At least," the officer mused, "at least things seem to be happening now. For so long nothing was happening at all."

Ernest nodded.

"This was inevitable, of course, sooner or later. But it won't be here in Italy that we shall be beaten of course," the German shrugged. "We shall hold you here, well not exactly here perhaps, but in Italy at least. We will hold you for a quite a while."

He turned again to the ruins of the monastery. "Though I suppose you have Rome now, once Cassino is in your hands, you will take Rome in weeks, perhaps less. Do you agree?"

Ernest nodded. "I suppose so." He sat down on a rock, carefully keeping his ankle away from the manoeuvre.

"You are injured, I see?" the German said, taking a long draw on his cigarette and blowing the cloud of smoke high into the air, his head tilted far back as he exhaled. "Poor you. Well, perhaps you will miss the battle for Rome in that case. A broken ankle should buy you a few quiet weeks of reading in a comfortable hospital bed. Lucky you." He flashed a smile.

Ernest winced as he attempted to settle his stricken foot on the ground. The German sat down beside him.

"Quite right," the officer said. "Let's stay here and wait for your friends to come to us. Of course, if you're happy to take the advice of your enemy, you would be best to winter here in the mountains. Not you personally you understand, your army I mean. The going will only get tougher in the next month or two. It would make sense to me for you to hold Cassino, and regroup here. That at least," he added a little sadly, "is what we had hoped to be able to do."

The sound of the battle was coming nearer all the time, with gun fire now within half a mile, Ernest reasoned.

"You know, if you like, we could walk back towards the Allied lines," Ernest said after a while. "If they see you helping an injured British solider back down the hill, it can only play in your favour."

The German thought about it for two more draws from his cigarette.

"I think you are right," he nodded after a while. "You my friend," he pointed at Ernest with his cigarette, "you're a smart young man. Come, let's get moving." The German sprung to his feet, and abandoning his butterfly net on the rocks, he put an arm around Ernest's back, and lifted him on to his one healthy foot.

"Okay soldier?" the German asked.

Ernest nodded through gritted teeth.

"Very good then, let's go."

The pair hobbled slowly back across the top of the mountain, towards the rumble and crackle of the battle below.

1988

Marjorie watched the dust particles dancing across the shafts of light that cut their way through the gap where the curtains didn't quite meet. She felt the pillow beneath her head and the soft duvet laying over her, nestled in either side of her body so she felt cocooned. This was her own bedroom. She knew that much. At least, she felt as if it was her own bedroom, but something was different.

The man – the man who read the newspaper each morning. He wasn't around so much. Her brother. No, what was she thinking, her husband. Yes, he was her husband, she realised. But his name wouldn't quite come. "It will come back to me in a minute," she told herself. Marjorie knew her memory played tricks on her these days. This was her bedroom, but she wasn't in her own home. She sensed she was somewhere else. On holiday perhaps? Yes, that must be it. The man, her brother, he had brought her away on a holiday. He was kind like that, her brother. "Oh, it nearly came to me then," she whispered. "Eric?" she tried the name aloud. "It might be Eric. Edward? I'm sure it begins with an E. It will come to me in a moment." She knew she was always like this in the morning. She would often complain about her memory to her brother when he was reading the newspaper. Not brother, husband. Yes that's it, husband.

Marjorie looked again at the shaft of light and tried to catch a glimpse through the gap in the curtains for a clue as to where they were on holiday. She would feel so silly if she had to ask her brother where she was. It made her feel such a fool, this condition, this problem with her memory. Where was he anyway? Must be having breakfast with mum and dad, she thought. Well, she wasn't going to get up just yet, she was going to lay here and enjoy this soft pillow and this warm duvet. They were on holiday in Cornwall. That was it. Yes, she could hear the seagulls. She was back in the guest house in Padstow. That was it. Oh, they did make a wonderful breakfast here. No wonder her brother was taking so long over it.

Marjorie heard a rattling sound from the door handle, and the next moment the door was being opened. She could make out the shape of a man, pushing the door with his back, while pulling a trolley. It must be her brother, her husband Ernie. That was it, Ernie, of course. Her husband.

"Hello my love, how was breakfast?" Marjorie called across to the figure.

"My breakfast was fine, thank you Marjie." But she didn't know that voice or that face. He was dressed like a nurse. Who was this, what was he doing in her bedroom?

"Who are you?" Marjorie shouted. "I'm going to call for my dad. My dad is just downstairs. Get out! Get out of my room! Dad! Dad! There's a man in my room!"

"Calm down Marjie love," the man said, as he started reaching for bottles from the trolley and measuring out pills into a little plastic container while ticking them off a list on a clipboard. "Time for your pills sweetheart."

"Get out of my room! My brother's just next door. He'll be here any moment."

Another person arrived, a woman, who also appeared to be dressed as a nurse.

"You can't come in here and start making my bed now," Marjorie cried. "I'm still laying in it. What kind of a guest house is this anyway? You can do my room when I go for breakfast. Who is this man?"

The man handed the clipboard across to the woman, who double checked the pills in the pot, and signed the document, before clipping it back on to the edge of the trolley.

"Don't worry Marjie," the woman called across. "You'll feel a bit better after your pills."

"I would feel fine now, if it wasn't for people barging into my room when I'm trying to enjoy my holiday. This is my holiday, you know? And will you both please stop calling me Marjie. How dare you call me Marjie? I shall be telling my dad about you two. Perhaps we won't be booking this guest house again."

The man failed to disguise a little laugh. "Alright Marjie, you calm down love. Now here's your tablets."

"My husband is called Ernie," Marjorie said, taking the glass of water from the man and dutifully taking each of the tablets in turn. "I'm not soft. I know my husband is called Ernie. He reads the newspaper at this time of the morning. He'll be downstairs reading the newspaper. We're on holiday here. It is such a lovely place."

"That's right my lovely, that's right."

The man followed the woman back out of the room, pushing the trolley and quietly whistling a jolly little tune. Marjorie heard the door bang shut behind him and she was left alone again. She looked back at the shaft of light cutting through the curtains, which caught the dust particles as they moved slowly through the air above her.

She sat up in the bed and idly ran her fingers through her hair.

"My brother must have gone down for breakfast with mum and dad," Marjorie said to herself. "They make such a lovely breakfast here."

Chapter thirteen
1993

Ernie and Rachele led each other to the dance floor. To Ernie's relief, the thumping dance music had long since finished and the DJ was working his way through a collection of slow pop ballads. The young girl leaned on the old man's shoulder, as they swayed gently across the empty dance floor.

"This takes me back," Ernie smiled, before adding, with a chuckle at the contradiction: "Do you know, I can't remember the last time I was on a dance floor. It's been decades I suppose."

"You can certainly move," Rachele beamed.

"Oh, I could strut my stuff in my day alright," Ernie laughed. "These days I'm doing well if I can shuffle to the kitchen to put the kettle on."

"Don't put yourself down," Rachele gave him a playful pat on the arm. "You've got some years in you yet and who knows, maybe you're at the start of a whole new stage of your life."

"The end stage?" Ernie grinned.

"No!" Rachele shrieked in frustration. "You know what I mean – the sort of new glory days."

Ernie pondered the idea.

"New glory days. Do you know, I quite like the sound of that. Maybe you're right," he nodded thoughtfully. "I do hope you're right. The new glory days."

"Are you nervous?"

"About dancing?"

"No," Rachele laughed again. "About tomorrow. Seeing Preghiera again after all these years. It's going to be strange for you both."

Ernie smiled. "You know my dear, the funny thing is, in some ways it feels like I never left her. She's always been close by somehow. She's always been here." He gently tapped his chest in rough estimation towards his heart.

"Oh, that's so nice," Rachele said. "But Ernie, why have you waited so long?"

Ernie looked down at Rachele's knotted frown and her imploring brown eyes, uncertain how to respond.

"What do you mean, my dear?"

"I mean how can Preghiera trust you? How can she know you won't just disappear from her life for a second time?"

Ernie looked puzzled and paused his dancing.

"Think of it from her perspective," Rachele went on, growing increasingly passionate. "You were there one moment, star-struck and head over heels in love. One quick screw behind a plane tree and then she doesn't see you again for what, weeks, months? Don't forget Ernie – she's not seen you for decades. How can she trust you? She wouldn't even recognise you in the street anymore."

Ernie shrugged, a look of sadness swept across his face, and he shuffled back towards the table in the corner, where he put his jacket back on and swiftly finished up his drink. Rachele approached him apologetically.

"I'm sorry Ernie, I shouldn't have spoken like that."

"No, that's quite alright my dear," Ernie said. "It's getting late. I think we're both a bit tired. Let's get back to the hotel."

Rachele picked up her handbag and took Ernie by the arm.

"Well, I am sorry if I upset you," she muttered.

"You see, it just wasn't like that," Ernie went on. "That's what I've been trying to tell you. Your life wasn't your own during the war. You had no control over anything, and then of course, by the time I got back..." his sentence tailed-off mid-flow.

"Yes?" Rachele tried to encourage him on. But Ernie just shrugged.

"Oh well, never mind," he laughed sadly. "It's all so long ago now. So very long ago. Let's not get ourselves upset over things that happened half a century ago. What would be the point? We should look to the future. Come on my dear, to the hotel."

"To the hotel and the future Ernie," Rachele smiled as they headed for the exit. "And thank you so much for this evening."

"It was my pleasure entirely my dear," Ernie said. "You've no idea how much fun I've had. I feel a good ten years younger. Though by the morning I will probably feel a good twenty years older. But it's a funny thing. It has been a very happy evening. Sometimes, you know, to get to keep happiness, you have to pin it down."

1944

Ernest rested on a rock, gingerly trying to find a comfortable position for his injured ankle.

"So, what do you get from catching butterflies?" he asked the German officer.

The German shrugged as if he had never thought about the purpose of his hobby before.

"It allows me to keep them, to capture beauty, to pin it down so you can retain it forever," he mused. "Otherwise, the beauty of the butterfly is so fleeting. It flutters past you one moment, the next it is gone. It might never have been. You have to catch it, keep it close."

Ernest stared at him blankly.

"I can see my friend that you do not understand."

"No, I'm not sure I do. Put a pin in a butterfly and you've killed it, how is that maintaining beauty?"

The German went silent awhile, before attempting to answer. "I've never thought of it like that before. You know, the butterfly would die anyway, with or without my pin. Why shouldn't I possess it for my own satisfaction?"

"I suppose," Ernest said quietly, "because the world isn't there to satisfy our whims as individuals."

"Or perhaps it is?" The German grinned warmly.

Ernest returned his long hard stare while he considered his response, but before he could speak again, he heard the sound of boots treading up through the scrubland and the bellows of American GIs shouting to each other. He looked up and a middle-aged American Colonel was walking brisky towards them, chewing on a cigar, the distinctive outline of a Colt M1911 in his right hand.

He walked up to the German and fired a single question at him. "Deutsch?"

"Yes," the officer said, raising his hands carefully. But before they were even fully raised, without a moment's hesitation, the American pulled the trigger. Ernest watched in dumbstruck horror as the rear half of the German's head appeared to explode, releasing all the butterflies he had ever possessed back into the crisp Lazian afternoon.

The American turned the barrel of the gun towards Ernest. "Deutsch?" he asked, his finger poised to acknowledge their differences without delay.

"No, no, no, fuck," Ernest screamed. "British! I'm fucking British!"

The American lifted the barrel of the gun a little skyward, without lowering the pistol altogether.

"What is a googly?" The American demanded.

"What?" Ernest sounded bemused.

The American turned the barrel back towards him, before repeating, "What is a googly?"

"It's, it's, it's cricket. Cricket! It's a ball bowled by a right-arm leg spin bowler."

The American lowered his pistol and placed it back into its holster with a smile.

"No fucking American could ever answer that question, let alone a God-damn Kraut," he grinned.

"It's all in the fucking wrist," Ernest muttered.

The American guffawed noisily and slapped him on the shoulder. "Will you get this guy," he said loudly to his compatriots. "It's all in the fucking wrist!"

Ernest looked over at the slumped remains of the German officer.

"You've killed him," he whispered.

"I have, that's right."

"Why? Why did you kill him?" he spoke with a profound sense of incomprehension.

"He was a German," the American reasoned. "I'm not taking any prisoners today. Period. You were God-damn lucky I didn't shoot you. What the hell were you doing passing the time of day with this Nazi piece of shit?"

"I'd been held prisoner, but escaped during the bombardment," Ernest said, still unable to take his eyes off the dead body beside him. "I don't understand. Why shoot him?"

"SNAFU," the Colonel reasoned with a shrug. "That's war for you."

"SNAFU?" Ernest sounded bemused.

"Sure, you know SNAFU – Situation Normal All Fucked Up," the Colonel grinned through his cigar. He seemed to be waiting on Ernest's laughter. It didn't come.

"Come on now son," the Colonel said, with a hearty pat on his shoulder. "Pull yourself together. It's like you've never seen a dead Kraut before. This here hill is a battlefield. What would Churchill have done? What would he tell you? What would..." he looked around for inspiration as he attempted to name another Englishman. "What would William Shakespeare have said?"

"The quality of mercy is not strained," Ernest replied pointedly, setting his eyes on the Colonel, before adding: "He was a decent man."

"Shakespeare?"

"No, him!" Ernest pointed towards the slumped remains beside him.

"A decent Nazi?" The American grinned as if he was missing a joke.

"He didn't shoot me for being British when he could have done. What does that make you, if he's the Nazi?"

The American frowned down at Ernest and chewed on his cigar.

"Listen here son," he drawled. "I'm not sure I like your attitude. When you address me, it's Colonel or Sir, got it? On your feet."

Ernest hobbled up to something like a vertical position.

"I think my ankle is broken, Sir."

The American gave the offending ankle a cursory glance and took the unlit cigar back out of his mouth. He turned to two of his own soldiers.

"Donnovan, Goldmann, take this man back to the British 56th lines. If he calls me a Nazi one more time, I might have to break his other God-damn ankle."

The Colonel did not make further eye contact with Ernest, but carried on walking purposefully up the slope. He turned to a fellow officer as he walked away, and Ernest heard the words being exchanged between them: "So what is a God-damn googly then?" "Search me."

Ernest took a slow, deep, deliberate breath.

"Thank you for not shooting me Colonel," Ernest called back over his shoulder, with a generous helping of sarcasm in his tone. "It was jolly decent of you." But the American had already gone out of earshot.

Ernest turned to Donnovan and Goldmann who were now supporting him on either side.

"He liked to collect butterflies," Ernest whispered to them, with emotion cracking through his voice.

"Is that so Mac?" Donnovan spoke humouringly, as one might speak to an over-tired child.

"You've had a tough time of it," Goldmann added. "Don't worry pal, we'll get you back to your guys in no time at all."

Ernest looked back over his shoulder at the body he was leaving behind. He thought of Patterson's body left behind further down the hill.

"Butterflies," he said again, more to himself than his two new companions. "Fucking butterflies."

1989

The service had passed by in a blur. Ernie felt a rising sense of panic as he looked towards the light oak coffin with its brass handles, and realised the vicar seemed to have finished his work and was walking away from the lectern. The little red velvet curtains were closing with a shuddering mechanism around the coffin. Ernie remonstrated with himself silently. 'I should be feeling more than this.' A hand came to rest on his shoulder, and he looked up to see that the undertaker was guiding him to be the first to leave.

Outside the crematorium complex was finished in the same sort of rough red little bricks that they built houses out of these days and a terrace was decorated with archways of these run-of-the-mill bricks. Ernie stopped to look at the flowers that lined the terrace. They might have been for Marjorie, he couldn't be sure as he didn't have his reading glasses to read the cards. Equally, they could have been there from the previous funeral. Or for the next one that would be following swiftly behind.

It wasn't a bad turn-out though for the old girl, Ernie mused. But then, she always had been so sociable. People liked her and it comforted Ernie a little to know that she hadn't been forgotten, despite being away from society for so long now. People around here didn't forget you. That was good. But there won't be this many people brushing down their winter coats to stand in this place when I go, Ernie thought to himself.

His gloomy train of thought was broken by Reg shaking his hand. Angela, who had her arm linked through Reg's was dabbing tears from her eyes theatrically.

"You must have taken great comfort from that Our Kid," his brother said.

"She was such a lovely girl," Angela sobbed, leaning forward to give Ernie a snotty kiss on the cheek. "Now you'll make sure you look after yourself won't you," she demanded, holding him by the cheeks and staring intensely into his eyes. "So many men wither away themselves after their wife has died. We don't want that happening to you."

Ernie nodded at the line of mourners filing behind Angela's ample rump. She used to be such a slim little thing, Ernie thought to himself, as he gazed intently at his sister-in-law.

"I'll look after myself Ange," he said. "You don't need to worry about me."

Reg slapped him on the shoulder. "Of course, you will Our Kid. You don't need to worry about our Ernie, Ange. He's as tough as old boots this one. Aren't you?"

Ernie nodded. "If you say so Reg."

"And under the circumstances," Reg went on cautiously. "Well, I suppose it must come as some kind of relief."

Ernie nodded once again. "It was no life for her in the end."

"Anyway lad," Reg slapped his upper arm joltingly. "Onwards and upwards, that's what I say. Let's get out of here and hit the buffet before that lot eat all the sausage rolls. I'm assuming there are sausage rolls."

"You'll be fine for sausage rolls Reg." Ernie smiled as his brother and sister-in-law walked away towards their car. He turned and looked up at the chimney above him. "Onwards and upwards Marjorie. Onwards and upwards."

Chapter fourteen
1993

After saying goodnight to Rachele in the hotel corridor, Ernie walked into his room, closed the door and leaned back against it for a moment. A moth circled the light. He couldn't remember the last time he felt this drunk. The room was unsteady around him. Silly old room. He stumbled across to the window, which he had left open in the heat of the day. It was late and the street outside was silent, but a refreshing cool breeze played with the edges of the net curtains. Ernie looked out at the deserted city, the streets orange in their lamplit glow, and wondered what tomorrow might bring. He closed the window.

The moth stopped fluttering and settled against the wall, its beautifully speckled wings now visible in its stillness.

What if Rachele was right? Ernie thought to himself, while he casually inspected the creature that had taken up residence on the wall. Perhaps when it came to it Preghiera wouldn't even recognise him. He turned his face to the mirror. After all, he had changed beyond all recognition. He ran a hand delicately across his own cheek and raised his chin unnaturally high in a vain attempt to remove the double-chins that had been a fixture of his neck in recent years.

But for that matter, what if he no longer recognised her? Don't they say that men age better than women? What if she turned out to be just another elderly Italian woman, perched on a wooden chair outside a Neapolitan doorstep. What if none of the feelings came back? A panic of butterflies began to rise in his stomach.

It was one thing to love somebody knowing that they existed out there somewhere in the world – that one day you might find them and live happily ever after. But to find them and find they have changed so dramatically that they no longer exist – at least, the person you had been yearning for no longer existed – what would that do to him, he wondered? How could he cope with the void it would leave?

Ernie sat down on the bed and slowly began to unfasten his shoe laces. Maybe he was being a fool. He addressed the moth. "Am I being a fool?" he asked. When no answer was forthcoming he groaned a little. "Aah, what would you know. Probably don't even understand English." He turned back towards the mirror. What was he doing out here in Italy at all? At his time of life, he should be doing sensible things like gardening and joining a crown green bowls club. Not travelling across Europe in search of his lost love. He suddenly felt ridiculous.

Ernie removed both shoes and placed them neatly side-by-side next to the bed. Perhaps the best thing would be to admit he had been foolish, but enjoy a few nice, nostalgic days in Naples, then climb on an aeroplane and head home never having attempted to meet Preghiera. Yes, that's what he would do, he decided as he filled the kettle to make a sobering cup of tea before heading for bed. In fact, he felt better already, he told himself convincingly.

Ernie flicked the switch on the kettle and sat back down on the edge of the bed. Watching the steam rise from the spout, he had another change of heart.

What if he did meet her and he still had those carefully cherished feelings? What if she still felt the same way about him? He walked back across to the mirror and gazed at his own reflection once more. What if they got their happy ever after moment after all?

1944

Ernest knew little of the journey back across the river other than the sensation of shaking uncontrollably in the boat. He remembered even less of being handed back over to his own commanding officer – the very captain who had sent him on the mission. *"Trust me, if you fuck this up Private, I'll make sure you bloody well suffer."* Had he "fucked it up"?

"Good man Green," the captain said, leaning against the side of the ambulance. Ernest reasoned to himself that he clearly hadn't "fucked it up" too badly.

He nodded. "Thank you, sir." He stumbled as he spoke. "I'm sorry sir, I'm still a little shaken," he added, feeling feeble. "You see, I didn't know they were about to bomb the abbey. It was upon us before I knew what was happening."

The captain gave another of his shark-like grins. "Frankly Green, we didn't know either. Our American friends didn't remember to tell the British ground troops that those B-25s were coming. Some of the chaps from the Royal Sussex were a matter of yards away, trying to capture Point 593. The blighters didn't know what had hit them when those Fortresses came over. Some of them have been carried back this morning with wounds from the flying rock splinters. Every bit as effective as the German defence."

Ernest shook his head, rubbing his eyes with his thumb and index finger, as was his habit in moments of confusion or bewilderment. "Unbelievable," he muttered. "Simply unbelievable. What chance do we have?"

"Only too believable I'm afraid Green," the captain grumbled. "They told the monks. They even told the enemy for Christ's sake. But they didn't tell us." The rising anger seemed to quell itself within the captain just as swiftly as it had arrived. He waved it away with a swift gesture. "Listen, never mind about all that now," the officer added leaning forward and patting's Ernest's shoulder with a thoughtful frown. "Get yourself on that ambulance and take it easy. It's going to take a while before you're back on your feet."

"Thank you, sir," Ernest made a vague attempt to salute, but his strength failed him mid-way and his hand only just made it to his cap badge, the fingers trembling a little. "Just one more question sir, if I may," he added. "What day is it?"

The captain gave a little laugh. "It's Tuesday, Green. But don't be concerning yourself with that sort of thing right now."

Ernest thanked the captain again and found himself being supported by a couple of men from his own unit as he climbed on to the back of the ambulance. He was glad of the support – he could feel his head spinning a little. The ambulance was filled with men in a much worse state than he was in. He took a seat and closed his eyes while the driver climbed into the cab and started the engine.

For the entirety of the bumpy ride back down to Naples, the groans of the other men kept his nerves frayed. Some seemed on the brink of giving up the ghost, omitting a disquieting variety of rasping sounds from their throats by the time they arrived at the military hospital. Others were well enough to whimper and grumble and wish aloud they had cigarettes.

As the orderly opened the back door, there beside him was stood the dark-haired boy, watching Ernest silently, his expression blank of emotion or concern. He just looked on. Nobody else seemed to pay him any heed.

"Will you get that God-damn kid away from the ambulance," Ernest complained to the orderly. He followed Ernest's pointed finger, and looked back at Ernest with a shrug.

"You feeling hot or sick at all?" he said, laying the palm of his hand on Ernest's forehead.

"Sick of this whole fucking shit show of a war," Ernest said.

"There speaks a sane enough man," the orderly grinned. "Come on let's get you inside." He supported Ernest as he struggled down the steps of the ambulance. The boy had gone.

"Is it true what they say about butterflies?" Ernest asked the orderly, who frowned at him with bemusement. "You know, that they only live for a day. Or that they only have very fleeting lives at least."

"Not sure pal," the orderly said. "Not having studied butterflies in-depth."

"Entomology," Ernest said, in a teacherly fashion. "It's funny, that's the second time I've heard that word in as many days. Isn't it strange how you can go your whole life without hearing a word, and then it crops up twice in two days."

"Yeah, queer that," the orderly mumbled, as he opened the heavy oak door of the hospital, and grappled with Ernest as he lowered him into a wheelchair.

"All yours Sister," the orderly pushed the chair a little in the direction of a dour-faced nurse. "Good luck with this one." He pointed with a spinning index finger to his own temple with a little whistle. He gave Ernest a comical pat on the shoulder and walked back towards the ambulance.

The nurse looked Ernest up and down.

"It's just a broken ankle Sister," he said apologetically.

"Perhaps young man, you will allow me to be the judge of that."

As she spoke, she was already wheeling Ernest along a series of corridors towards a triage bay.

"I'm told you've been a little confused in the ambulance – not quite as chipper as one might expect when you're being driven away from the battlefield with a broken ankle." the Sister said. "Have you suffered any head injuries?"

"I watched a man having his brain blown out yesterday," Ernest said. "That was head injury enough for me for one week."

"We all see trying things in times of war," the Sister said without lifting her eyes from her note-making. "You mustn't let yourself get fixated on such things. It's a little self-indulgent isn't it? Anway, you could always pray for his soul, if you're feeling so inclined. Now, have you ever had malaria?"

"No.

"Typhus?"

"No."

"Venereal disease?"

"No."

"Venereal disease honestly?"

"Honestly I haven't Sister. The chance would be a fine thing."

The Sister frowned up at him. Ernest mumbled an earnest apology under his breath.

"My goodness, aren't we the very picture of health young man," she said suspiciously. She walked across the room and put down the clipboard. She then turned on her heel and headed towards the opening in the curtain. "The doctor will be along to check out that ankle just as soon as he can. It may be a while. He is terribly busy, as I'm sure you can imagine. I would get settled in for the night and perhaps we will get you to the ward in the morning."

She turned to leave, looking less dour as a smile flashed across her face. "Welcome to the 300th General Hospital – your home for the next few weeks," she looked again at the swollen ankle, "Yes, a few weeks I should imagine." With that she bustled away.

The days passed slowly on the ward, with only a copy of the *Gideon's New Testament* and a two-month-old edition of *The Times* for company. After much nagging from Ernest, one of the young Italian nurses agreed to ask around the other wards to see if any of the men had an actual book that he could borrow. He had lent his copy of *David Copperfield* to a lieutenant at the barracks before they left for Monte Cassino, and it had not yet been returned to him. Eventually the young nurse appeared with a dog-eared copy of *Burmese Days*, which Ernest consumed with relish.

"You've got yourself a cushy little wound there ain't ya?" a Cockney corporal grumbled from the neighbouring bed. He had lost an eye, so Ernest felt duty-bound to concede the point.

"You might say that pal," Ernest grinned. "Hurt like fuck, mind."

"Still, worth it eh, for a few weeks with your feet up and pretty Italian nurses bringing you cups of tea and novels to read."

Ernest looked at the skyline of Naples spread beyond the window.

"I can take them or leave them to be honest," he said. "The Italian nurses I mean. I'm just looking forward to getting back on my feet and getting out there."

"What do you want to go out there for? The place is an absolute hellhole."

"I know," Ernest nodded. "But even that hellhole has the occasional angel walking through it."

"Randy bugger," the corporal chuckled.

"No, it's not that," Ernest frowned. "There's one in particular I would like to see again."

"That so? Smitten are we? Quite the Romeo aren't you?"

"Something like that I suppose."

"Well, watch yourself sunshine, you'll be back in here with a broken heart instead of a broken ankle if you're not careful."

Ernest smiled. "Not sure I'd get much treatment for that."

"Plenty of Italian girls out there in the back alleys that would treat you for it if you can spare them a couple of bob."

Ernest laughed, but raised his eyes to the heavens in disgust at the same time. He turned his head and looked back to the window. Come on, you bastard ankle, heal, he thought to himself as he gazed out across the rooftops and wondered what Preghiera was doing at that very moment.

"So near, yet so far," he said aloud. "So near, and yet so far."

The corporal in the next bed gave a dirty little laugh. "Like I said, you're a randy bugger Romeo."

"Yeah, well I'm not the one winking all the time," Ernest muttered with a grin.

1989

It had been the sort of day when the sun seemed never to have properly risen. The rain clouds had swept over in the morning, discharging their downpours, and leaving the ground glistening. Ernie carried his mug of tea into the lounge and looked at the small cardboard box on the coffee table. He stared at it for a long time, before he finally took a sip of his tea, and placing the steaming mug on a coaster, his fingers reached out for the box, but paused in mid-air. He let out a long sigh and rubbed the stubble on his cheek.

He looked up at the framed photograph on the mantelpiece – a picture from their wedding day. It captured him looking up at a cloud of confetti, while Marjorie was looking straight out of the picture, straight down the camera lens – straight at him as he sat there before her box of ashes. "Well Marjorie, it's about time we did something with you."

He steadied his nerve and opened the box. Inside, was a small black plastic jar. It had a screw-on lid, like a tea urn, only somehow more clinical. "Come on then my dear, little urn and Big Ern are going for one last walk. He carried the urn into the hallway and placed it down on the telephone table. He sat on the little pleather seat that adjoined the table and put on his walking boots. He got back to his feet and wrapped a scarf around his neck and put on his winter coat. He then turned back to the urn and picked it up carefully. "Come on my dear, it's just you me. One last walk."

Ernie walked along the road holding the urn in two hands, as if it might break at any moment. It was a cold day, and the street was empty. He could see his breath hovering as a cloud of vapour before his mouth as he walked. He moved through each of these little clouds, leaving them hanging on the air in his wake. The entrance to the woodland was only a few hundred yards away. He pushed his way through the kissing gate, and gave the urn a little peck on the cheek. "One last time my dear," he whispered.

The autumn had taken hold of the woodland and a layer of auburn leaves had scattered like a red carpet for Marjorie's last walk. Above his head the branches of the trees swayed and creaked in the wind. A pair of crows cawed at each other as they circled high above the highest branches. Ernie's feet crunched along deeper and deeper into the woodland. He turned a corner and could no longer see the entrance. Now he was surrounded by only trees, their presence tangible and benevolent as they groaned and moaned in what seemed like mourning.

Ernie trampled away from the main footpath, deeper into the woodland, where the holly bushes offered flashes of green and red, and the birch trunks stood to attention neatly placed at regular intervals. He found a place that felt right – where moss had grown and taken over the trees' roots, giving this little glade a luminous glow in the watery light. He brushed aside the leaves at the base of one of the silver birches and opened the lid of the jar.

Ernie cleared his throat and spoke hoarsely as he allowed the ashes to scatter out of the jar and on to the damp ground: "And so you return to the ground, for from it you were taken; For you are dust, and to dust you shall return." With the last of the ashes settled, he returned the lid to the jar and carefully covered the little grey pile with leaves in a wealth of autumn colours – from burning reds to deep earthy browns.

"You can rest here now my dear," Ernie said aloud and picking up the jar he held it to his side as a sportsman might hold a rugby ball. He stood back and looked upon the place at his feet, now returned to autumn carpet. "You'll get some peace here my dear. You were ready for some peace weren't you?" His gaze followed the line of the birch tree, leading straight upwards, pointing without deviation towards the heavens where the wisps of cloud were being swiftly blown by overhead.

"You sleep tight," Ernie muttered, wiping the dewdrop that had formed at the end of his nose. His boots crunched across the leaves as he made his way back to the path.

1944

Ernest's mother was making her usual rounds for a Saturday – a stroll around the market and a few of the department stores, before calling in at Boots to change her books, then heading straight to the Savoy. There was such comfort in the familiarity of the routine.

She bought her ticket as usual after a brief chat with the young girl in the box office. "Any word from your boys Mrs Green?" She shook her head with a smile. Then she made her way up the sweeping staircase to her usual balcony seat. She had been running slightly later than usual – there had been a queue at Boots' counter – but she just managed to slip into her seat in time for the start of the Pathe news reel.

The elderly woman took out her handkerchief and dabbed at the perspiration that had gathered on her forehead in the walk across town and gazed up at the screen. "CASSINO MONASTERY BOMBED" it began, with the three capitalised words set in white against a black background, and the shadowy cockerel emblem of British Pathe silhouetted in the corner. It then faded to a shot of the abbey itself, in silhouette against a bright sky. *"The abbey on the crest of Monte Cassino,"* a plummy voice chirped up. *"Before we take you through replays of its bombing, we visit an abbey in Kent for an exclusive interview granted by the Lord Abbot of Pershore and Nashdom, head of an Anglican community of Benedictine monks, the Abbot makes these observations..."*

Ernest's mother gazed intently at the screen. She sensed careful propaganda was afoot.

"Benedictine monks all over the world will regret the destruction of the abbey on Monte Cassino," the Abbot addressed the cinema goers directly standing in a monastic garden, his arms folded inside his cassock. *"For it was there that Saint Benedict wrote The Rule which is that of all Benedictine monks. Regrettable though the bombing and shelling of the monastery may be, it would appear that our military leaders had no choice in the matter. If its preservation would have meant the prolonging of the war, and the loss of perhaps hundreds of our soldiers, its destruction was more than justified."*

With that, the news reel returned to the sun-bleached hills of Italy, and a shot of the abbey still standing tall in its final moments. Just one thought was echoing through the old lady's head – I wonder if Ernest was there at that moment?

The newsreel showed warning leaflets being dropped over the building, written in Italian and English, before it cut to the sight of bombs being prepared and loaded on to the flying fortresses. *"German soldiers were known to be using it as an observation post – a bastion of the Gustav Line,"* the news reader went on, as the old lady once again dabbed her forehead, suddenly feeling queasy at the thought of the destruction that was to come.

"On the following day, Fortresses, Mitchells and Marauders, a squadron at a time, showered high explosives on the abbey every twenty minutes or so," the news reader went on, and the screen before the old lady was filled with a scene of enormous destruction – great plumes of dust and smoke rising, wiping the abbey's ancient walls from the landscape. *"With careful deliberation and every reluctance, the decision was executed,"* the news reader added. His words echoed emptily around the cinema, with its rows of faces gazing in disbelief at the brutality of what they were witnessing on the screen. Stirring music crescendoed in the background, as if a second-rate orchestra had been on hand in the Latin Valley that morning. *"Another wave comes,"* the newsreader said, but the old lady was no longer looking at the screen. She held her head in her hands, suddenly feeling as if she was going to be sick.

She leaned forwards in her chair, then backwards, writhing in the seat as an all-consuming pain tore across her chest and down her left arm. The people either side of her began to shuffle in their seats, awkwardly, in a terribly English manner, for a moment or two everyone pretended not to notice – nobody wanted to cause any fuss. But as the old lady let out a hollow rasping sound from her throat and slid like a deflating balloon down into the footwell between the rows of seats, the two people either side of her finally plucked up the courage to intervene – waving over at the usherette, whose torch appeared through the darkness as the screen flickered on with scenes of devastation at Monte Cassino.

A group of elderly men and young women left their seats to help to carry the old woman out of the darkness of the cinema and into the light of the little landing area at the top of the staircase, surrounded by the framed posters advertising all the latest films. Clark Gable, Cary Grant and David Niven all glared down from the posters at the scene unfolding before them.

The young girl from the box office caught wind of the commotion and left her cubicle to run, two steps at a time, up the sweeping staircase and stopped with horror at the top step. She stood still for a moment, her hands over her mouth. Then she knelt beside the old lady, took hold of her hand, and hissed at the blank-faced usherette to "go fetch a doctor!"

But she knew, from the moment she touched that ice cold hand, and looked down into the lady's blank staring eyes, she knew that she was already gone. "Oh Mrs Green, Mrs Green," the girl rocked backwards and forwards a little in her distress, and clung on to the old lady's hand until the doctor arrived.

Chapter fifteen
1993

Ernie lay back in the bed and closed his eyes. His head was spinning with the face of Rachele appearing one moment and morphing into the features of a young Preghiera the next.

Preghiera smiled at him, her olive brown eyes alive with warmth. Ernie felt the warmth radiate from her and seep through his very fabric. He cast his eyes lustily down the contours of her throat and towards the supple landscape of her chest. She reached out a hand to touch his cheek, but as she did so, this young beauty morphed again into an old hag who cackled with a caustic breath into his face and then erupted into a puff of dust that hung in the air before him and sprinkled his face with ash.

He could taste the degradation in his sleeping mouth, then he was falling and falling until, as he grappled to lean forwards amid the freefalling air, he was sitting bolt upright and screaming into the darkness of the hotel room.

"Oh God, oh dear God," he muttered to himself, as he refamiliarised himself with the room, before laying back down and turning comfortingly on to his side. "Dear God," he muttered one more time. He spent a moment taking long, deep, calming breaths.

"What am I doing? What on Earth am I doing?" he muttered into his pillow. With the question still hanging on his lips, he slipped into a more peaceful sleep, which settled across him like a blanket, until the first beams of a warm dawn cut their slanting route through the hotel room, illuminating the dust that hung in the air above him.

1944

The Sister came into the ward and glowered at Ernest and the corporal in the neighbouring bed as if conversation wasn't to be encouraged. She approached Ernest. "Telegram for you Green," she said quietly, handing it to him, before turning on her heel to leave. "I'm afraid it's date stamped some days ago," the Sister added. "They must have struggled to track you down."

"Telegram? For me?" Ernest said, but the Sister was already walking back down the corridor.

Ernest frowned down at it in his hands, wondering who could be sending him a telegram here?

"Love letters?" the corporal chuckled from the next bed.

His eyes scanned the flimsy paper. It was from his brother Reginald. "Mother buried with father yesterday. Sorry we could not get a message to you sooner. She died peacefully. Reginald."

Ernest took a deep breath, and turned to the corporal who was watching his face expectantly.

"My mother's dead."

The corporal frowned down towards his own blanket. "I'm sorry to hear that pal."

"You know, my mother once told me something very true," Ernest said at last, emotion already dampening his eyes. "She said that a loving heart is the truest wisdom."

The corporal's face was no longer painted with his usual fixed grin. He was nodding silently.

"She sounds like a clever lady, your mother," the corporal said. He gave a compassionate smile to the young soldier holding the telegram.

"She was," Ernest said quietly. "She was a remarkable woman my mother."

It was a week after receiving the news of his mother's death in that single-line telegram before Ernest heard again from his brother. A letter arrived at his hospital bed. Ernest recognised his brother's scrawling hand before he had even opened the envelope. His fingers fluttered a little as he tore it open.

Hello Our Kid, the letter began.

I hope this finds you well and still in one piece. Sorry about the telegram lad. It was tough to break it to you like that, but I wanted you to know as quickly as possible. She would have wanted you to know. I knew you wouldn't be able to get back for the funeral, but it seemed right that you found out as soon as possible.

It was a blessing that I was here in England when she went. The ship had only reached Portsmouth a couple of hours before. I'd not even disembarked when I got the call to go up to the bridge to see the captain himself. He had received the news onboard. Broke it to me nice and gentle, he did, then before I knew it, I was being bundled on to a train at Portsmouth station heading north. Decent bunch in the Royal Navy, you know. I'll be back down in Portsmouth tomorrow. I can't say where we're off to, but it's going to be a long one, so you may not hear from me for quite a while.

She died at the picture house. Well, there's nothing like going doing what you love best. She'd loved going to see a film every week ever since father died. She said she went for the Pathe news reels – to find out what was happening with you and me. But I think it was to see Clark Gable or Cary Grant mostly. Fair play to her.

The funeral was all done nice and proper – just like mother would have wanted. The vicar mentioned you – said you were away bravely fighting for king and country. Didn't mention the spaghetti and the Neapolitan ladies, so you did alright there. Mrs Fairclough next-door-but-one did the spread in our back room. She's a lovely lady. She did mother proud. Cucumber sandwiches with the crusts cut off – all posh like. She's buried with father now – mother that is, not Mrs Fairclough.

Hope you're enjoying the vino out there.
All the best Our Kid, Reg

Ernest read the letter through three or four times, smiling a little, before he folded it and placed it carefully back into the envelope. He hobbled across from his bed to his kit bag, where he squirrelled it away with the last letters he had received from his mother. They felt like sacred relics now somehow, too precious to throw away. Occasionally he would take one out at random and read it, pretending a little to himself that she was still around. It was a funny thing, not having been there when she died. Not having been there when she was buried. Not having been there for Mrs Fairclough's cucumber sandwiches with the crusts cut off. It was almost like she hadn't died and sometimes he would almost forget and half wonder what she was doing back home that day.

Ernest was still hobbling when they discharged him. It had now been so long since he last saw Preghiera and he was desperate to get out of the hospital and across the city to find her and let her know that he was still alive – broken ankle, or no broken ankle.

What must be going through her mind, he thought to himself as he walked carefully across the Neapolitan cobbles, past the stencil of Il Duce and the streets of shame where women still lined themselves up like pieces of meat in return for tins of meat. But he paid no attention. The 'Green by name, green by nature' Ernest was gone forever. Now, with his edges hardened to it all, he didn't bat an eye lid to any of it. He hobbled across the city with a real sense of determination. The street was still filled with American GIs, whooping and leering and drunkenly pushing their comrades towards a woman to enquire about her services.

"What's the fuckin' problem?" he heard one gum-chewing American say to another angrily. "These wops went to war against us, I reckon we're owed our pound of flesh." With that the American raised one fist-capped arm into the air in a provocative gesture that suggested an erection and brought about a cacophony of dirty laughter from his friends. But the other, dark-haired GI he had been arguing with, was looking increasingly angry and it struck Ernest as he watched the scene that things could rapidly turn nasty.

"You're disrespecting these people," the dark-haired GI said angrily. "You forget Mitchell that for those of us with Italian heritage, these are our people."

"Our people my ass," the other retorted. "You'll fuck a wop for a tin from your C-ration, just like the next man."

With that the fists started flying. The bewildered-looking women whose honour had been the subject of the disagreement shuffled back their wooden chairs and price list boards in an attempt to draw away from the fracas. Ernest briefly considered stepping in to separate the pair, but quickly thought better of it. By the time he turned the corner, he could hear the jeering and rhythmic clapping of the wider group of GIs, who cheered on their two drunken comrades like a pair of prize fighters.

Ernest turned the corner from the bustling street and cut deliberately down a narrow alley to escape the furore. He thought he had a vague idea of where the little alley came out, but from experience knew that if you became lost in these labyrinthine back streets, it could take a while to extract yourself back to the main roads. The alley smelt like a latrine, and the few high windows in the houses here had long since been shuttered, as if turning a blind eye to the degradation.

Ancient washing lines were cast between the buildings at regular intervals, but here there wasn't a single garment pegged out to dry. The alley curved a little to the left, and as Ernest turned the corner the sound of the Americans began to fade into the dull drone of the city. A little way further down and the lonely alleyway turned sharply to the right. It was a dead end. A few feet above his eyeline, in this forgotten corner of the city, a pair of feet in well-worn leather women's shoes were hanging, rocking backwards and forwards in the cool breeze. A tall wooden A-framed stepladder lay on its side a few feet away.

Ernest slowly allowed his eyes to lift, up the line of the stockinged legs, up the cheap flowery cotton dress, to see the face, once loved, once the respected head of a household, now bruised, discoloured and twisted grotesquely into a horrible mask. Ernest immediately recognised it as a woman he had seen when he first entered the city, selling her honour on the nearby street. Her one glass eye stared down at him from the lofty perch, where she hung – a rope tied precariously to the ancient washing lines that criss-crossed the alleyway.

Ernest dropped to his knees and caught his face in his hands. He rocked backwards and forwards, disorientated and uncertain what to do next. For a moment he thought he might vomit, but the wave of nausea crashed over him and passed on down the alleyway from where he could hear a pair of boots running.

He turned his head, still on in his knees, as if in prayer. The GI who had moments before been instigating a fist fight with his Italian American comrade, skidded to a halt. His bloodied face betrayed the fact he had lost the battle and had taken his chance to escape from his irate friend's fists down the nearest alleyway. The American wiped the blood from his nose with the back of his hand, and looked at first at Ernest and then up at the swinging corpse. Tentatively, he started to walk forward.

"Fucking hell," he whispered, before turning to Ernest and stating the obvious, but as yet unspoken fact: "She's dead."

Ernest nodded sombrely and got to his feet. He reached into his pocket and pulled out a packet of cigarettes. He lit one, his hands still shaking, without attempting to offer a cigarette to the American. The GI didn't notice the slight. His eyes were still fixed on the twisted face of the woman hanging before them. He took a step closer. "I knew her," he said. "I knew this woman. I mean, I fucked her," he turned to Ernest as if feeling the need to explain. "She had my C-rations a few times this one."

He took another step closer to the corpse. He was now so close that if he had reached up, he would be able to lay his hand on the well-worn leather shoes and stop the body swinging in the breeze. But he kept his arms by his side. The American shook his head and without turning back to Ernest or taking his eyes off the sight of the dead woman, he asked softly: "Why the hell did she do this?"

Ernest stepped back and took a long drag on his cigarette before he answered: "Why the fucking hell do you think?" He turned and wincing at the pain from his ankle, he walked away back into the nightmare landscape of the alleyways, leaving the suddenly sobered American gazing up at the woman's body in disbelief.

Ernest walked on through the city, recomposing himself and slowly regathering his thoughts. By the time he reached Torre Annunziata, a thin film of perspiration glinted across his forehead, dripping slowly with each step through his brow. The butcher's shop, standing on the far side of the square, looked as it had ever done – even down to the queue of locals shuffling in and out. But there was no sign of Preghiera in her usual place by the door, counting them in four at a time.

He pushed his way past the queue and entered the shop itself for the first time. It smelt crisply of blood and mincemeat. It felt icy cool compared to the heat of the streets. An elderly man stood behind the counter, wiping his hands in his white shop coat.

"Preghiera's father?" Ernest ventured. The old man stared back at him. "Voglio vedere Preghiera," Ernest said, his voice raised awkwardly in his pidgin Italian.

The old man leaned forward across the counter, and speaking English with surprising ease, muttered in a hoarse whisper: "You will not see Preghiera." He picked up a knife and started to hack at a piece of meat on the counter as he spoke. "You will not see Preghiera again." He looked up and pointed the tip of the blade across the counter at Ernest, before adding, "Ever."

"Where is she?" Ernest sounded suddenly frantic, his voice quavering a little, like a child who had seen his toys snatched by the neighbourhood bully. He looked over the old man's shoulder at the doorway and the staircase beyond. "Preghiera!" he shouted. "Preghiera!" But Ernest's voice echoed emptily back to him through the hidden rooms behind the shopfront.

The old man's stubbly face flickered and flowered with a malevolent smile. "You waste your breath soldier. She is not here. She has gone to stay with …" His sentence tailed off, and he looked down at the raw meat before him.

"Where?" Ernest demanded. "Where have you sent her?"

"She is with family, she will not see you again ever." He glared across the counter for a moment, before adding: "You come here again, and I will kill you myself." He spat on the floor as if to seal the threat. Ernest shook his head with a sad smile and walked out.

He sat on the edge of the fountain in the middle of the square and looked back up at the room that had been Preghiera's, its shutters closed. His mind wandered back, her words echoing in his memory: "I can't go anywhere – my father..."

As he gazed at the house with damp eyes, a gnarly-faced old lady, dressed all in black, emerged from the butcher's shop, clutching a shopping basket. She shuffled across and sat down beside the young soldier.

"He says it's beef, but I know it's horse," the woman tittered quietly. "We must take what we can in these times."

She was silent for a moment, before turning to face Ernest. The sunlight landed on her face, illuminating every crease and wrinkle.

"Young love," she whispered, "is the finest, noblest thing you will ever feel young man."

Ernest turned to the elderly woman. "You wouldn't understand."

She laughed a little. "Now, now, soldier. Don't forget, we were all young once. San Bastiane," she added.

"What's San Bastiane?"

"Preghiera was taken to San Bastiane by her father. Her uncle and cousin live there."

"San Bastiane? Where is San Bastiane?"

"Not so far," the woman muttered, gesticulating towards the distinctive outline of Mount Vesuvius on the edge of the city.

"San Sebastiano al Vesuvio?" Ernest asked. "You mean San Sebastiano al Vesuvio?"

"Si, si, San Bastiane. Just a little village on the slopes of the mountain. She will be safe there with her uncle."

Ernest swiftly got to his feet, wincing at the sharp pain from his ankle. He reached into his pocket and pulled out a US bank note. He patted it into the old woman's hand. "Thank you," he whispered. "Thank you so much, you dear old dear." With this, he kissed the woman's venerable forehead, generating a sound between alarm and excitement from her throat. She brushed him away affectionately, "Go, get away from me you crazy Englishman," she laughed, carefully pocketing the bank note as she took to her feet. She balanced the shopping basket on her forearm, and walked away across the square muttering to herself.

Ernest hobbled happily back across Torre Annunziata, sensing Patterson walking beside him all the way. "I'm going to get her back Sarge, you fucking watch me. I'll get her back." He turned his head as he spoke, and realised he was addressing the warm and fetid evening air alone.

The barracks felt empty without Patterson's booming voice. Smudge and Mouse were still somewhere around Cassino and he had a room to himself. It felt hopelessly empty. There were a few officers dotted around the building and the occasional man hobbling around on crutches. But mostly, the echoing corridors were deserted.

A young lieutenant, who was keen to be liked by the men, took Ernest to one side the next morning.

"I say Green, you're an educated chap, teacher and all."

Ernest shrugged. "As far as it goes Sir, I enjoyed a little education before my call-up."

"Yes, yes," the Lieutenant nodded. "I figured you might as well do something enjoyable during your recuperation. I thought you might like this." He handed him a pass. "So you can get out and visit Pompeii. I went a few weeks ago with Captain Cartwright. It was quite something to see. Seems they had a rum old time, back in the day."

Ernest looked at the pass he had been handed.

"Thank you, Sir, I appreciate that," he said. "It's somewhere I've always wanted to go. Though I would have preferred better circumstances of course."

The Lieutenant beamed and nodded in his dim but pleasant way. "Good, good. I thought you would be keen. Just a little thank you, for the loan of *David Copperfield*. Ripping yarn. Listen Green, you can take the Land Rover that's parked up at the Sally Port Steps. It has a full tank and if anyone asks where you're going, tell them you're running an errand for me."

"Sir," Ernest nodded, "thank you, Sir."

"Happy to help Green," he smiled. "Always happy to help."

The next morning, the Lieutenant stopped Ernest as he was leaving the mess after breakfast. He handed him a small, red leather-bound book – *The Last Days of Pompeii* by Sir Edward Bulwer Lytton.

"I thought you might like to borrow this," the young officer said. "It was awarded to me for proficiency in the School Certificate Examination." As he spoke, he took the book back from Ernest's hands and pointed out a school prize frontispiece certificate that had been pasted into the book on the inside cover. It was dated "Speech Day 1941" under the scrolling, self-important signature of a headmaster.

Ernest looked back up at the Lieutenant and realised for the first time just how young the officer was. "Congratulations Sir," he smiled. The Lieutenant nodded in a pleasantly self-satisfied way and handed the book back to him.

"Thought it might just help to bring the old place to life for you," the Lieutenant said. "Jolly brainy chap, this Bulwer Lytton."

"That's very kind Lieutenant," Ernest said, waving the book in thanks. "I shall take very good care of it."

The Lieutenant beamed at him as Ernest turned to leave the room.

It was a short, but invigorating drive along the Salerno road. It was largely empty and with each mile, the Neapolitan suburbs gradually evolved into a classical, dusty landscape dotted with acacia and fir. He followed the battered signs that pointed twisted fingers towards Pompeii. How long he had wanted to follow those signs, and excitement fluttered through him as he at last was able to make each turning that pointed towards the doomed town.

When he reached his destination, it was at first a little unclear what he had come here to see. Ernest pulled up and stepped out into the dusty, empty parking place and tried to gaze through the windows of a locked-up building, which he imagined had once housed an exhibition or museum before the war. There was nobody about, so Ernest walked slowly around the outside of the building, before finding his way into the archaeological site itself. There, suddenly, the glories of the ruins were unfurled before him in all their splendour. Nothing had prepared him for the scale of Pompeii, which stretched out, street after street, a relic of so many centuries past.

"Welcome Sir, welcome!" he heard a voice approaching from behind. A crumpled-looking Italian in an archaic three-piece suit, strode towards him, grubby but somehow timeless with his watch chain hanging in a debonair fashion from the pocket of his waistcoat. Behind a stubbly white beard, Ernest saw the creasing eyes of a smiling middle-aged man.

"I am the keeper of the treasures of Pompeii," he beamed grandly, holding out a hand in greeting. "You must be Private Green?"

Ernest gave him a mystified look as he shook his hand.

"The young Lieutenant telephoned just a few minutes ago to say that I should be expecting you," he explained. "I shall be your guide Private Green."

"Ernest, please."

"Ernesto? Thank you – Ernesto. You may call me Lorenzo." He presented his name with multiple vocal embellishments that made him sound like the chorus introducing the first act of a Shakespearean play.

"I didn't expect anybody to go to any trouble," Ernest stammered. "I was just going to take a wander around the ruins."

"It is absolutely no trouble whatsoever," Lorenzo smiled, "è interamente mio piacere." He tapped himself on the lips by way of apology, before slipping back into his sing-song English. "It will be my pleasure entirely Ernesto."

Lorenzo began to lead the way along an ancient pavement lined with ornate columns and the occasional Roman statue still standing, with blank eyes staring up to the great towering volcanic mountain that loomed over the place.

"There were warning signs for those who lived in this city in 79AD when Vesuvius erupted so dramatically," Lorenzo explained. "The eruption lasted for two whole days – first it rained pumice stone out of the sky. Many took this as their cue to leave and escape this place."

"Absolutely," Ernest smiled. "When it's raining pumice stone, that's always a good moment to make for the exit."

"But some did not leave," Lorenzo said. "Those who were still here when the high-speed, dense, scorching ash clouds rolled down from the mountain. They stood no chance. No chance at all. Within moments they were buried in ash – 20ft deep in some places. Their bodies cast in ash for all eternity in the throes of death."

Lorenzo continued: "The archaeologist Giuseppe Fiorelli came up with an idea for reconstructing the bodies in the 18th century. After discovering the air pockets that indicated the presence of human remains in a street dubbed "the Alley of

Skeletons", Fiorelli decided to pour plaster into the voids. They let the plaster harden, then chipped away the outer layers of ash, leaving behind a cast of the victims at their moment of death."

"Incredible," Ernest muttered. "The ultimate death masks."

"Exactly that," his guide nodded sombrely.

Lorenzo led the way into a courtyard, in which were lined up 13 grisly casts of ancient bodies frozen in various states of writhing and agony, but some with their head resting on their palm as though in peaceful repose.

"You have read the words of Pliny the Younger?" Lorenzo asked. Ernest shook his head. Lorenzo continued: "Pliny said 'You could hear the shrieks of women, the wailing of infants, and the shouting of men; some were calling for their parents, others their children or their wives, trying to recognise them by their voices. Many besought the aid of the gods, but still more imagined there were no gods left, and that the universe was plunged into eternal darkness for evermore."

Ernest gazed ashen-faced at the casts of the bodies as Lorenzo spoke. Where once were people, now they left a void, a shadow of having once existed. Ernest knelt beside one of the figures and ran his hand across the cast's recognisably human face.

"Where be your gibes now?" Ernest said to the plaster cast figure, "your gambols? your songs? your flashes of merriment, that were wont to set the table on a roar?"

"Ah, you English," Lorenzo tutted. "Always so obsessed by William Shakespeare."

Ernest shrugged. "He captured the emotions around life and death better than anyone else has ever done in our language."

"Si, si," Lorenzo conceded. "In any language perhaps." He knelt beside Ernest and also looked closely at the face of the cast. "And where now is Shakespeare too? Quite chap-fallen himself, rather like this chap? Yes?"

Ernest laughed. "True enough Lorenzo." He knelt back beside the blank ashen face of the figure.

"Fear no more the heat o' the sun," he began, now more in a whisper. "Nor the furious winter's rages." He ran his hand across the cheek of the plaster cast face. "Thou thy worldly task hast done, Home art gone, and ta'en they wages."

Ernest thought for a moment of his mother and father, dead and buried in his absence, and now lingering in their graves back home. He got back to his feet with the flicker of a smile. He brushed down his knees. "Golden lads and girls all must, As chimney-sweepers, come to dust." Lorenzo returned his smile.

"Shakespeare, eh," Ernest mused. "What a man ..." His sentence was interrupted by a curious sensation that coursed through Ernest, a sort of vibration at first, followed by a deep rumble, and a sense of rippling movement beneath the ground. He cast his eyes up to Lorenzo. "Bomb?"

Lorenzo shook his head decisively. "Earthquake. Just a little one."

"Really? I've never felt an earthquake before. Should we be worried?"

"Just a tremor," Lorenzo waved it away, but his eyes frowned up towards the summit of the volcano. "But not a concern," he added. "Just a tremor. You were talking poetry I believe my friend." Lorenzo seemed suddenly keen to change the direction of the conversation.

"Ah yes, Shakespeare," Ernest smiled. "But tell me Lorenzo, do you know the poems of Edwin Atherstone?"

Lorenzo shook his head and frowned. He was still studying the silhouette of Vesuvius in the distance, while feigning some interest in English poetry.

"No, he certainly wasn't a Shakespeare. But he had his merits," Ernest added. "He wrote a poem you see called *The Last Days of Herculaneum*."

"Ah Herculaneum, yes – just down the road from here."

"That's right," Ernest smiled. "Atherstone wrote: 'The city sinks as in a sepulchre; Deep down it sinks in that tremendous pit, Remains a dark-hued plain alone, whose rugged face The lessening lightnings plough; o'er which the flood of lava slowly settles in a lake. Years – ages – centuries – shall pass away, And none shall tell where once that city stood."

Lorenzo nodded thoughtfully, as if allowing the words of the Victorian poet to settle in his mind. The breeze caught the lapel of his jacket as he stood in front of Ernest considering his response.

"I think perhaps I must try to remember that one myself. You certainly know your poetry."

"I was a teacher in peacetime," Ernest explained. "At least, I was training to be a teacher before all of this." He indicated his uniform with a flourish of his hand.

"Ah yes, this war," Lorenzo mused. "It has altered the course of many lives." He turned for a moment into the breeze as he considered his own words, before sharply bringing himself back to attention with a click of his fingers. "And now," the guide added, leaning in towards him conspiratorially, "like all the young soldiers who come here, I suppose you will want to see the rude mosaics?"

Ernest raised his eyebrows in amusement.

"I thought you'd never ask."

"Of course, of course," Lorenzo grinned. "Step right this way my friend."

1990

It had been a lonely Christmas and New Year period, but Ernie wasn't glad to see the arrival of January – which he felt had always been the bleakest time of year, even at the best of times. And this certainly wasn't the best of times for Ernie.

Although Marjorie had been in a care home for the last months of her life, there had been a comfort to knowing she was there. Even though she often wouldn't recognise Ernie when he visited. Yet still he came to see her every other day. But now she was gone altogether, the loneliness took on a different texture. It was a tranquil but biting sort of loneliness. The days seemed to take an age to pass. By the time he had read the newspaper from cover to cover, it would be late morning, but that still left great swathes of time to sit alone and think, listening to the ticking of the clock on the mantelpiece.

Always a bit of a bookworm, since Marjorie's death he hadn't been able to settle to read novels. They always seemed so weak and limp with their inevitable happy endings. *'Reader I married him.'* Yes, but then what happened my dear?

Sometimes Ernie would take a walk out through the woods, just as Marjorie used to do each day. It brought him closer to her somehow. Now he understood how this place eased her anxieties, with its gentle sounds, its whispering of the leaves and the creaking of the trees. To know she rested here among the peace and harmony of the trees, was a source of great comfort for him. It was almost as if her soul had entered and mingled with the spirits of the trees themselves. As he walked through the woods, Marjorie was everywhere around him – alive in every creaking branch and fluttering leaf.

Apart from the occasional dog walker, Ernie would rarely see anybody else on these walks, and that was how he liked it. He would always pause, of course, near the silver birches where

Marjorie's ashes were scattered. He would often have a word with her in this quiet place. That way neither of them would ever truly be alone. He would still get to visit her every other day, and she would still be as aloof to him – with Ernie never really knowing whether she knew he was with her at these times. Just as it had been in the care home.

Then, if it wasn't too muddy, he would walk home the long way, through the fields – just to delay the inevitable moment when he turned the key in the door and stepped back into the silent house. As the weeks turned to months, Ernie settled into a sort of comfortable routine throughout the week. On a Sunday he would get up and drive to the local supermarket, where he would order a cooked breakfast and a frothy coffee. He would pick up a copy of the *Sunday Times* to take home – that would see him through the afternoon.

Occasionally he would go to church after his supermarket breakfast, sitting at the back in a lonely pew, and listen to the vicar speak of God and faith and the teachings of Jesus. But it wasn't the words of the sermon that comforted him, it was the familiar words of the Victorian hymns, the Pater Noster, the Gloria Patri, the call and response of the liturgy. The bits that tripped off the tongue without having to think too deeply about them. It was knowing when to join in with an Amen that created a sense of fellowship, even in this church where nobody ever attempted to speak to him or invite him for a cup of coffee at the end of the service.

Then they started to change the words a little here, a little there. A modernised version of the Lord's Prayer, new hymns that sounded more like pop songs, and Ernie no longer felt the connection in quite the same way. He increasingly felt like a fish out of water.

The vicar would always be standing by the door when it was time to leave inviting empty compliments. Ernie hated having to queue up to get out. There was no slipping past anonymously, he would have to shake the priestly hand and smile and say thank you, what a lovely service, while the vicar would nod with a fixed smile that betrayed no interest in Ernie's life. He was just another elderly man who sat at the back and had known the words of the old liturgy, but increasingly looked a little lost, even here.

Chapter sixteen
1993

The early morning sun was breaking through the gaps in the shutters and illuminating Ernie's hotel room with an intensity he would normally never see back in England. He could hear the sounds of the streets waking up outside – a delivery of barrels being rolled off a lorry, the chatter of men standing outside a coffee shop, the ever-present buzzing of the Vespas. Ernie lay in bed and took it all in.

"So, today's the day," he murmured to the still room. He lifted his arthritic fingers to his face and rubbed at his eyes. The excesses of the night before echoed around his head with a dull ache. "But am I doing the right thing?" he asked himself silently. "Perhaps it's just too late in life to complicate everything again?"

He reached out a hand towards the bedside table and felt about for his glasses. Finding them, he replaced the frames on his face and slowly sat up. Creaking, grunting and growling all at once he raised himself to his feet and stretched luxuriantly, with a cat-like dedication to serving every inch of his back with a twist or a shudder.

Ernie walked to the window and moving the shutter aside looked out at the alleyway below, still cast into darkness by the long early morning shadows. He reached into his jacket pocket and pulled out a packet of cigarettes. Drawing a cigarette from the packet, he fumbled around for a lighter, before taking in a long, slow, deep lungful of nicotine, tar and smoke, allowing the ash to build up steadily at the end of the cigarette like an ashen finger of one of those Pompeii casts pointing at him accusingly. "Where be *your* gambols now, old man?"

Ernie watched the smoke rise through the room in the morning sunlight.

"I shall write a note to say I came, but realised just in time that it would be a mistake," Ernie reasoned to himself. "Preghiera will understand if I explain properly. She's bound to understand. After all, it is better that we remember each other as we were then, not as we are now." He looked over to the mirror. "Decrepit." He tapped the ash into an ash tray that had been left on the windowsill.

Ernest took another drag and walked closer to the mirror, stopping to gaze at his reflection for a moment.

"But it is what I always wanted," he added quietly. "A happy ending. Am I robbing myself of that final happiness? That happy ending?" He thought quietly for a moment, tears of frustration forming in his eyes. He didn't know what to do. He took in another lungful of smoke and looked back to the mirror and addressed himself directly.

"Decision made," he announced aloud to the room. "No snivelling little notes. No last minute apologies. I will meet her. No expectations. But I will go and meet her. Darling Preghiera. How long have you waited too for this day?"

He examined his face even closer. "I shall need to shave. I'm going to have to make the best of a bad job. Come on then, you bloody old codger. There's no fool like an old fool." He made his way towards the ensuite bathroom, pausing to stub out his cigarette firmly in the ash tray.

1944

"Thank you so much for this," Ernest said as he handed the book back to the Lieutenant.

"Keep hold of it if you would like to read it," the officer beamed. "Just pass it back when you're finished. I know you'll look after it Green."

Ernest gave the cover a gentle brush with the palm of his hand. "Thank you Sir, I will read it."

"I have finished your book though," the Lieutenant lifted the familiar red leatherbound *David Copperfield* from a sideboard and handed it to Ernest. "Thank you so much for the loan. It really," he paused as if struggling to articulate the thought, "it really took me out of this war for a while. Maybe that sounds silly. It was a reminder that our lives are more than just this." The Lieutenant looked to the window as he thought. "It was a reminder that we can dream."

"Yes, it's a good book Sir," Ernest nodded, weighing the old book in his hands. "What is it Dickens says? 'Dreams are illusions, and we can't let go of them because we would be dead.'"

The Lieutenant nodded sombrely. "That's right Green. Yes, I think that's spot on. Anyway," he added, brushing his melancholy away with a rubbing together of his palms as if it was cold. "What did you think of the old place?"

"Pompeii?" Ernest asked. "I thought it was extraordinary Sir. Truly extraordinary. Just as you said. It was like stepping back in time."

"Yes, it is extraordinary, isn't it?" the officer enthused. "And Lorenzo? How was Lorenzo?"

"Excellent Sir – thank you for setting that up. I had no idea. It was very thoughtful."

"Think nothing of it Green. Dear old Lorenzo. He gave us a tour and I thought he was superb. Brought the whole place back to life for me. If he'd not been there, I wouldn't have had a clue what I was looking at. Pile of old ruins as far as I was concerned. Always been a bit of a duffer, truth be told."

Ernest smiled.

"I do hope he showed you the smutty bits Green?" the Lieutenant grinned for ear to ear as he spoke.

Ernest nodded and gave a little laugh. "He did Sir. Extraordinary what those ancients got up to."

"Wasn't it indeed? I rather think they had all the fun in those days," the Lieutenant's eyes betrayed a wandering mind.

"Up until the sudden suffocation in ash Sir."

"Yes, up until that moment Green. Up until then, I rather suspect they were having the most marvellous of times. Still," the officer looked out of the window. "The old devil is waking up again I believe."

"Sir?" He followed the Lieutenant's gaze out of the window to the outline of Vesuvius in the distance. A distinctive wisp of smoke was rising from its crater. "Oh, an eruption? It's not actually an eruption?" Ernest turned to the Lieutenant, with sudden concern.

"Not sure I'd go that far," the Lieutenant chuckled. "More a bit of a grumble as far I can see Green. I wouldn't be too concerned. Not sure we're all going to be plaster casts before the day is out."

He laughed again, but Ernest didn't join in. His mind was now elsewhere.

"I wonder Sir," Ernest ventured nervously. "I know it's a lot to ask, but I wondered if I might be able to take the Land Rover again today?"

"The Landie? Whatever for Green?"

"I need to go back."

"To Pompeii? Why?"

"Lorenzo ran out of time Sir, he said I er, missed most of the best bits. He had to dash off to a meeting fairly early."

"Damn and blast him," the Lieutenant grumbled. "I asked Lorenzo to spend the whole day with you."

"Not his fault, I'm sure Sir. But he did say I could go back today, if you cleared it."

"Of course, of course," the Lieutenant waved his right hand towards Ernest, as if to brush away the very idea of him not returning. "You really must see the whole thing while you're here – an educated chap such as yourself."

"Yes Sir."

"After all, you'll be wanting to tell the boys when you get back to teaching."

"That's right Sir."

"Not the smutty stuff I hope," the Lieutenant gave a mischievous grin. "Though I daresay school boys today get up to far worse in their own dorms."

"One never can be sure, Sir."

"Quite, quite," the Lieutenant's mind was clearly wandering once again. "Young rascals eh Green. Damned young rascals."

The Land Rover was still waiting as he had left it outside the barracks the night before. He climbed in and grabbed a map from the glove compartment. He ran his hand over the map to flatten out the creases.

"San Bastiane? Where the hell are you?" he muttered to himself casting his eyes around the great circular void in the map that represented the volcano. "Hang on, San Sebastiano al Vesuvio. That's it – San Sebastiano al Vesuvio." He hurriedly worked out a route, then casting the map down on to the passenger seat, started the engine and careered away from the barracks, kicking up a cloud of dust in his wake.

As the road took him away from the Neapolitan urban decay, he followed a winding lane from farmhouse to farmhouse, with the Bay of Naples rising up as blue as the sky in his rear view mirror. But there was now no escaping the sight of the great mountain and the gathering cloud of rising black gases bubbling above it.

Not for a moment did Ernest consider his own safety, even as the lane began to chicane backwards and forwards in a winding S pattern with an incline that clearly indicated that the vehicle had already begun its ascent up the volcano's slopes.

He passed through a scattering of villages, where people stood leaning on their rakes or simply standing outside their homes, watching the deadly wisp of cloud gathering overhead. Their faces were creased with concern.

"Preghiera," Ernest muttered beneath his breath. "What the hell are you doing up here my love?"

He drove on, increasing his speed, even as the dusty road became narrower and harder to negotiate. He stopped at a fork in the road, confused and losing all sense of direction. He carefully re-examined the map, cast it back on to the seat beside him and skidded away.

San Sebastiano al Vesuvio was a remarkably unassuming place, perched on the mountain's western slopes. Ernest barely realised he had reached the village, even as he drove through the centre of it. A few houses, a school, a shop and a modest church – but little more. He parked the car on what appeared to be a central square, and put on his cap. 'How difficult can it be to find her in a place as small as this?' Ernest thought.

He stepped out of the vehicle and looked up again at the mountain, with its crater now looming perilously close. What had been black wisps of smoke, had now evolved into billowing grey clouds of ash, which seemed to be barrelling over themselves to escape the mouth of the crater. A pungent smell of sulphur hung in the air. He grabbed a handkerchief from his pocket and held it to his mouth.

Ernest walked around the village and on first inspection, struggled to find anybody. But a young teacher was busy fastening shutters to the outside of the school building.

"No school today?" Ernest asked as he approached.

"No school today," the young woman nodded. "The children will have a real life lesson in geology today I think. Are you here to evacuate us all?"

"On my own?"

The woman shrugged.

"No, I'm not here to evacuate you all. Though, I suspect it's advisable to get away from here. I'm looking for somebody."

"Who?"

"A young woman."

"Any young woman?"

Ernest smiled. "Preghiera de Rosa."

"de Rosa? You sure about that?"

"Yes. Preghiera de Rosa."

"There is a Preghiera – house on the end. She's expecting?"

"No," Ernest said, suddenly beaming. "She's not exactly expecting me. But thank you." He took to his heels down the path.

"No, no," the young teacher shouted after him as Ernest dashed across the square, still limping against his afflicted ankle. "That's not what I meant!" But he was already too far away to hear.

Ernest banged on the old green door of the end house without even considering what his next words might be when the door opened. But nothing prepared him for Preghiera opening it herself. There she stood, wearing a neat little pinafore, her hair tied up in a bun. Preghiera stared at Ernest in disbelief and her eyes immediately filled with tears.

"No, no, no," she said, pushing him away from the door. "You can not come here."

"Preghiera," Ernest tried to speak, but the young woman's rising panic was poured out over his words.

"No, no, no," she gushed. "You can not, you must not be here. Oh my love, my love, my love." With this, her passion seemed to falter and she half collapsed into Ernest's arms on the doorstep. She wept desperately into the shoulder of his uniform, as she whispered, "no, no, no, you can not be here."

She lifted herself away from him and gestured towards the church across the square. "They are all in there. The village is meeting to decide what to do. Vesuvius is awake you see."

"I know," Ernest nodded, coughing once more into his handkerchief on the sulphurous air. "So why are you here?"

"It is cooler up here on the slopes of the mountain," she muttered. "And they wanted me away for a while."

Preghiera glanced back across towards the church, its sturdy oak doors were still firmly shut against the world.

"But you must go," Preghiera went on. "They will kill you. My uncle will kill you. My cousin will kill you." She let out one long, gruesome groan of sheer suffering, before adding in a low voice, "my husband will kill you."

Ernest stood dumbfounded like a statue deposited on the doorstep. It seemed like an age of silence passed between them before he spoke again.

"Your *husband*?" he repeated.

"My cousin, my husband," Preghiera seemed to balance the two words in either hand as she spoke. "They are the same – they made me marry my cousin." Her voice broke again, and she sobbed bitterly into her slender hands, which met her face in the gesture of a prayer.

"No, no, no," Ernest repeated Preghiera's own phrase back at her. "This cannot be. Why? Why would they do this? Marry your cousin? Why?" he demanded.

Preghiera reached down and untied her pinafore and let it slip to the floor. It revealed a distinctive bump across her abdomen. It was not yet huge, but its globe-like rise and fall could mean only one thing.

Ernest slumped to his knees. Now he appeared to be the one in prayer.

"No, this cannot be!" he said angrily. "It cannot be."

He looked up at Preghiera's grief-stricken face.

"But when did you marry him?"

She could not offer him an answer through her mournful sobs. She raised her hand again to her mouth, and Ernest saw now the golden band on the fourth finger of her left hand.

"My love, my love," she intoned softly. "I am so, so very sorry."

Ernest raised himself to his feet in a single, sudden and swift movement. He turned from Preghiera, his face crimson in rising anger.

"You should leave this place," Ernest said sharply. He glanced down at the bump beneath her clothing. "Both of you."

He walked quickly towards the waiting vehicle, crunched the gearbox into submission, and skidded away from the village square as tears began to flow down his face stinging like lava-flows against his skin. He careered back down the side of the mountain, tearing through the dusty lanes he had passed with so much optimism less than an hour before.

Now the city and Bay of Naples stretched out before him, while the increasingly ominous cloud of ash gathered in the skies of his rear-view mirror. Ernest could barely breathe for sobbing as he drove. So, it was over, finished, forever. He had lost his love, his one true love, and now, bound before God and her own people, there was no way of getting her back. No redemption for either of them. No escape from the misery that seemed to stretch ahead of him through time, undiminishing down the years. Never again could he be happy. Never again would he feel the lightness of love, the sense of ease of being close to the love of his life. It was all finished and he would fight on through this God-forsaken war, but with no happy ending to fight for any longer.

By the time he reached Torre Annunziata and parked up the Land Rover outside the barracks, all he felt was empty and suddenly devoid of emotion. It was as though it had all sluiced from him on the drive back down the mountain. He had handed it over to that great, angry deity that now rumbled across the bay, groaning and growling as the skies rapidly darkened from the billowing bile that flooded out of the top of the volcanic crater high above the scene.

Chapter seventeen
1993

A bar tender fiddled with the steaming coffee machines, before handing over a cappuccino and nodding half-heartedly to Ernie. He gestured towards a plate of sweet pastries on the far end of the bar. Ernie chose one and carried it on a tiny plate, together with his coffee to a small table by the window.

He looked for a moment at the view of a brick wall on the opposite side of the street and the occasional flash of a speeding Vespa driver passing by, before tucking into his breakfast. He reached into his pocket and took out the postcard from Preghiera. He read it over two or three times: "Domani è adesso, amore mio. Preghiera x"

"Tomorrow is now," he muttered to himself. "Tomorrow is now. It's actually now my love."

He was halfway through the pastry when Rachele appeared at the archway that led into the restaurant. She smiled towards Ernie and flashed her hand in the briefest of waves, before negotiating the room on nimble feet to join him.

"Morning my dear," Ernie beamed. "The coffee is good."

"Fantastic," Rachele said. "I'll grab something. How are you feeling?"

"A little nervous I suppose," he smiled, lifting his right hand to show its subtle shake.

Rachele leaned across the table and gave his shoulder a gentle squeeze.

"You'll be fine. You're doing the right thing. You do know that you're doing the right thing, don't you Ernie? If you didn't do this, you would always regret it."

"Absolutely," Ernie nodded. "Happy endings."

"Happy endings," Rachele agreed. "Here's to happy endings."

1944

Ernest awoke to the sound of the rapid movement along corridors of many boots. At the very moment he opened his eyes, the Lieutenant burst into the dormitory.

"Sorry for the rude awakening Green," he announced with a little cough. "I hope you got to see everything you wanted at Pompeii?"

Ernest rubbed his eyes and nodded. "Yes Sir, absolutely. I saw as much as I needed to see."

"Good, good. Well today I rather think you are going to get a better understanding of the lived experience of its inhabitants."

"Sir? I don't understand your meaning."

"The blasted volcano has been going hell for leather all night," the young officer explained. "Surprised you slept through it actually Green."

"I was rather tired Sir. The volcano Sir? The eruption has worsened?" Ernest rubbed his eyes to try to properly shake himself from his slumber.

"It's caused all kinds of problems for those American johnnies with the little US Air Force base just outside Pompeii. The ash or the dust or whatever it is spurting out the top of the blasted thing has grounded half of their aircraft. Completely totalled some of them apparently. Now listen, we have been given a bit of a task today," the Lieutenant spoke briskly. "I have two units working on the evacuation of a series of villages that appear to be directly in the path of the lava flow."

"Lava Sir?" Ernest suddenly sounded alarmed.

"Yes Green, lava, of course lava – it is a volcano erupting out there. Were you expecting custard?"

"I hadn't realised it was quite that serious an eruption."

"Oh yes, it's a big one I'm told," the Lieutenant beamed mindlessly. "Quite the spectacle I believe. It should be quite an experience. Anyway, I know you're getting rather used to driving that Land Rover. Truth is, my driving is hopeless. Worse than hopeless in fact. Self-taught you know. Between you and me Green, I'm more likely to kill myself than to be killed by the volcano if I drive. Wondered if I might trouble you to be my driver for the operation?"

"Of course, Sir, I'll be very happy to help," Ernest said as he twisted his body out of bed and started to put on his uniform in a hurry.

"We need to evacuate a place called San Sebastiano al Vesuvio," the Lieutenant explained, as he strode across to the window and looked out at the scene dominated by the eruption on the horizon. An inky grey streak smudged across the sky out into the bay.

"San Sebastiano al Vesuvio? The lava is heading to San Sebastiano al Vesuvio?" Green cried, panic rising in his voice.

"Yes, that's right, do you know it?" the officer said absently.

"Yes, San Bastiane. I do know it," Green speeded up his preparations visibly. "Oh my God, Sir, San Bastiane. Why does it have to be San Bastiane?"

"Crickey Green, you really have been assimilating yourself into the local culture haven't you," the Lieutenant said merrily. "You sound almost like a native. Most impressive, I must say. Jolly good, jolly good indeed. I can't follow any of it. The language all sounds like double-Dutch to me, and frankly, everywhere looks the same. Dusty. Down at heel, if you know what I mean. Shambles of a place as far as I can see. Bloody shambles. And now this," he turned back to the window and the epic scene of tectonic vitriol bursting forth on the horizon. "Can you imagine? Poor buggers eh Green. Poor buggers."

Ernest pulled on his boots, jumped back up, and swiftly placing his cap on his head, stamped his right foot to attention.

"All present and correct Sir," he formally announced.

"Splendid, splendid," the Lieutenant nodded. "Good Lord, you are speedy, aren't you? Most impressive. Let's be off then, shall we?"

Before he had finished speaking, Ernest was leading the way out of the door.

"Quite right, that's the spirit, no time like the present," the Lieutenant chuntered as he tripped along to keep up with his subordinate. "Let's go and get these poor dagos to some sort of safety."

Ernest drove with equal determination, in a manner that rather alarmed the young officer. "I say, I know it's an emergency Green, but let's get there in one piece, shall we?" the Lieutenant said, holding on to his cap as Ernest weaved the Land Rover in a series of ambitious manoeuvres to overtake the lorry loads of British and American troops that were lumbering up towards the evacuation villages.

"Keen to get this done Sir," Ernest said brusquely.

"Quite right, I suppose," the Lieutenant nodded. "But let's have a care for the Landie. We can't afford to lose her. I say, you really do know these roads well Green. Are you sure you've not been here before?"

"Intuition I suppose, Sir. Like you said, all these places look the same."

"True enough I suppose," the Lieutenant muttered, silently wrestling with the logic of this in his mind.

Before long the scale of the disaster unfolding ahead of them became gruesomely apparent. The horizon was glowing with a false second dawn, while the two men twisted their faces against the overpowering smell of sulphur.

"Bloody hell fire Green, look at the place. Just take a look at the blasted place." The two men gazed up at the sight of the magma in the cauldron of the crater giving the peak of the volcano an other-worldly glow, which reflected on the bottom swirls of the thick, insipid black clouds of ash that now hung over the scene.

"It looks like Dante's blasted Inferno," the officer whispered to himself.

Ernest slowed the car to an almost standstill and leaned forward to take in the scene, his mouth dropping open in wonder. "It's like the very gates of hell," he whispered, before crunching the gears and careering on towards the angry mountain.

When they arrived at the sulphurous village, Ernest parked the Land Rover in the same place as he had on the previous day, and climbed straight out of the vehicle. The Lieutenant eyed him with wonder.

"You're certainly keen," he laughed.

"I'll start with the house on the end, Sir," he announced, before the Lieutenant had even found the door handle of the car.

"Good chap," the officer called after Ernest, still a little shaken from the drive. "Carry on Green, carry on."

Rounding the corner on foot, Ernest was confronted by the strange and awe-inspiring sight of a great wall of lava moving with an odd rolling flow down the slope. It wasn't red, as he had imagined it would be, but black and crusty, with the texture of burnt porridge. Great mountains of it, moving as one on a scale that was hard to take in. But there was no denying its unnegotiable force – trees, cars and the whole sides of houses were being swept up in this slow-moving river of darkness, sparking into blazes as the wooden surfaces were enraged by the unimaginable heat of the molten rock. It was tracking down the mountainside just yards from the edge of the house in which Preghiera was living. Ernest stood a moment and gazed in horror.

A small dark-haired boy sheltered in the ley of the houses, watching Ernest nervously as the soldier tried to make sense of the scene. Ernest sensed the child, catching glimpses of him from the corner of his eye, but when he turned the child was gone. He shook his head from side to side for a moment, as if to try to shake the apparition from his mind. He then looked up again at the gargantuan lava flow, and steeled himself for action.

Ernest ran up the path and banged on the door. An elderly man, whom Ernest immediately took to be Preghiera's uncle, opened the door and squinted out at the young soldier. He looked desperate, like a frightened child who had been left alone to tackle a danger far beyond his capacity to escape.

"You are all being evacuated to safety," Ernest said, pushing past the old man without another word. He immediately set about dashing from room to room, apparently looking for occupants – but all the time only thinking of one person. He found Preghiera in an upstairs bedroom. Her face was contorted in fear. Ernest reached out a hand. "You're coming with me."

"But my," she paused a moment, "my cousin will return soon."

"You mean your husband?" Ernest gave a bitter little flash of a grin. "Where is he?"

"He went into Naples."

"Naples? He left you and your uncle here? In this?" Ernest laughed angrily. "He left you here to die?"

"He is coming back," Preghiera said meekly. "He did say he would come back."

"Not bloody likely," Ernest seethed. "But don't worry, there are two whole units of soldiers making their way up here to get everybody out. If he does come back, he'll be taken to safety. But you are coming with me, now."

Grasping her hand firmly, he pulled her to her feet and led the way forcefully down the stairs, his hand still clinging to Preghiera's as she ran behind him. Ernest brushed straight past the old man, who was still standing by the door.

"Women," Ernest paused and looked down once again at Preghiera's domed midriff. "And children first." The old man nodded and encouraged Preghiera out of the house with a flurry of hand gestures.

Ernest almost dragged Preghiera away from the house and manhandled her into the passenger seat so recently vacated by the Lieutenant. The Lieutenant himself wandered around ineffectually tapping his swagger stick in his gloved hand, as he waited for an opportunity to command some element of the evacuation, which with the arrival of the first lorry load of soldiers, seemed to be taking place perfectly well without him.

"This woman is pregnant Sir," Ernest called across. "I'm taking her straight back down to safety. The fumes," he added by way of explanation.

"Of course, of course," the Lieutenant agreed. "Rather. Good show Green."

At that moment a loud creaking sound growled behind them. Ernest turned to see the river of slow-moving lava had suddenly swelled, as if in rage, and was now skirting the base of the far side of Preghiera's uncle's house.

"The old man!" Ernest shouted.

"He's still in there?" the Lieutenant cried.

Preghiera let out a frantic scream as she turned in the car seat to look back at the house, which now seemed to be swaying like a sapling in a gale, its wooden gable end dancing with the flow of molten rock that was careering through its foundations.

Ernest ran back towards the house. The old man was still standing looking down absently at the Land Rover, apparently oblivious to the danger.

"Let's get you the hell out of here," Ernest shouted, taking hold of the old man by the shoulders, and pulling him down the path. His elderly legs gave way and his feet kicked to find a purchase on the ground, as Ernest strained and the man's weight transferred suddenly into his arms. He pulled and dragged the man down the path in a sort of ungainly rugby tackle. The Lieutenant had reached the edge of the gate, and dropping his swagger stick on the floor, he grabbed the old man's legs and helped to manhandle him out of danger just in time.

Behind them the old house gave one final crackling howl, as it broke crisply down the middle like a communion wafer, and half of the building appeared to glide in its entirety down the mountainside, helplessly riding the growling wave of lava.

They lowered the elderly man on to the floor and instinctively dusted him down as they helped him back to his feet.

"Get him in the car, for God's sake," Ernest cried to the Lieutenant, who ran on ahead to open the Land Rover's back door. With her bewildered uncle seated in the vehicle, panting and chuntering in an unintelligible flow of Neapolitan dialect, Preghiera turned to pat and caress the old man with a flurry of concern, brushing at the sides of his face with overpowering tenderness.

"He's fine, he's fine," Ernest said, calming her swiftly.

"The house! The house is gone!" Preghiera could hardly get the words out as she struggled to find her next breath.

"Calm yourself," Ernest reassured her. "You're safe. Everybody's safe. We're getting out of here now."

Ernest took to the driver's seat and started the engine. The Lieutenant looked over in horror at the gaping hole where the family's house had stood until a moment before. Every piece of timber, every piece of masonry, every door and every window had in seconds been folded up and consumed by the merciless molten flow. He turned to Ernest, and wiping his forehead with his handkerchief, he quietly mused, "You know, I think I'll come back down with you. Best placed to lead this sort of thing from HQ. And you might need a hand, with the old man and such like."

"Quite right Sir," Ernest nodded as the Lieutenant climbed into the back of the Land Rover beside Preghiera's uncle.

"It's all going to be fine now Sir," the Lieutenant reassured the elderly man. "British Army," he added, pointing at his regimental cap badge. "Everything's all in hand you know."

The passengers were plunged back into their seats as Ernest thrust his foot towards the accelerator and made his way swiftly out of the village. Ernest drove with his blue eyes fixed on the winding road, swerving occasionally to avoid another lorry load of soldiers making their way up the mountainside. Preghiera occasionally looked across to him, wringing her hands in her lap nervously, opening and closing her mouth unable to find any words. Both were acutely aware of the Lieutenant's presence in the back seat, but the silence between them was tangible and for both of them, it was almost more than they could bear.

"Terrible business," the officer babbled. "Shocking, shocking." But neither Preghiera nor Ernest nor the old man even heard him. They were all deep in their own thoughts.

Back in Torre Annunziata, the Lieutenant leaned forward to make himself heard. "Better drop the civilians off at the hospital before we head back Green."

Ernest nodded.

"I hope you will be okay my dear," the officer added, speaking unnaturally loudly in the confused hope that it would allow the Italian woman to understand English if he shouted it at her.

Ernest parked the vehicle outside the hospital entrance and walked around to help Preghiera out of her seat. He then helped her uncle out of the car.

"Do you feel okay?" he said. Preghiera nodded. "Still," he added softly, "best to get everything checked out. Under the circumstances."

"My family?"

"We'll make sure they know where to find you," the Lieutenant shouted through the open window of the car. She flashed a little smile at the officer.

"Come, I'll take you both inside," Ernest offered, taking her hand more gently now.

"No, you should carry on," Preghiera looked up at Ernest with her eyes glinting with emotion. "We need to take our own paths. We have no choice."

Ernest's eyes implored her silently to allow him to take her hand, but she pulled it away. "We have no choice. We must go our own way from here. You know it as well as I do."

The Lieutenant watched on, thinking how terribly dramatic the Italians can be. "It's like a scene from a Puccini opera," he muttered, only half under his breath.

Ernest looked down at Preghiera's hand in his, slender, soft and warm. "I know," he said quietly. "I know we must."

"Yes, that's right, you must, best of British luck my dear!" the Lieutenant chirped from the back of the car.

Ernest reached into his pocket and took out an old letter from his mother. He tore off the top corner, where his mother had written their home address. "If you ever want to find me, when all this is over," he whispered, placing the scrap of paper in her hand.

Preghiera glanced at the address and folded it in her slender fingers. She reached out and took Ernest's hand once more and held it for a long moment. Their eyes were locked together, glistening in the sunlight. Preghiera nodded and gently slipped her hand from Ernest's hold. She took a single step back.

"But I want you to always remember," her voice broke with emotion, "there will always be domani, domani, domani." With the last domani, she crumpled with a sob.

Ernest watched Preghiera turn and walk towards the hospital beside her uncle, who had reached up to take her arm and support her every step, his old face creased with concern. Ernest stood and drank in her features and her shape, the flow of her body and her olive skin that softened at the nape of her neck where her long dark hair settled. She turned one last time before opening the hospital door and looked for a final moment upon Ernest, those big eyes fixed on his, then she turned and went.

The soldier stood a moment longer, watching the heavy oak door close behind her, and feeling more hopelessly alone in the universe than he had ever felt in his life. He took a long slow sigh, and turned on his heel to walk slowly and despondently back to the driver's seat.

"Next to creating a life, the finest thing one can do is to save one," the Lieutenant said quietly from the back seat, before adding, by way of explanation: "Abraham Lincoln. Now there was a chap who knew how to write a decent quotation."

The Lieutenant gave Ernest a pat on the forearm. "And incidentally Green, you just saved two."

Ernest nodded. "We saved three lives Sir."

"Oh yes, of course. She did look a few months gone. Good show indeed," the officer agreed.

"Three lives saved and so much lost. What will it profit a man if he gains the whole world, yet forfeits his soul?" Ernest quoted back to the Lieutenant, who nodded sombrely while frowning to himself as he secretly struggled to understand the soldier's meaning.

"Well quite," the officer sounded bemused. "Really rather profound Green. As ever, good chap. Nail on the head and all that. Quite the philosopher. I admire you for that. Terrific capacity to see the bigger picture, if I may say. Jolly well done. That will get you far. But listen here Green. You mustn't go beating yourself up too much. I'm tip-top, 100 per cent sure that the chaps will get everybody out of that God-forsaken place," he said by way of comfort. "You have my word of honour on that. You needn't trouble yourself at all on that count. Not at all. They have His Majesty's Army to thank for their lives mind you. And you've certainly done your bit Green, and more. You can be damned proud of yourself Green. Damned proud. There are men who go through their whole Army careers without having the opportunity to demonstrate valour of that magnitude. Crickey, when that lava flow swept down. Crikey indeed eh? You were challenged in the field and you showed your grit, as they say. I admire that in you Green," he patted his forearm with pride. "And it certainly won't go unnoticed in despatches. You have my absolute word of honour on that point." The Lieutenant climbed into the front passenger seat, having worked himself up to a lather, positively bristling with pride in the entire British Army. He settled into the passenger seat as Ernest started the engine with a shake of his head. The Land Rover grumbled back into life and Ernest cranked it into first gear.

"And another thing. You know what, Green," the Lieutenant mused as the car rumbled along the street, "I think that woman rather had eyes for you."

"Do you really think so Sir? How extraordinary."

"Yes Green," the Lieutenant chuckled. "I rather do actually Green. I tend to pick up on this sort of thing, and I really rather do."

Chapter eighteen
1993

A waitress shuffled out from a back room and cleared away the breakfast plates and cups in a cacophony of clattering. Ernie took the last sips of his coffee and smiled at Rachele across the table.

"It really has been very kind of you to keep me company like this," he said with a tissue paper thin smile. "I don't know what I should have done if we'd not met. I'm sure I would have been moping about alone worrying about whether or not I was doing the right thing."

"But now you know you are," Rachele said. "That's the important thing."

"Yes indeed. Now I'm certain it's the right thing," Ernie agreed.

"I do hope this isn't a goodbye?" the young girl added.

"No? I'm sure you must have better things to do with your time in Naples than keeping an old fogey like me company."

"Not at all," she added tersely. "What else would I be doing? Anyway, you're not going to get rid of me that easily. I'll be joining you today of course."

"Oh no, you mustn't do that."

"Somebody's got to walk you to your meeting."

"Really?" Ernie grinned. "I'm sure I could manage alone. I've done so for quite a while you know my dear."

"Don't be silly. I'll come with you, make sure you're safely delivered to Preghiera, then of course I'll step away and leave you two old love birds to it."

Ernie laughed and put down his empty coffee cup. "I'm really not sure it'll be like that. After all, as you say, we're old people now. Where's the romance?"

"Oh Ernie, there's always romance," Rachele enthused, clinging to her mug of coffee like an embrace. "There has to be. There always has to be romance."

"And what about you? Where's your romance my dear?"

Rachele swept the idea away with her napkin. "Oh, I'm far too young for all that."

"You're too young, I'm too old. I wonder when the romance should be arriving in our lives?" Ernie mused quietly.

"I suppose whenever it arrives," the young woman said with a pat of his hand on the table. "We must be open to love whenever love arrives."

"That's true enough my dear, because I can tell you from experience, even in a long life, true love doesn't visit very often."

"I know Ernie." Rachele nodded. "That's why I'm going to make sure you get safely to your meeting. Just call me Cupid." She winked at the elderly face that smiled at her across the table.

"Cupid indeed," Ernie scoffed. "Funny sort of love story if you ask me. Where's Cupid been all these years?"

1944

The barracks was alive with activity when Ernest and the Lieutenant arrived back in the Land Rover. Two ambulances and two troop transporters were parked up outside the main entrance.

"Looks like the unit is back from the front," the Lieutenant said. "Some of them at least. What a moment to get back to Naples."

The first person Ernest saw as he walked into the lobby of the building was Smudge. He was sitting quietly on a small wooden bench waiting for something or somebody. His face still looked acutely familiar, despite the addition of a black patch over one eye.

"Ernest, you're here too?" Smudge sounded surprised. "We didn't know whether you'd got out of it or not. And Patterson?"

"Patterson bought it at Cassino," Ernest whispered with a pained expression, as he sat down beside his old friend.

Smudge nodded sombrely. "Do you remember little George Durrer?" he asked. "He stood on a mine on the side of Monte Cassino. There was nothing of him to bury."

The two men pondered the idea silently for a moment, before Smudge decided to lighten the mood. "You look well though?" he said.

"I'm in one piece, broken ankle was about my limit."

"Well done, glory wound," Smudge laughed. "As you can see, and I can't, I am returned not quite in one piece." He tapped on the eye patch. "Lost it on the third day. Bit of shrapnel found its mark in my face. They had to operate and remove the eye. That was the end of my battle right enough."

"You can still see from your right eye though?"

"Oh yes, perfectly fine out of the right eye, so you know, mustn't grumble. Think of the money I'll save on glasses over the years. I quite fancy myself with a monocle."

Ernest smiled warmly at the no-nonsense resilience of the man.

"And Mouse?"

"Lost both legs I believe," Smudge shook his head as if he was still trying to compute the implications of the fact. "Poor bastard. I've not seen him yet, though I believe he was in the ambulance that came down in front of us."

"Poor Mouse," Ernest muttered, staring at his boots.

Smudge gave him a pat on the back. "Don't be glum about it all old chap," he smiled. "Mouse was always at his best when he was legless."

Ernest took his head in his hands in mock despair at the awfulness of the joke and gave a resigned little laugh. "I suppose you're right. It'll be the end of his war anyway."

"True enough," Smudge nodded. "He can enjoy getting back to Blighty and getting to know some pretty nurses while we battle on out here."

"You're not being sent home?"

"No, wouldn't hear of it," Smudge dismissed the idea with a wave of the hand. "It's only an eye. I've got another one. I'll hang around to claim my eye for an eye and all that. Now if I was in the navy, that would be more of a hindrance."

"How's that?" Ernest looked confused.

"Well, everything's 'aye, aye' in the Navy isn't it?"

Ernest groaned. "That's terrible – even for you. Is there anything you don't joke about?"

"Not if I can help it pal," Smudge grinned. "If you can't have a laugh about it all, well it's poor hopes then isn't it?"

Ernest nodded. "That's the spirit Smudgy. That's the spirit. What are you waiting here for? Let's go for a drink."

Smudge looked at Ernest with his single smiling eye. "I'm supposed to be waiting for eye drops, would you believe. Fuck it, let's go for a drink," he agreed.

But it felt strange for Ernest and Smudge when they took their places at the usual cast iron table outside their favourite bar. They shot back the Strega, time after time, but the two other chairs looked despairingly empty. Once, not so very long ago, those two chairs would have housed the restless rump of Mouse and the great garrulous bulk of Patterson. Now they looked stark in their emptiness.

It was the thought of replacing one of these voids that caused Ernest's stomach to flutter with a little pleasure at the sight of the Lieutenant turning the corner into the square.

"Will you have a drink with us Sir?" Ernest shouted across to him. The Lieutenant looked touched beyond measure at the invitation.

"Well, that's jolly decent of you Green," he gushed. "Don't mind if I do. Just a quick one. They'll be wanting to close up at this time I would have thought."

The Lieutenant turned to Smudge before taking a seat. "Evening old chap. I say, I was terribly sorry to hear about the eye."

"Not to worry Sir," Smudge grinned. "I'm a dab hand with a telescope these days. Binoculars, less so."

The Lieutenant nodded, uncertain of the joke. Ernest whistled at the waiter, who instinctively brought the Strega bottle from the bar as well as another glass for the officer.

"Has Green been telling you of his derring-do in the face of that volcano?"

"No Sir," Smudge said. "The only eruptions coming from Green this evening, I put down to the garlic that the mess has started using."

The Lieutenant nodded, once again uncertain if Smudge was being serious or not. "Yes, it can have that effect on a chap."

The conversation ebbed and flowed in this staccato vein for an hour or so, before the men relaxed properly into the evening.

"I believe you were a teacher, Green?" the Lieutenant said eventually, relaxing back into his seat and sipping at his glass of Strega.

"Training to be a teacher Sir."

"And will you go back to teaching, when all this is over?"

"I suppose I will," Ernest said. "Although, I'm not sure I will be able to teach anything I've learnt out here."

"What have you learnt out here?" Smudge asked, sniffing at the rim of his glass.

"I've learnt that humans are horribly flawed," Ernest said with a faraway gaze. "We're all past redemption, even the best of us."

"That's a gloomy thought to end the evening indeed," Smudge said with a whimsical little raising of his eyebrows.

"I'll go and pay the bill," Ernest slurred. "Tonight Smudgy, the drinks are on me."

"Cheers Ernest," Smudge said. "I'll see you right, when I get my glass eye."

"Yes, much obliged Green," the Lieutenant added. "Next time, they're on me."

The three men ambled back across the crumpling and bruised neighbourhoods of the suburban wasteland in the darkness, over the rubble-strewn bomb sites and down the piss-stenched alleyways. Ernest was momentarily aware of a dark-haired child hovering behind in the lamplight, but when he turned back the boy was already gone. He flapped his hand around his face, as if brushing away a mosquito.

Rounding a corner into another dark back road, Ernest became conscious of another shadowy figure. But this one was much more burly, leaning against the wall, lit only by the tip of his cigarette. The bulbous broken nose, and greasy mop of wavy black hair were disconcertingly familiar.

"Buona sera Ernesto," the figure spoke in a gruff voice.

"What the fuck do you want?"

"What you've done to Preghiera is not good, not good at all. I thought you were a good Christian boy?"

"Go fuck yourself," Ernest barked back into the darkness. "She's gone hasn't she. I'm not the one married to her."

Ernest carefully patted his trouser pocket, feeling for his bayonet in the darkness.

"I say old boy," the Lieutenant whispered.

"Let's get the hell out of here," Smudge agreed. But in the next moment the figure had pounced and was holding Ernest, twisting his arm up behind his back with one grisly hand, while the other grabbed his forelocks and pulled his head backwards.

"Get off him!" Smudge bellowed, leaping at the figure in the darkness. The next sound Smudge made was a hollow roar, as if all the breath had been sucked from him. Smudge slipped to his knees, clutching the crimson flow oozing from his abdomen where a knife now emerged from him, buried up to the hilt in his flesh.

"Smudge!" Ernest shrieked. At the end of the alleyway, half a dozen more figures appeared, but in moments Ernest realised with relief that these shadows were dressed in British Army uniform. At the sight of them, Ernest felt himself being released. As he slumped to the ground, he heard the big Italian boots running off into the darkness.

Then a single gunshot burst out. The hulking figure of the Italian crumpled to the cobbles. Beside Ernest, the Lieutenant was standing, his pistol shaking in his hand.

"Bloody hell," the Lieutenant whispered. "First time I've ever properly used this thing."

Ernest reached over and grabbed hold of Smudge.

"Is it growing darker, or is my eye patch on the wrong eye?" Smudge grinned up at Ernest, blood coughing up from his mouth with every word.

"When will you ever stop cracking fucking jokes Smudgy?" Ernest smiled sadly, his eyes filling with emotion. He turned to the group of soldiers who had now reached them. "Get help – he needs a medic! He's been stabbed!" Ernest bellowed. Two of the men ran back down the alleyway to raise the alarm, the others helped Ernest wrestle Smudge on to his back.

Three Geordies, who seemed to know what they were doing took charge. They were shouting instructions to each other, placing pressure on the wound, ripping up bits of uniform to try to stem the bleeding and clearing his airways with their stubby fingers. But Ernest knew it was already too late. Smudge's body had lost its glow, the sparkle had gone from his face.

"He's dead pal," the oldest of the three Geordies eventually said, as he rocked back on his heels, wringing the blood from his hands. "Sorry pal, but your mate's gone."

"I know he has," Ernest said. He could see Smudge's shadow taking to its feet and standing beside him out of the corner of his eye. He turned, but there was nothing there. Ernest buckled to his knees, and took Smudge's lifeless body by the shoulders. "Not you too Smudgy, not you," his voice cracked with the bare emotion. "It was me he was after. You'd done nothing Smudge. You'd done nothing wrong."

Chapter nineteen
1993

Ernie patted an extra splash of after shave lotion on to his cheeks and straightened his tie in the bathroom mirror. There was a knock at the door.

"Just coming my dear!" he shouted, as he made his way through the hotel room, picking up his tweed jacket on the way through. He opened the door and was met by Rachele's smiling face.

"Ready for this?" she asked.

"Born ready," Ernie nodded, as he slipped his jacket on and stepped out into the corridor. Ernie held out an arm to Rachele. "Thank you for supporting an old man on his last crack at a love story my dear."

"It's my honour Ernie," she purred, linking her arm through his and leading him towards the archaic lift.

Outside the streets were bustling and lively. The couple walked through the city, with Ernie looking at the windows of the swish designer clothes shops and craning his neck at the sight of a glass-fronted tower block.

"It's changed a little since my day," he muttered. At the taxi rank, Rachele opened the door for Ernie and helped him inside.

"Torre Annunziata," she called to the driver, as she climbed into the car beside Ernie.

"You know, I can't believe this is happening," he whispered as the car started to move away. Rachele reached out and wrapped her young hand around his. Ernie looked down at the slender olive-coloured fingers and smiled.

1944

Ernest pushed the wheelchair along Via Vincenzo Ianfolla. Mouse had barely spoken for the whole journey across the city.

He stared persistently at the absence where his legs should hang beneath the crisply ironed creases of his uniform.

Ernest followed the Padre through the gates of the military cemetery and the three men waited beneath the whispering branches of a tree, beside the gaping hole in the ground that waited for Smudge.

Six soldiers formed up as coffin bearers, while others lined up beyond the graveside with service rifles primed for their own show of honour. Silence enshrouded the scene as Smudge's coffin was carried into place and lowered into the earth, while another pair of fresh-faced young soldiers carefully folded the Union Flag that had been draped across the coffin.

The Padre spoke solemnly in a gruff, weary voice: "Give rest, O Christ, to your servant with the saints: where sorrow and pain are no more, neither sighing, but life everlasting."

Ernest heard no more, the words spoken faded to a background hum, while his mind flashed back to his friend's smile and laughter, to the happier times drinking Strega with Patterson and Smudge and Mouse in the Neapolitan sunshine. He looked at the crumpled silhouette of Mouse, his head deeply bowed in his wheelchair, his chin resting on his chest.

The volley of rifle shots jerked Ernest from his reverie.

"They shall grow not old as we that are left grow old..." the Padre went on and a bugler stepped forward in eager preparation for the Last Post.

As if lost in the moment a while, Ernest jerked his head once again to find minutes had passed, the grim-faced performance was at an end and the soldiers were falling out around him.

"Fancy a drink Mouse?" Ernest whispered.

"Christ yes," a small voice came from the wheelchair in front of him.

The Padre closed the black leatherbound book and placed a reassuring hand on Ernest's shoulder.

"It gets no easier," the Padre muttered. He looked suddenly older somehow, as if he had been wearied in his soul by one too many of these burials. Ernest knew that in reality they must be a similar age, but the Padre still seemed hopelessly old. He shook his head once again. "Yes, it never gets any easier," the Padre repeated, as he began to fold up the black-fringed stole from around his neck and slowly walked away from the open grave.

1973

Ernie pushed the wheelchair along Whitehall, eyes left as the parade passed the Cenotaph.

At the end of the ceremonials, the old soldiers tailed off, some appearing as if they didn't want to stop marching, others looking as if they wished they had never started. Ernest leaned down towards the wheelchair, his Italy Star medal wilting on his chest as he did so.

"Fancy a drink Mouse?" Ernie asked.

"Christ yes," the small voice came back from the wheelchair.

"You boys heading off?" a voice interrupted. It was the Lieutenant, looking as cheerful and mindlessly jolly as ever.

"No Sir," Ernie stammered. "We were going to grab a drink."

"Fine idea Green. The Italy Star Association lads are having a bit of a do at the Army and Navy Club in Pall Mall to mark the 30th anniversary of the Salerno landings. If you fancy joining me?"

Ernie looked at Mouse. Mouse looked back at Ernie and shrugged his shoulders.

"Why not," Ernie said to his former commanding officer. "After all, we rank and file were all there too, eh Sir?"

"Absolutely Green. You chaps did all the real graft, if I remember rightly."

"Do you think they serve Strega at the Army and Navy Club?" Mouse asked with a glimmer in his eye.

"Now then, not sure about that," the Lieutenant mused, still never certain when men were joking. "I'm sure we could ask."

"Don't worry Sir," Ernest said, "perhaps a stiff whisky for Mouse and I?"

"Now that sounds more like it Green," the Lieutenant nodded, and with a minor adjustment of his bowler hat, he led the way through the crowd of old men, all rattling with medals in the November drizzle.

1993

Ernie reached back into the taxi driver's window and handed over a colourful handful of lire notes.

"Good to see the locals are still robbing us blind," he grumbled to Rachele as he took her arm and they walked along the seafront of Torre Annunziata. "Still, this place looks a bit better than it did in my day."

Rachele laughed softly as the Mediterranean breeze caught her long brown hair and made it dance lightly around her face.

"What happened to Mouse and the Lieutenant, Ernie?" she asked.

"Oh, they're both long gone I'm afraid," Ernie said. "Mouse died of lung cancer about 15 years ago, and I don't know about the Lieutenant. He stopped appearing at the Cenotaph parade a few years back. I imagine he shuffled off this mortal coil in his own buoyant sort of way. 'Can't be helped chaps' he would have said."

Rachele laughed softly. "Bless him."

"Yes, bless them all," Ernie said. "Bless them all."

Ernie stopped and looked around. "I think it was this way my dear," he muttered, as he led Rachele off the seafront and down a series of cobbled pavements, passing buildings still crumbling, shops blindfolded by their shutters that looked as if they hadn't opened their doors for years. The shutters were daubed with spray can graffiti. Ernie raised his eyebrows at the outline of a large and alarmingly excitable male member, painted in a shocking fluorescent green.

"Maybe this place doesn't look much better than it did in 1943," Ernie chuckled. "Well, perhaps a little better. But there's not much in it. There's really not much in it at all."

They walked on and on, taking shortcuts through alleyways and cutting across small residential squares of apartment buildings.

"You know Rachele, the extraordinary thing is I can retrace my steps here, though I increasingly get lost trying to drive to Sainsbury's back home. But this place, this place is ingrained on my mind, as if somebody had burnt the map of these streets on to my brain."

He looked down at his wristwatch. "We should be on time," he muttered. Rachele squeezed his hand comfortingly.

"Of course we will Ernie. Of course, we will. There's still plenty of time."

Ernie led them down a side alleyway, cutting at right angles from a square. It was cluttered with large commercial bins for a bar that fronted on to the other side of one of the buildings. A rat scattered at the sound of their approach and slipped effortlessly into a drain. Ernie paused and looked down at the grubby paving slabs beneath his feet.

"This was the place where Smudge died," he whispered. Rachele nodded and then rested her head for a moment on Ernie's arm. They stood silently for a few seconds, with the sound of Vespas buzzing down the nearby main road providing a constant background hum. Ernie reached into his pocket and took out a small paper poppy, which had been in his jacket since the previous November. He stretched down and laid the single poppy with all due ceremony at the side of the pavement. He bowed his head and then nodded.

"I've not forgotten you Smudge my old mate," Ernie whispered. "Come on dear, let's carry on," he said, raising his head and wiping his hands together. "Let's carry on."

A few more twists and turns in the roads of Torre Annunziata, and Ernie pointed at a crumbling old building that had been blinded by breeze blocks built up in all its windows. "That was the barracks," he told Rachele. "That was the nearest thing we had to a home out here."

Ernie walked on with Rachele clinging affectionately to his arm.

"So long ago my dear," Ernie muttered, "it was all so very long..." But he couldn't finish the sentence. His words were taken from his mouth by what felt like a punch to his stomach.

"Down there," he gestured and led the way down an old alleyway. Ernie felt a familiar presence following just behind, just out of sight.

"This is where it happened – the blast," Ernie said. "I told you about the blast, didn't I? The dark-haired boy. He was holding the door handle one minute, gone the next."

Rachele put her hand across her mouth at the thought of it.

"Come on sunshine," Ernie called behind his shoulder. "You're home now. You stay here now, do you hear? You stay here now. Your people are here. You don't need to cling on to me anymore." Ernie thought he felt a gentle touch of a tiny hand on his palm. "You stay here now son," Ernie said again, his voice breaking. Rachele watched Ernie uncertainly.

Ernie didn't quite see the boy anymore. But he sensed that he was present in the air around him and he knew as he moved away the boy was remaining behind in this familiar place. The boy was setting himself down contentedly amid the rubble, flashing one final smile for the old man who was walking away into the labyrinth of back streets. Ernie couldn't see the smile, but he sensed it. He quickened his pace, and whispered to Rachele, "Come on my dear. Please don't ask me to explain. I have lots of loose ends to tie up on this trip. Some of them I just can't really explain."

The pair walked on in silence for a while, then turning one final corner Ernie stopped a moment to gather his thoughts. There before him was the square where he had so long ago first met Preghiera. He struggled to catch his breath. A group of teenagers stood in the nearest corner, slapping each other on the back affectionately and engrossed in florid conversation. They parted like reeds to allow the old man through. Ernie gazed across to the former butcher's shop in the far corner. It now appeared to be a shambling little place selling cigarettes and newspapers. But there, standing beside the entrance, was a familiar slender outline.

Those olive eyes caught his from across the square. Ernie stood still and felt Preghiera's gaze lock on to his. Those eyes – they were unchanged by the decades. Around them Preghiera's face had creased into wrinkles, and her once dark hair was brushed down into a grey bun with just a few wisps curling down around her temples.

Ernie felt a hand on his shoulder pushing him gently onwards. "Go on then," Rachele whispered. Ernie gathered his nerve and began to walk, never for a moment losing contact with that ancient and excruciatingly familiar face. Rachele followed closely behind. Before he realised the moment had arrived, Ernie found himself standing before Preghiera. She smiled with her eyes at the old man and reached out an elderly hand beyond him, placing it on Rachele's cheek.

"Thank you my dear," the old lady whispered. "You brought him back to me."

Ernie turned from Preghiera to Rachele, a puzzled frown creasing his forehead.

"So, my love, here you are, and you have already met my dear granddaughter I see," Preghiera said.

Ernie looked again at Rachele and nodded. "You know, I thought those eyes seemed familiar my dear," he smiled.

"I'm sorry, I didn't say, I thought it would scare you," Rachele said. "But I wanted to make sure you got here."

"But we met on the aeroplane..." Ernie seemed bewildered.

"Sure, I booked the tickets," Rachele smiled. "Yours as well as mine."

Preghiera turned her slender old fingers to Ernie's face, touching his cheek as lightly as she had ever done all those years before.

"I thought we would never meet again," she said softly.

"Yes," Ernie nodded. "It seemed that way. But I think I always knew we would be together once more, before the end came. I always hoped so anyway."

"I prayed for that too, so many years," Preghiera smiled. "And now here you are."

"Here I am."

"And no father to chase you away," Preghiera laughed, with a glance back towards the shop.

"I certainly hope not. My running days are long since behind me."

Preghiera reached forward and with the lightest touch of her lips, kissed Ernie's cheek.

"Thank you for coming back to me. Domani, domani, domani," she grinned. "Finally, today is tomorrow."

Ernie nodded and struggled to find the words to express his emotions. He reached for them in the air around him, before finally deciding on something easier to say: "Shall we go and get a drink?"

"Let's do that," Preghiera said, linking her arm through his.

"I'll leave you two young love birds to it," Rachele said with a smile. Ernie gave her a wave as Rachele backed away from the couple. "And hey," she added, as she skipped back into the crowd, "don't either of you do anything I wouldn't do."

Chapter twenty
1993

Ernie leaned forward across the table and gazed at the elderly face of Preghiera, ignoring the sounds of the bustling restaurant.

"Look at you," he beamed. "Look at you."

"Well, look at you," Preghiera shrugged. "Not so bad for your age."

A waitress arrived at the table and placed a glass of white wine and a beer on the table before them.

"Thank you," Ernie nodded to the waitress, before turning back to his companion. "It should be a Strega really, if I'm going to do the nostalgia thing properly, but it's a bit too early in the day for me. Anyway, Rachele and I drank quite a lot of it last night and my head isn't fully recovered."

Preghiera smiled.

"She's marvellous," the old man added. "You know, it never dawned on me for a moment who she was. I thought I'd met her out of the blue. Still, we did get on like a house on fire."

"You still don't get it do you?" Preghiera leaned forward and took Ernie's hand in her own. "Rachele isn't just my granddaughter. She is your granddaughter too."

It took a very long moment for Ernie's face to register the implications of what Preghiera was telling him. He sat for what seemed like an eternity with his mouth hanging open, as if he had lost all muscular control of his jaw.

He eventually broke the silence with a funny little laugh and then took a long slow drink from his beer. Finally, he took a deep breath and seemed ready to respond.

"You were pregnant when last I saw you," Ernie whispered. "Are you telling me the baby was mine all along?"

"Of course," Preghiera said. "I never said it was anybody else's child."

"But we only, you know, just the once, didn't we?"

"Sometimes, it only takes the one time," Preghiera shrugged expressively.

"You're sure? It couldn't have been your husband's child?"

"Of course not, my father only made me marry my cousin when he found out I was pregnant." Preghiera leaned forward and tenderly kissed Ernie's hand before holding it closely to her cheek. "There was nobody else my love."

"Does Rachele know?"

Preghiera nodded. "She does. And her father knew too."

"Her father?"

"Your son my love. Ernesto."

"Ernesto?"

"They couldn't stop me naming him Ernesto – though my father called him by his middle name, Giovanni."

"And he knew about me?"

"Not for a long time, but thankfully I had told him when we lost him. Just a few weeks before."

"Lost him?" Ernie asked.

"He died. He came off his Vespa. He was only 48. It nearly broke me."

Tears were escaping from Ernie's eyes before he realised they were even forming.

"I am so sorry," Ernie said. "He must have hated me."

"Of course not, why would he hate you?"

"To him, I must have been the man that made the memory of his father no longer the memory of his father," Ernie said. "I also must have seemed like the man who left behind his mother when she needed me most."

Preghiera fixed her eyes on Ernie's eyes.

"That's not how it was," she said. "I know that, you know that – and he knew that too. I made sure he understood."

"But all these years," the words seemed to choke Ernie.

"I couldn't tell you," Preghiera said. "First there was my father, then there was my cousin – my husband."

Ernie, suddenly feeling self-conscious, reached into his pocket and produced a handkerchief and started to dab his eyes.

"I am sorry Ernest, really I am."

Ernie smiled. "It's been a long time since anyone called me Ernest."

"Well," Preghiera grinned mischievously. "It's been a long time since anyone took me for a drink."

"Your husband?"

"He died in '89," she said swiftly. "I never loved him, not as I have always loved you."

"My dear, you shouldn't say that."

"It's true," she muttered. "No more secrets."

Ernie nodded. "No more secrets."

"But my love," Preghiera paused and looked down at her lap a moment. "I do have one more secret to tell you."

"Yes?" Ernie raised his eyebrows.

"I can't stay too much longer."

"Oh, ok," Ernie glanced at his watch. "That's quite alright. I can get you home whenever you like. Perhaps we could meet again tomorrow, or this evening?"

"No, my love," Preghiera smiled a bitter-sweet smile. Now it was her turn to be taken by surprise by the tears. "You don't understand me. I can't stay too much longer in this life."

Ernie's face turned the colour of ash. "You don't mean..." his words trailed away to silence. Preghiera nodded.

"Today must be our tomorrow."

"Our domani," Ernie nodded. There was a long, staring silence between them. "But why? I mean, what is it?" Ernie gushed.

"Cancer."

"Cancer?"

"In my breast," she placed a hand on her chest as she spoke. "But also then the, how you say, lymph nodes?" She tapped her neck. "And bones. And liver. And lungs. And," Preghiera took in a sharp intake of breath, "And brain."

Ernie buckled before her. "No my love," he whispered. "No, no, no, this can not be. This can not be."

"We must enjoy what time we have left given to us," Preghiera calmed herself and gave a smile of reassurance. "Can you stay a few weeks?"

"Yes," Ernie said. "Of course, I can stay forever."

Preghiera laughed a little. "I'm afraid that will not be necessary. A few weeks will do it, you see. That's what the doctor said – a few weeks at best."

"Weeks?"

Preghiera nodded.

"Weeks," Ernie repeated to himself, before making a visible effort to pull together his emotions. "We must," he nodded. "We must make them the very best weeks of our lives my love."

Preghiera smiled. "They will be my love." She gripped his hand once again. "You are with me. We are together. They will be the best of times. The very best of times."

"And the worst of times," Ernie thought to himself. But he hid the thought away behind another smile.

1944

Ernest pushed the wheelchair to the railway station, carrying Mouse's bag on his back. Mouse spoke sullenly from the chair as they negotiated the broken cobbles of the street.

"Now the Jerries have left Rome, do you think the unit will push north then Ernest?"

"I shouldn't be surprised," Ernest nodded. "I suppose they'll be wanting to chase Jerry all the way back to Berlin. I'm supposed to be returning to the front line in a couple of weeks. They reckon my ankle has healed sufficiently now for me to get shot."

"I wish I could stay and fight," Mouse grumbled.

"I reckon you've done your bit pal."

Mouse nodded silently and looked up at the skeletal remains of the buildings around them.

"Still, it'll be good to get home to my Mrs," Mouse added. "Prove to her that it's all still working down there, even without the legs."

Ernest laughed and heaved as he pushed the chair up to the station platform. "That's good to know." The railway carriage had been daubed by the squaddies with their own piece of ironic graffiti - "D Day Dodgers".

Mouse gave a bitter laugh. "That's what they called us. That's what that bitch Lady Astor called us."

Ernest broke into a flurry of song from behind him: "*We are the D-Day Dodgers, Out in Italy, Always on the vino, Always on the spree.*"

Mouse clapped along and took on another verse: "*Dear Lady Astor, You think you know a lot, Standing on a platform, And talking tommy rot. Dear England's sweetheart and her pride, We think your mouth is much too wide, From the D-Day Dodgers, Out in sunny Italy.*"

The locomotive let out a burst of steam ahead of them. Their singing had stopped and left behind it a tangible silence. They weren't smiling any more. The two men were still, gazing ahead down the tracks with their memories raw.

Ernest broke the silence, speaking, almost whispering another verse of the song under his breath: "Look around the hillsides, Through the mist and rain, See the scattered crosses,

Some that bear no name. Heartbreak and toil and suffering gone, The lads beneath, they slumber on. They are the D-Day Dodgers, Who'll stay in Italy."

Mouse nodded in agreement, lit a cigarette, took a long drag, then handing it back to Ernest for a draw, added a line of his own making: "Fucking Lady Astor, come and look at me. One of the D Day Dogers, Out in Italy." He looked down at the limp ends of his trousers where once his legs had been. "Fucking come and look at me. Nothing below the knee. Fucking come and look at me."

Ernest handed the cigarette back to Mouse and gave his shoulder a gentle squeeze. Mouse reached up and patted the hand on his shoulder.

"You'll be alright old pal," he said softly. "You'll be in Civitavecchia in a few hours, then on a troop ship home."

"That's when my battles will really begin, I suppose," Mouse muttered. "Living my life like this."

"You'll find a way."

"I know," Mouse nodded. "I will find a way. We'll all find a way."

The locomotive let out a long blast of the whistle.

"Come on sunshine," Ernest said. "Let's get you on the train."

Chapter twenty-one
1993

Ernie looked across Preghiera's kitchen table. Rachele was sitting opposite him, smiling through the rim of her wine glass. Preghiera was clattering pans at the hob.

"So, you knew everything all along," Ernie shook his head.

"Of course," Rachele said. "Of course, I knew everything. Well, most of it anyway."

"You had some nerve. The way you befriended me," Ernie grinned a little to show he hadn't taken it badly. "But why?"

"I wanted my grandmother to spend some time with you before," she paused and took a sip of wine. "Before it was too late."

Ernie nodded and looked out of the window at the garden beyond.

"And I wanted to get to meet my grandfather," she added. "And make sure he was suitable for my grandmother."

Ernie smiled. "And what did you make of him?"

"I liked him. A lot."

"I've not been much of a grandfather to you."

"Well," Rachele waved it away. "I've not been much of a granddaughter to you. Until now."

"Until now," Ernie agreed. "You know, I couldn't have wished for a finer granddaughter. You can certainly hold your liquor too. I guess you get that from me."

"You've obviously not seen my grandmother at Christmas."

Ernie laughed, but after a moment the laughter turned to a thoughtful frown. "That's true. I've never spent a single Christmas with your grandmother."

"You will."

"God willing," Ernie whispered, his gaze turned to the elderly lady serving out reams of spaghetti from a steaming pan.

"He will be," Rachele gave a sad smile. "He will be willing."

"I hope so, my dear."

Preghiera delivered two plates of spaghetti bolognaise and began to shuffle back to the other side of the kitchen to collect a third.

"I'll get it," Ernie said, rising to his feet." Preghiera waved him back down. "No, no, I'm not an invalid yet my love." She collected the third plate and joined them at the table.

"You know Rachele, Ernest and I were talking," Preghiera said. "We're not getting any younger, so we want to spend some time together."

"Of course," Rachele enthused, picking up the Chianti bottle and refilling the three glasses. "What the Americans call 'quality time'."

"That's the thing," Ernie agreed.

"So anyway, we are going to go away for a while."

"Away?" Rachele tilted her head towards her grandmother. "Away where?"

"Well, we thought Lake Como perhaps."

"Como would be nice," the young woman sounded relieved and took a sip of wine. "I thought for a moment you were revealing a suicide pact to me."

Preghiera laughed loudly.

"Oh, my dear!" Ernie shook his head. "Nothing so drastic, I can assure you."

"You need never fear on that front," Preghiera's eyes glinted, though her laughter had ebbed away. She grasped a silver crucifix that hung from a necklace and rested on her chest. "My father was too religious, but having a religious father wasn't altogether such a bad thing. Some sins I have committed. But that is a sin I would never consider."

Ernie touched Preghiera's shoulder with affection.

"Why did your father hate us so much my love?"

"Hate who?"

"The British. Soldiers generally."

"You were an invading army don't forget," Preghiera said lightly. "But my cousin Pietro was shot dead, we think by a British Intelligence officer when he was being questioned."

"About what?"

"His links to the camorra I imagine," she shrugged. "They were always asking about links to the camorra."

"But why shoot him?"

"Who knows," Preghiera thought about it a moment, before repeating "Who knows – lots of people were being shot in those days. Lots of people went out and never came home. You never knew anything of these kinds of atrocities?"

"No," Ernie muttered. "No of course not." But his mind was already echoing back to a single gunshot heard on the streets of the city long ago. "They were dark days my love."

Preghiera smiled up at him. "Thank heaven it is in the past. Ancient history."

"Ancient history," Ernie agreed. "But now, we must decide if we are going to Lake Como or not."

"Of course, you should go to Lake Como," Rachele beamed.

"You will be okay here if we go?" her grandmother stroked the table top with anxiety.

"You know I'm a grown woman now, don't you?"

"Si, si," Preghiera smiled. "I know you are a grown woman."

"Well, that's sorted it then," Ernie said. "We're going to Lake Como."

"Ha, a holiday, at my age," Preghiera shook her head. "Crazy, crazy."

"Not crazy my love," Ernie looped his spaghetti carefully around his fork.

"Can you just stay here in Italy, indefinitely?" Rachele asked Ernie. "I mean, do you not have things to get back to in England?"

"I don't see why I can't just stay on," Ernie said. "I don't have any pets. I might have to phone the UK to cancel the milkman and the newspaper deliveries, but otherwise, I'm a free agent."

"Do I have the right clothes to stay up in the North?" Preghiera wondered aloud.

"I will take you shopping," Ernie reasoned. "We will visit Milan enroute."

"Milan! The cost!" Preghiera smiled, and instinctively moved a hand to her face so her slender fingers covered him mouth. Her olive eyes glistened playfully and suddenly she seemed like the 17-year-old Preghiera once again.

"Today is our tomorrow," Ernie said, touching the top of her arm with affection.

"Listen to you two," Rachele laughed. "You'll have me crying again in a moment."

1944

Ernest walked back through the broken streets and fractured alleyways of Torre Annunziata alone. His palms still longed with the indentation of the handle bars of Mouse's wheelchair. He had never felt so alone. Patterson lay on the slopes of Monte Cassino. Smudge was buried on the outskirts of the city. Mouse was sailing for home broken and dejected. And Preghiera had released him from her life.

He wandered back to the most familiar streets around the barracks, and settled on a cast iron chair outside the bar. He called for a Strega, before shouting back to the barman to bring the bottle. The barman delivered it without a smile.

"You are alone today signore?"

"I am indeed quite alone," Ernest nodded.

"It's not good for a man to drink this stuff alone," the barman looked concerned.

"Are we ever truly alone?" Ernest asked enigmatically.

"Maybe you would prefer a beer?"

"No thanks. The Strega please. You're not the greatest salesman are you?"

The barman gave a shrug. "Please yourself, of course." He gave the glass a polish with the rag that hung from his belt, before laying it down on the table next to the bottle. "Your good health," the barman added, before sullenly ambling back towards the bar. Ernest sat and looked at the shapely contours of the bottle before him, removed the cork and poured out a generous slug of the nectar-like liquor.

A small dark-haired boy watched him from the shadows. Ernest knew he was there, but didn't turn towards him.

Are we ever truly alone? Ernest thought again to himself with a smile. He slowly lifted his glass, and raising it towards the empty square in a solitary toast, he muttered: "To happy endings," before knocking it straight back like medicine.

1993

Preghiera and Ernie walked along the promenade arm in arm. Rachele walked alongside them working her way through an ice cream in a wafer cone. Ernie was gazing at the gargantuan presence of Vesuvius, which had the setting sun illuminating it like a pantomime villain taking centre stage.

"It really is an extraordinary thing when you look at it," he said. "This great mountain connecting this bay with the very centre of the world."

"It's a hero and a villain, a god and devil all rolled into one," Preghiera added. "It gives us this rich farmland that has fed our people for generations, but it can turn to anger at any moment."

"Amazing to think you were both here for the eruption in '44," Rachele said, as she took another circular lick of her ice cream. "You must have been terrified."

"I don't remember being afraid, but it was an awesome sight," Ernie recalled.

"La colata lavica," Preghiera added with a sharp intake of breath. "Ricordo il flusso di lava."

"She remembers the lava flows," Rachele translated for Ernie's sake.

"How could we forget," Ernie nodded. "Such power. So non-negotiable." He looked back to the mountain. "I wonder what it's like up there at the top?"

"It's a great big crater, no lava on show these days though," Rachele said.

"You've been to the top?"

"Oh yes of course, it's not so tough a climb. More of a steep walk. The biggest problem is avoiding all the tourists. You should do it while you're here."

Ernie looked again at the mountain and stopped walking to consider the idea. "I'm not sure," he said after a while. "Surely it's dangerous."

"Not at all," Rachele smiled. "Vesuvius is pretty quiet these days. You would need to worry more about heat stroke than lava flows."

"I'm not sure," Ernie said again.

"Well, I for one am certainly not climbing that mountain," Preghiera added determinedly.

"Of course, not Nonna," Rachele smiled. "You're not well enough. But Ernie could do it no problem. I'll do it with you."

"Yes well, perhaps tomorrow."

Preghiera laughed a little. "Always domani with you." She turned to her granddaughter. "Men are all talk, you'll see."

"All talk indeed," Ernie blustered. "We'll do it, won't we Rachele? I'm not so old that I can't climb a volcano."

The following morning Rachele locked her car door and smiled at Ernie – an uninspiring sight in his rolled-up shirt sleeves, carrying a bottle of water, a bottle of sunscreen and a hastily cobbled together cheese sandwich in a small plastic bag.

"Time to put my money where my mouth is I suppose," Ernie grinned and headed towards the dusty path out of the car park. Before long, they found themselves trudging along as part of a snaking line of tourists, many of whom appeared to be a contingent of Japanese middle-aged couples who had been on the same luxury coach. The ladies walked beneath umbrellas, which they were using as parasols against the morning sun.

The heat was gradually rising as the day wore on, but the higher Ernie and Rachele got, the more they enjoyed the salty breeze that whipped in warmly from across the bay. A couple of ropes tied between wooden stakes provided the only edging to the dirt track. As it wound its way higher and higher, with the Bay of Naples ever more resplendent below, Ernie became increasingly more nervous about walking on the outer side of the path.

"If that dirt crumbles there would be nothing down for us," he grumbled to Rachele, who gave a little laugh.

"It's perfectly safe Ernie."

"And what if it did start erupting?" he said, as he paused to wipe his brow. "What would we do then? There would be nowhere to run."

"These days modern technology means they can see an eruption coming weeks in advance," Rachele reassured him.

"They would have stopped us climbing the path if there were any concerns. It is perfectly safe Ernie."

Ernie paused again to read a sign: "Attenzione caduta massi."

"It means beware of falling rocks," Rachele said, still smiling. "But as I say, it is perfectly safe Ernie."

Ernie withdrew into a period of quiet walking, and Rachele imagined that his mind must be casting back to seeing the volcano in full vitriol as a young man. In fact, Ernie was thinking not about the mountain, but about the friends he had left behind when eventually he had been able to return home from Italy. Patterson's death in particular continued to trouble Ernie. Leaving the Sergeant's body there on the hillside had felt wrong then, and it still felt wrong now – though he knew the body had been eventually recovered and the Sergeant now lay peacefully in a Commonwealth War Graves Commission cemetery nearby.

"I would like to revisit Monte Cassino too while I'm out here," Ernie said aloud. "Perhaps when I take your grandmother to Lake Como, it might be possible to call there enroute."

"Yes, you should do that," Rachele agreed. "It's good to lay all those old ghosts to rest."

"That's right," Ernie looked at Rachele and wondered at the young woman's extraordinary sensitivity and empathy. "That's exactly what I thought."

By the time Ernie and Rachele rounded the final corner to be greeted by the peak of the mountain, it came as something of a surprise. Suddenly they were standing at the very rim of an enormous crater. It wasn't what Ernie had imagined – no bubbling lava or geysers of seeping steam. It was just an enormous bowl of dust and dirt. Some edges were sheer and seemed to be cut into the fabric of the mountain, others were sloped with scree slides, and the occasional hardy bush grew up from the ground.

"I warned you it wasn't too dramatic a sight these days," Rachele said, catching her breath.

"No, but it's what lies beneath the surface isn't it my dear," Ernie took a swig from his bottle of water and offered it across to his young companion. "Looks can be so deceptive. Things can appear old and benign and shabby around the edges from the outside, so you would never have any idea of what passions lay beneath the surface. Passions can run deep, even when something is so ancient. Bubbling up over the years, waiting for the opportunity to rise up to the fore."

Rachele squinted up at Ernie in the heat of the midday sun. She no longer knew if he was still talking about the volcano.

1944

Ernest was drunk. Being drunk felt different when you were alone. There was a dreamlike sensation for him as he kicked back the chair and left the bar behind, slapping a random collection of coins and bank notes on the table as he went.

He staggered through the city streets that he had grown so vividly to despise, scowling at everyone he passed and hurrying through the alleyways with one purpose in mind. Moments later he found himself standing outside the butcher's shop on the little square. The place felt so empty and derelict knowing that Preghiera was not in there.

Ernest picked up a rock and threw it at the upstairs shuttered window in the centre of the building.

"Come out, you God-damn son of a bitch," Ernest slurred. "You want to fight me, well come out and fight me. You're a God-damn coward, getting big ugly thugs to do your dirty work. Come out here, you God-damn coward."

Eventually a light came on behind the shutters. They opened and Ernest could make out the little silhouette of the old butcher in his pyjamas. "You're drunk! Get out of here!"

"I'm sober enough to do you over, you old bastard! Come down here right now!"

The shutters closed and Ernest saw the light come on downstairs. A moment later the front door of the shop opened. The butcher appeared and squinted out into the darkness at Ernest.

"Oh, it's you," he muttered with contempt. "Preghiera is not here."

"I know Preghiera is not here. It's you I've come to see."

The old man walked out into the dimly-lit square and stood before Ernest. He placed a hand on Ernest's shoulder.

"You invade my country and demand my daughter."

"We liberated your country you dimwit," Ernest growled.

"Well, that all depends on your point of view now doesn't it," the butcher said. "We paid heavily for the honour of being liberated. You English and Americans don't know what the Germans did in those final hours before they left the city. The reservoirs were drained, the sewers dynamited, the coal reserves all set alight. The Germans torched the fishing fleet, wrecked the trams, burnt down the oil refinery and the brewery and the tannery. They blocked the main railway tunnel coming into the city by crashing two trains together head-on on the same line. My neighbour, he tells me, one German battalion broke into the library at the Italian Royal Society with cans of kerosene and they burnt all the books, shooting dead the guards who tried to stop them. They did the same at the University of Naples and again in Nola, where they say 80,000 precious books, and precious paintings from the old masters, were all torched. How can you call this a liberation? It's a decimation."

"You were happier with the Nazis in charge?" Ernest felt an anger rising within him.

The old butcher shook his head sadly in the night air. "You're just a silly young fool," he muttered. "You may have taken possession of this great land of ours. But my daughter is no longer available. You may not take possession of her. She is married in the sight of God."

"God-damn you. I love your daughter."

"Then I will pray for you," the old man smiled sarcastically. "I will pray for you and I will pray for Preghiera. For she has sinned greatly. I am sorry for your heartbreak. But the broken hearts of youth are quick to mend."

"I'll fucking kill you, you evil old fool," Ernest's words seemed more slurred than ever. He started to lunge towards the old man.

"You lay a hand on me, and I will call for the military police," the butcher shrugged, taking a quick step backwards. "You'll enjoy your time in solitary confinement. I will enjoy your time in solitary confinement. Anyway, you might as well get used to this solitary life, because you'll never see my daughter again as long as I live."

"I'll live to see you dead and laying in your grave," Ernest growled, grabbing the old man by the collar. "And Preghiera and I will be together again, if it's the last thing either of us ever do. We'll be together. Do you hear me? Do you hear me old man?"

The old man lifted his chin and spat into the drunken soldier's face. "And my curse on you, drunken English fool, my curse on you and any woman who finds herself with you." He spat again, this time on the floor. Ernest reached up and wiped the spit from his face. The butcher laughed a little. "We may be poor here," he said, "but we are families of honour. You dishonour my daughter and you disrespect me. A thousand curses upon you, stinking English soldier."

Ernest felt his own right fist tighten. Then he paused and saw Preghiera's face before him, hidden within the contours of the old man's features. He loosened his fist and released his hold on the man's collar. He staggered back a few steps and wiped his cheek. Ernest laughed a quiet, embittered little laugh.

"You, sad old man," Ernest whispered. "You claim to fear God, but love nobody here on Earth. You are a sad, unhappy old man, who wants only to pass on his unhappiness to all those around him."

The butcher tutted and shrugged away Ernest's remark. "You are a drunkard. You are just a drunken soldier. Pathetic."

"Not half as pathetic as you old man. So maybe I'll pray for you," Ernest called after him as the old butcher walked back into the shop and closed the door. "I'll pray for you, you sad, sorry old fool."

Chapter twenty-two
1993

Ernie followed a few steps behind Preghiera as she walked into the flickering darkness of Naples Cathedral, pausing to touch the holy water from the stoup and lifting it to her forehead, before genuflecting swiftly before the distant altar.

"Thank you for coming with me," Preghiera whispered to Ernie as she guided him towards a side chapel that was alive with candlelight. Ernie allowed his eyes to adjust to flickering darkness. Slowly the details of the chapel emerged. "It is important I think that we ask for San Gennaro's protection before we make our journey," Preghiera added softly.

"We're only going to Lake Como," Ernie smiled. "It's hardly a war zone."

Preghiera scowled at him playfully in the darkness. "It once was," she whispered. "And anyway, we always need the protection of our blessed saint. It is not for we mere mortals to know our fate."

Ernie wandered deeper into the chapel and started to examine the paintings. "Do you know that Naples has more than 50 patron saints?" he mused.

Preghiera nodded irritably. "Yes, but San Gennaro is, how would you say it, he is the main man. For we Neapolitans, he is the main man. He is watching out for us, you see?"

Ernie chuckled beneath his breath. He didn't see at all, but didn't wish to undermine Preghiera's devout convictions. "He certainly is my dear," he muttered in a humouring tone. "He certainly is the main man here in Naples."

Ernie took a step back as Preghiera lit a candle and then knelt before an oversized side altar. She lowered her head, closed her eyes, and seemed to be enveloped in prayer. Ernie turned his eyes to the ground a moment, and then looked back up and started once again to examine the interior of the chapel. The former bishop-turned-saint was depicted in an ornate polished statue recessed above the altar. The saint's blank eyes looked down at an enormous silver crucifix, which glistened in the middle of the altar.

Ernie cast his eyes back to Preghiera. He could see her lips moving in silent prayer. He wondered what she could be troubling the saint over in such detail. He shook his head a little with a smile and strolled away, placing his hands behind his back. He stopped a while and took in an enormous oil painting of the saint. The scale of the painting alone was quite something to admire.

The figure of the saint was wearing his resplendent mitre as Bishop of Naples, but looking over his shoulder like one who already knows that his days are numbered. Ernie then noticed the rope that was binding the bishop around his arms and waist. He was surrounded by armed men falling in wonder at his feet, and a group of cherubim had taken to the skies above the bishop's head.

Ernie read a little plaque and discovered that the bishop was depicted having just emerged unscathed from a furnace. Without turning, Ernie sensed that he had been joined again by Preghiera.

"Sounds like he wasn't treated very well this saint of yours," he whispered, with a raise of his eyebrows.

"That was nothing – he was beheaded eventually at the orders of Diocletian," she said softly. "His body is buried in the crypt," she added, with a nod towards the high altar, before adding, "both his body and his head that is."

"Naturally," Ernie grinned. "Wouldn't want to be seen to have lost his head."

1944

Ernest found his own faith severely and regularly challenged by his experiences of a world at war. But to his constant bewilderment, it seemed that the war only served to fuel the Italians' faith in just about everything and anything. There was a sort of group hysteria to the fervour in which the city would regularly become fixated on the latest crying statue, bleeding crucifix, talking icon or sweating fresco.

But the city's biggest supernatural obsession revolved around a phial of blood in Naples Cathedral, said to be that of San Gennaro. Three times each year – in September, December and May – the blood in the glass ampoule apparently miraculously liquified. The blood failing to liquify was seen to be a very ill omen indeed. The miracle had failed in three of the previous four years, leaving the Neapolitans' nerves in tatters.

By March fears that the blood would not liquify again in May had reached fever pitch. It was amid this state of mass nervous exhaustion that Ernest found himself alone in the city – his friends all either dead or invalided back to Blighty, while Preghiera was lost to him. He was propping up the bar at his usual Strega-drinking establishment, when he got chatting to a British Intelligence officer by the name of Lewis.

"This place is absolutely crazy," the officer grinned. "At the weekend crowds of them flocked out to Campi Flegrei to watch a 12-year-old to whom the Virgin Mary had apparently appeared with messages of comfort."

"What was her message?"

"Christ knows," Lewis said, and took another mouthful of beer, before almost spraying it across the bar when Ernest's wry smile pointed out the irony of his words. Instead the beer dribbled a little from his lips on to his uniform as he attempt to swallow the liquid while repressing the laughter.

Ernest laughed along with the officer. "You would hope He would, if anyone would."

The officer eventually found his composure and the laughter ebbed to smiles. "They had a band and all manner of festivities to keep the faithful entertained between messages from the Virgin, so I'm told," Lewis said, reaching for a handkerchief and drying himself off. "Then at Pomigliano we have a flying monk who simultaneously demonstrates the stigmata."

"By flying monk, do you mean he has a pilot's license?"

"No, levitation," the officer shrugged a "what-can-you-do-with-these-people?" sort of shrug. "The monk claims that on one occasion last year he levitated up to catch a pilot of a stricken Italian plane shot down in a dogfight. I've spoken to very well-educated Italians who believe every word of it."

Ernest shook his head in disbelief.

"So, what do you make of this place?" the officer turned his piercing eyes towards Ernest.

"The whole place is crazy," he said at last. "I know they've been through the mill, but it's like these people do everything they can to stop themselves being happy. This so-called passion of theirs, it gets in the way of their lives."

The officer nodded.

"I don't know," Ernest said. "But from everything I've seen and heard while I've been out here, I can't see how anybody will ever do anything with these people. They're a bunch of gangsters being ministered to by another bunch of gangsters in the churches, if you know what I mean."

Lewis nodded, silently taking it all in, fitting Ernest's thoughts into the greater jigsaw puzzle in his intelligence officer brain that was trying to make sense of the city around him.

Ernest put his empty glass down on the bar, wished the officer well and walked back towards the barracks considering the apparent miracles that had taken such a hold over the city. For him the biggest miracle of all was that he was still there in Naples working as a driver for a Lieutenant who hardly ever left the barracks. But all that was to change – the previous evening he had been given his papers to accompany the Lieutenant back to the front line. He wondered if his run of luck had run out. He thought of Preghiera and his lost pals and wondered if he would ever feel happiness again.

Pausing outside the imposing frontage of a church bearing the resplendent name of Complesso Monumentale San Lorenzo Maggiore, Ernest said to himself, 'well what harm can it do to ask?' and he gingerly went inside.

He had expected to be enveloped by the darkness of the space, but this was unlike so many other churches in the city that were shadowy and cold. This magnificent building had high clear windows above the nave, which allowed the sunlight to flood in, warming the backs of the faithful as they prayed. A single, mighty Romanesque archway framed the high altar, with an eerily lifelike wooden crucifix hanging above the scene.

Ernest sat down and gazed at the figure hanging on the cross, with ribs showing around His emaciated torso. The divine head was slumped to one side as if in deathly repose, but the dark brown eyes were open and staring directly at Ernest with calm benevolence.

"I know I don't do this often enough," Ernest began silently. "But I am asking now, as I have never asked before. In this world of inhumanity, please Lord, allow me one last straw to clutch as I go off to battle. Let me return one day to be with Preghiera, that we might be together for our final days. Give me that final hope and that is prayer enough that I may survive all that life can throw at me until then. Let me cling on to the idea of a happy ending." Ernest closed his eyes and allowed his right hand to lift to his forehead, from where it made the sign of the cross down to his chest and then from shoulder to shoulder – a movement that felt at once alien and comforting to him in this sacred place.

A moment later, he opened his eyes and glanced swiftly over one shoulder, then the other – to check that nobody had been watching him. He looked back towards the crucifix. "Let's keep this between you and me Lord," he muttered, before rising to his feet and walking back out towards the sunlight that glowed through the open door.

Chapter twenty-three
1993

Ernie was driving along with a beaming smile that appeared to stretch from ear to ear. He had figured, if he was going to drive Preghiera from Naples to Lake Como, then he was going to do it in style. He had hired a pristinely polished red 1970 Alfa Romeo Spider and shrugged off Preghiera's panic about "the cost". Now they were working their way along the A1 highway with the roof down, the engine growling and the wind in their grey hair.

"I was there you know," Preghiera said as she watched the road rolling out ahead of them. "I was there the night you came to threaten my father."

"You were?"

"Of course, they didn't keep me at the hospital for more than a few minutes. I had nowhere else to go, so I went home. I was back home for months. It was years before they started rebuilding the village and by then my cousin – my husband – had bought a little apartment here in Torre Annunziata. So we never left again."

"You were there when I spoke to your father?"

"Yes, I was listening behind the shutters of my room."

"You didn't come to me?"

"You were drunk."

"I was drunk," Ernie nodded as he drove. "That's true enough. I was very drunk. I think your father cursed me that night, I seem to remember."

"I'd have cursed you if you'd woken me by throwing a brick at my window."

They drove on for a few minutes in silence, both deep in their own thoughts. The silence was eventually broken by Ernie.

"Why did your father so take against me?" he asked, keeping his eyes carefully on the road ahead.

"I've told you. You were an outsider," Preghiera shrugged. "You don't understand Italians at all do you? Neapolitans particularly. If you're not in, you're out. If you're out, there's no way in. You stay out. You were always out. You were always going to be out. It wasn't actually personal. It was just the way he was. He wasn't as bad as he seemed you know. He thought he was doing the right thing for me. I can see that now."

They drove on for a few more minutes in silent thought, each working their way through distant memories. Once again it was Ernie who finally broke the silence.

"And your cousin was an insider I suppose?"

"Of course, he was my cousin. He was my father's nephew. He was the ultimate insider."

"Makes sense I suppose," Ernie said with a raise of his eyebrows. "What was he like, your cousin, that is, your husband?"

Preghiera considered the question carefully, before answering. "What was he like? He was just a simple man. A country man really. He wasn't, how do you say in English, sophisticated?" She nodded. "He wasn't in any way sophisticated. But he wasn't such a bad man. He was kind in his own way."

"But you didn't love him?"

Preghiera shrugged. "There are different levels of love, it's not just an on/off switch. I loved him as my cousin. I loved him differently as my husband. But I suppose I was never in-love with him. Not in the way," she paused and changed the direction of her sentence. "Not in that way. But he was a good man really. He married me because he was told to marry me. I couldn't hate him for that. He was never a cruel man. Just a simple man. None of it was really his fault. And when he died, I missed him. It was strange to not have him around. It would have been a lonely life for me without him you know?"

"Maybe, maybe not," Ernie said, keeping his eyes on the road. "Maybe you would have been able to marry somebody you really were in love with?" He coughed a little, and glanced out of the side window at the landscape speeding past the car, before turning back to the road. "Perhaps you might have married me?"

"True," Preghiera whispered. "That is true. Perhaps in an ideal world, we might have married when we were still young and in love." She ran her fingers through her long grey hair. "I would have liked that best," she added softly. "But I can't regret my life. It was my life after all. It is what it is."

"I do understand," Ernie said. "I don't regret my life either. If we had been allowed to get married back then, I never would have met Marjorie. Lives are so much more complicated than love stories you see. Things can be good and bad, both at the same time. Life is funny like that."

"Perhaps things are neither good nor bad, they just are what they are. It's just life," Preghiera flicked open her empty palms in a theatrical gesture.

"You know what Shakespeare said, don't you?" Ernie added. "Nothing is either good or bad, but thinking makes it so."

"He was a clever man, your William Shakespeare I think."

"Yes, he was for all the ages, as they say. I think he knew a thing or two," Ernie chuckled and pushed the accelerator closer to the floor, driving the cool breeze through the car so that Preghiera whooped with sheer joy, holding her hands aloft to catch the force of the air. She smiled at the man sitting beside her, with tears forming in her eyes. He looked young again in that moment – and carefree in a way he had never been able to be when he was a young man when war had tainted everything.

The landscape rolled on ahead of them – like an endless series of stunning photographs being projected on to the windscreen. A few hours later and Ernie found himself driving through the town of Cassino – nothing was recognisable to him from the last time he was here. Nothing that is, except the great craggy mountain that loomed overhead and its monolithic monastery perched on the top, which appeared to have regenerated itself like an octopus' arm in the years he had been absent. To see it once again, rising brilliant white in the afternoon sun felt like he was experiencing a curious time shift.

"Well, this is very peculiar," Ernie muttered, as he turned on to the track that wound its way up the hillside. Preghiera smiled sympathetically. "It's certainly easier to ascend the mountain this time than it was back in '44," Ernie laughed.

The couple parked up and walked hand in hand towards the abbey. Neither Ernie nor Preghiera spoke as they made their way up a long marble staircase, enclosed by a midnight blue ceiling embossed with silver stars. The building stretched out before them like a palace.

"This is extraordinary," Ernie whispered. "The last time I was here, the whole place was almost entirely reduced to rubble. There was a German, who collected butterflies. Can you believe it – butterflies."

Preghiera shook her head and smiled. She could see that Ernie's eyes were no longer seeing the landscape around them, but were now focused on long ago, another existence in this same sun-baked plot of land. She didn't speak, afraid to encroach on his reminiscences, so merely squeezed his hand reassuringly, giving it a gentle pat with her other hand as he spoke.

"It's the strangest thing to be back here my love, the strangest thing of all. In some ways, it feels like only yesterday that I was here. But in a way, it was altogether another world back then. So long ago now. So very long ago."

Ernie paused to turn and take in the view. The silence of the place was almost audible. From this vantage point the town of Cassino itself looked like a model village, with the main road stretching out from it like a pencil line on a map.

"What you call Highway Six, was known as the Via Casilina when the Romans first laid it two-and-a-half thousand years ago," he said to Preghiera, unable to help himself from turning once again to his "school teacher on a school trip" mode. Preghiera just nodded and smiled. "It is one of the great roads of history," he added. "It was down this very road that the Romans marched to fight the Samnites in the fourth century. It was down this road that General Fabius arrived to resist Hannibal. It was down this road that General Belisarius marched to recapture Rome from the Goths in the sixth century. It was down this road that Gonzalo Fernandez de Cordoba and the army of Isabella of Spain came to fight the French in 1503.

"You know your history," Preghiera laughed.

"It's always been my great interest," Ernie nodded. "My father encouraged us to read a lot. 'If you know where you came from, you'll know where you're going', he used to say, in his more sober moments. But it's always stayed with me – that sense of walking in the footsteps of those who came before. We're always walking in others' footsteps you know my love."

He turned and led the way across the courtyard and stepped inside the twinkling darkness of a chapel. He sensed Preghiera genuflecting habitually towards the tabernacle, taking a pinch of holy water from the stoup at the side of the doorway and making the sign of the cross over herself with theatrical devotion.

It took a moment for his old eyes to adjust to the darkness after being out in the warm Italian sunshine, but the incense seemed to gather around him and infuse his lungs as he walked on. He stopped and looked down towards the altar, his memory alive with the last time he had seen this place with the resilient prayers of two monks spiralling heavenwards out of the wreckage. Could he have imagined it or were there really two monks here praying throughout the bombardment? Was it just a trick of his memory? But he could see them there still so vividly in his mind's eye. The way their bodies were shaking with terror as they interlinked their arms together in mutual fraternal support.

Ernie took a long deep breath and brought himself back to the present day. He was beginning to feel strangely disorientated by the whole experience.

"I'm going to sit awhile," he whispered.

"Of course, my love, you take as long as you need," Preghiera said. "I will wait outside, in the sunshine." She flashed that smile that had melted him so profoundly as a young man and still hit like an arrow to his heart all these decades later.

Ernie closed his eyes and felt the blanketing sensation of being alone within this sacred space. When he reopened them, he realised he was no longer alone. A figure was walking slowly down the aisle. He didn't turn his head, but sensed the presence of an older man, with breath rasping a little as he walked. The figure stopped alongside him, just out of his line of vision, so he could partially see a black shirt and grey trousers out of the corner of his eye. Even before he had turned his head to make eye contact with the figure, there was something in that combination of dull hues that meant he already knew instinctively he had been joined by a priest.

"May I join you, do you suppose?" the priest asked.

"Of course, of course," Ernie flustered and shuffled along the pew to make space.

"I knew you even from the back of your head," the priest said. "So, you've come back here too?"

Ernie turned sharply and studied the face in the flickering shadows. It was strangely familiar, now he came to take a closer look, but Ernie couldn't place him at first.

"The last time we met we were laying poor old Smudge to rest," the priest said, smiling in the knowledge that he was helping the penny along as it was about to drop.

"Padre?" Ernie whispered. "Oh, my word, Padre. It is you. How extraordinary. I'm so sorry, I didn't recognise you."

"It's been a very long time. Our memories aren't what they were. It was Green, wasn't it?"

"Well, your memory seems to be working fine," Ernie smiled and reached out to shake the old priest's hand. "That's right, Ernest Green. Ernie."

"Ernest, yes of course, I could remember Green, but the Ernest was escaping me."

Ernie gazed at the old man smiling benignly beside him. In many ways, he somehow appeared younger now than he had done when he was laying Smudge to rest all those years ago. It was as though there was a lightness to him now that wasn't there before. "What an extraordinary coincidence to be here at exactly the same time," Ernie said.

"Not such a coincidence as you might think," the priest smiled. "Whenever you'd come you would have probably found me here. In fact, I live here now. I have done so for a long time. I converted to Catholicism after the war. The things I'd seen, well they never left me. So, I thought the best place for me was here. I came back to help rebuild this place. I wanted to be a part of rebuilding. Putting the whole place back together again after all that destruction. Such terrible destruction. So after the war, well this place felt like the right place for me to be."

"Incredible," Ernie could hardly find the words to convey his emotions. "That's absolutely incredible."

"You know when we bombed this place, we pretty much flattened it?"

"I know," Ernie said. "Oh yes, I certainly know."

"The devastation spared almost no part of the monastery, apart from some of the underground chambers," the priest went on. "But amazingly this chapel and the cell used by St Benedict himself unaccountably escaped. It was almost as if there was an invisible hand giving the bombs a little nudge to the left or right as they fell."

"It's amazing," Ernie nodded.

"What's even more amazing, is a high calibre artillery shell landed within a foot of the Saint's tomb, but failed to explode. Or perhaps, declined to explode, depending on how you view these things." The old priest smiled. "Much here was destroyed, but somehow the key things survived. Curious isn't it?"

Ernie nodded. "I know. The chapel where the monks were praying, survived completely intact. It raises more questions than it answers in a way. What was it Voltaire said? If there was no God, it would be necessary to invent Him."

The priest just smiled knowingly. Ernie continued: "Of course, this place has been sacked four times in its history. The war was just the latest time it has been almost destroyed. But each time it has grown stronger."

"Very true," the priest nodded.

"I was reading recently about when it was sacked by the Lombards just 40 years after Saint Benedict's death," Ernie added. "The abbot and monks fled to Rome, but it was while there that the fugitive Benedictines so impressed the Papal authorities that they were given the apostolate of the Germanic countries."

"Very true," the priest repeated. "After all, Benedict only conceived of the order as a self-contained local community, but it became this influential global missionary movement because history forced its hand."

"Ah, history is always forcing our hand," Ernie nodded.

"Talking of history, I suppose you're doing the war graves tour are you?" the priest asked, brushing some dust from his grey trousers as he spoke.

"No, well," Ernie became flustered again. "That is to say, I suppose I will visit the cemetery while I'm here. After all, I should go, shouldn't I? It would be good to try to find Patterson's grave. Do you remember Sergeant Patterson? We lost him here. I had to leave him behind on this mountain. His body crumpled like a doll that had seen its strings cut and I just had to leave him in a pile on the side of the mountain. That was such a terrible feeling. Such a terrible feeling."

"I'm sure it was Ernest, I'm sure it was." The priest was listening carefully. "But you're not here on the war graves tour then? You must be here for something else?"

The priest looked at him keenly with those calm all-knowing eyes. Ernie looked away from the priest for a moment, and gazed at the chapel ahead of him. It looked so beautiful, with the amber glow of the votive candles either side of the altar, with the goldwork of the hand-embroidered altar-frontal glinting magically within the half-light. He turned back to face those benevolent old eyes that were waiting patiently for him to answer.

"It was love that brought me back I suppose," Ernie said after a while. "Foolish I know, at my age."

"Not at all my friend," the priest said, laying a reassuring hand on Ernie's shoulder. "It was love that brought me back here too you know. There are so many different kinds of love, but what they have in common is that they can draw you back to where you feel you must be."

Ernie nodded. "That's very true Padre."

"What was it Saint Paul said," the priest added thoughtfully. "Do you recall? Love is patient, love is kind …"

"Oh yes, that's right," Ernie nodded once again.

The priest smiled and added quietly: "It bears all things, believes all things, hopes all things, endures all things. Love never fails." He squeezed Ernie's shoulder once more, moved closer to Ernie's ear and said again even more softly, "It endures all things. Love never fails."

Ernie smiled back at the priest's words and felt his own eyes dampen unexpectedly. After a moment of looking into that weather-worn all-knowing face, he patted his hands together and said: "Padre, you must come and meet Preghiera."

"Preghiera?" the priest grinned. "Now that really is a wonderful name."

1945

The rugged tips of the Alpine foothills appeared as silhouettes, foreshadowing the greater peaks that stood beyond. The mountains ranged like blue and white clouds for as far as Ernest could see. It was an almost fantastical landscape for a young soldier from the back streets of Birkenhead to take in.

Ernest felt completely wearied by all these years of war. They had taken the battle to the Germans time and again during the previous months, and many of their enemies had finally withdrawn back to their Fatherland to face their final battles. Others had surrendered more amicably and were interred by the Allies as prisoners-of-war all over the north of Italy.

Italy's own deposed dictator, the always absurdly prancing Benito Mussolini, had enjoyed his final strut. He had been captured by partisans in April and executed, later being strung-up for public viewing outside a petrol station in Milan – like a prancing cockerel with its neck pulled, finally silenced, finally revealed as the ridiculous creature he had always been. A couple of days later and the news broke that Hitler himself was dead. It felt like the last straw for the conflict. For Ernest and his comrades, there was a tangible sense that the fighting was done. Without their Fuhrer, surely the German battalions would now crumble like a pack of cards? It was in this moment, in a final act of benevolence from the top brass – at the recommendation of the good old Lieutenant – that Ernest and the other surviving members of his unit had been given leave at Lake Como, far in the north.

Although he could hardly bring himself to think of it, Ernest sensed that he would soon be going home. It was almost impossible to believe. Home had become something like a fiction in his mind. The long bumpy journey up to the north in a three-tonne truck had given Ernest plenty of time to think and reflect. He had worked slowly and methodically through his experiences of the last few years – the moments of horror, the moments of happiness, the total withering exhaustion of these final months. By the time he arrived at the resort, he felt strangely calm. The lake gleamed like a polished piece of lapis lazuli surrounded on all sides by steep, verdant mountains.

Ernest left the truck and shouldered his bag. He strolled aimlessly through the resort, crossing an ancient stone bridge and gazing awhile at the reflection of the tall, ivy-covered lakeside houses in the water.

He checked in to his accommodation and told his friends he would catch them later in the bar. He wanted to spend some time alone in this tranquil place. He walked back to the lakeside and lit a cigarette. The clouds of smoke moved away from him in a graceful motion across the gentle waves of the lake. A duck came in to land awkwardly on the water a few yards in front of him. It gave a grumpy call to the birds around it bobbing on the surface of the lake, before dabbling around the edges where the rocks provided green crags in which to search out scraps of food missed by the others. Ernest watched the duck, as he breathed in great big lungfuls of smoke and wondered how this place could feel so calm when the rest of Italy had been so frantic.

He walked on in silence, ambling at a leisurely pace, taking in the sights and sounds. He was surrounded by other solitary soldiers on leave, wandering similarly, with a sort of mindless expression on their faces as they, like Ernest, took this much-needed opportunity to be alone and to come to terms with everything they had been through.

At the jetty, Ernest discovered you could hire a rowing boat to make your way across the edge of the lake to a pleasant spot where the NAAFI was serving cups of tea. He reached around in his pockets, to see if he had enough change on him. Something almost primeval seemed to be calling him to get out on to the water, where the world seemed even calmer still.

Ernest paid the little Italian in the wooden hut and was directed towards a rowing boat painted garishly, but patriotically, in the colours of the Italian flag. He stepped into the boat alone and began to cut the oars through the still waters. It was the first time he had rowed a boat since that fateful day when they had lost Patterson. It seemed so long ago to Ernest now. Almost like another lifetime.

As he pulled slowly on the oars, the mountains rose up around the city, and Ernest was struck by a reassuring sense that he was not entirely alone, nor had he ever been entirely alone throughout his war. Perhaps, Ernest thought to himself once again, perhaps we never are.

He looked towards the shore, expecting to see a figure watching him, such was the sensation of being observed, but there was nobody in sight. Ernest took a deep breath of the crisp air and rowed on, soaking in the tranquillity, just as he had imagined he would be able to do on the water.

1993

Ernie and Preghiera settled themselves on a wooden bench with ornate cast iron arms. They had walked along the lakeside through Varenna, on the opposite side of Lake Como to that he had visited during the final days of war. But the sense of tranquillity of that place had stayed with him through all the years, and he felt it again now, gently massaging his tired old soul. The sun was slowly setting behind the mountains and the lake's still surface mirrored the pink hues of the sky. For Ernie it was as if time had simply stood still in this place. It could just as easily be 1945, except now, Ernie had the great happiness of not being alone – of having Preghiera beside him. It felt as if the final piece of the great fumbling jigsaw puzzle of his long life had been put into place. It all felt so right.

The drive up from Monte Cassino had been relaxed and quietly joyful, including an undreamt-of visit for Preghiera to the boutiques of Milan, where Ernie delighted in getting her kitted-out in an elegant outfit at great expense to the great wodge of lire bank notes in his wallet. Then there was the easy drive on from the sprawling city of Milan to Como itself. They had checked into their plush hotel room overlooking the sprawling lake late in the evening, but awoke the next morning to what Ernie had immediately told himself was the perfect day. It was the day he and Preghiera had always waited for – their domani. It had come at last and Ernie could almost feel the sensation of happiness careering tangibly through his veins like a hit of morphine. Now they rested on the wooden bench and allowed their happiness to permeate gently through their sinews.

Preghiera settled her head against Ernie's shoulder. Ernie looked at the wisps of grey hair, and nuzzled his face against the top of her head. It had indeed been the perfect day. A long lazy morning in the hotel room with the sun streaming through the window. A relaxed lunch in one of the lakeside restaurants, filled with laughter and fine Chianti. They had then taken a boat trip across the lake and enjoyed an afternoon strolling through the pristine gardens of the Villa Carlotta, laughing and joking, arm in arm like a pair of young lovers. And now there was this moment to take in.

Ernie closed his eyes and listened to the flapping wings of a swan, the singsong of children playing nearby and the distant thud-thud of a motorboat ambling across the lake. There would never be a better moment than this, Ernie thought to himself. This was the tomorrow – the domani – he and Preghiera had always longed for he kept telling himself, time after time, like an incantation. It was as if it was the only way he could make himself believe it had all really come true – this long-held dream of happiness.

"I have just one question to ask you now," Ernie whispered, to Preghiera. She did not respond. Ernie opened his eyes slowly and took in the beauty of the place once more. He reached a hand down and placed it on the slender fingers of Preghiera's hand. "You feel cold my love." Preghiera remained motionless.

Ernie lifted his head slowly. He closed his eyes. No. Not this. Not now, he prayed. He opened his eyes again, and took a deep breath.

"My love," he said, turning towards Preghiera, who slumped to the side as he moved. He touched her cold cheek with his hand, and lifted her face towards his. That face had retained the innocent beauty of so many decades. The olive eyes that had preserved the playfulness of the 17-year-old now stared blankly through him, beyond him to another place.

"Oh, my love." Ernie settled back on to the bench and allowed Preghiera's head to fall once more on to his shoulder. "Oh my love, my love, my love," he rocked backwards and forwards, as he felt the pain knotting in his stomach. "Oh my love. Here's to happy endings," he whispered, as he took hold of her hand. "Here's to happy endings."

Christmas 1993

Ernie tucked into his fried breakfast with relish, pausing only occasionally to idly turn the pages of the newspaper that was laid out on the table before him. It was his usual spread – fried egg, bacon, sausage, mushrooms, tomato, hashbrown, black pudding, a steaming mug of tea. Occasionally he would raise his eyes to watch a trolley-pushing family move by on the nearest aisle of the supermarket, fractious children, fractious parents – your standard happy family.

A single strip of shiny green tinsel had been hung in half-hearted swags across the top edge of the servery, and the greasy steam from the breakfast buffet was causing it to move from side to side with a perpetual motion that captured Ernie's attention for a long while as he swept a piece of toast around the now nearly empty plate, carefully collecting the combination of flavours, before chewing the edge of the toast with his mind wandering far from the simple charms of the little supermarket café.

With his main fried breakfast complete, he took his second piece of white toast and carefully spread butter and marmalade upon it. He wasn't in a rush. He wasn't so much reading the newspaper that rested on the table beside his tea and toast as he was occasionally just looking at the pictures. His mind was elsewhere, working through the events of the past few weeks, culminating in that grand Italian funeral mass, which he had sat through at the back of the church like a distant acquaintance of the deceased.

Rachele had tearfully promised to keep in touch. He was expecting a Christmas card any day now.

He finished the last of his tea and the café attendant walked across in her crisp supermarket uniform and gave him a polite smile as she took his plate.

"Busy day ahead?" she asked.

"Not so busy," Ernie admitted and thanked her for taking the plate. "It's always such a great breakfast." She nodded and smiled and took the plate away. Ernie patted at the pockets of his overcoat, which was hanging on the back of his chair, to reassure himself that his car keys were still there. He felt the keys and his fingers also found the old red leatherbound book that he had been re-reading recently. It was his father's pocket edition of *David Copperfield*. He weighed the book in the palm of his hand. This little book, with its embossed golden scrolls on the spine, had been all through the war with him, and yet it looked untouched somehow, as if it was still pristine and new. It was still a thing of wonder to him. He opened it to the frontispiece with its ornate title surrounded by little drawings of cherubs and an odd etching of an elderly man reading a book in an armchair long ago. He turned another page and ran his own old fingers across the words '*The personal history and experience of David Copperfield the Younger*'.

"The personal history and experience of Ernest Green, the much, much older," he whispered to himself, closing the little book and returning it to his pocket. His mind rushed for a moment back to his father. The book-lined room with the little fireplace crackling away. The library books being flung towards him. He thought of his mother, pious and timid, hiding upstairs like a shrew. Life, he had come to realise, was all about the people one met along the way. His mind worked its way through a series of long familiar faces – Patterson, Smudge, Mouse, Captain Wright and Choo Choo, the Lieutenant looking cheerful and bumbling. He thought of the German with his butterflies and the little dark-haired Italian boy, both now so long gone and lost to the shadows. He thought of dear Marjorie and lovely young Rachele and most of all, he thought of Preghiera with her olive eyes and gentle benevolence and that word always playing on her soft lips for eternity: "Domani, domani, domani".

A tap on his shoulder woke him from his reverie. A tubby little woman was smiling down at him. Ernie frowned up at the face. He didn't recognise it.

"It is you Sir, isn't it?" the woman grinned. She was in her mid-30s, but she exuded the dull lustre of a hard life, which made her look at least ten years older. Ernie still didn't recognise her, but whenever any adult stopped him and called him Sir, he always politely pretended to remember their childhood incarnation from decades before.

"It's Lil," she said, leaning in towards him conspiratorially. "Lilian. Lilian Grimshaw."

A smile erupted across Ernie's face. He did remember Lilian Grimshaw.

"So how are you Sir? All ready for Christmas?"

Ernie took to his feet and patted the woman affectionately on her stocky shoulders. "You know how it is with Christmas Lilian," he smiled as he reached down for his overcoat. "Disappointment can leave that awful hollow feeling in your stomach."

The woman gave him a vacant look and nodded a little. "Well," she muttered. "You have a good one Sir."

"You too my dear, you too."

Leaving the supermarket with his newspaper folded beneath his arm, he dashed across the car park in the rain and sat back in his steamed-up car breathing heavily. The rain pattered noisily on the roof. Ernie closed his eyes for a moment and listened to it. So gentle, but so visceral. Somehow that sound seemed to reverberate through his whole being. Such were the simple pleasures that he had grown to love and to give their due attention. Reopening his eyes, he leaned forward and fastened his seat belt. He started the engine and Radio 3 sparked into life from the tinny old speakers. A tenor was singing *Che gelida manina* from La Bohème. Ernie turned up the volume dial and drove away.

He didn't have far to drive. He left the supermarket car park and pulled up a few moments later around the corner from the church that had become his usual Sunday morning haunt. Today was a Saturday, so it felt a little odd to be heading to church. But it was Christmas Eve, so the world was working a little differently. He dashed across the pavement, avoiding the puddles as best he could, and swiftly made his way inside the old building. Shaking the rain from his coat he nodded at the smiling church warden who was standing at the door.

"Not very festive weather for Christmas Eve," the warden said, rising up and down between his heels and toes, with his hands clasped behind his back.

"Not at all," Ernie laughed, and taking an order of service and hymn book from a second usher at the end of the aisle, he made his way to his usual place on the back pew.

As the organ rumbled into life, the families filed in one by one in festive spirits. Ernie gazed ahead at the altar and the brass cross that stood at its centre. It was gleaming and devoid of a Christ.

"I suppose I have to hand it to you," Ernie prayed silently. "You did what I asked, didn't you? I was with her at the end. A little more time would have been nice, but I suppose you hear that from everyone."

The young vicar took to the lectern – they had long ago stopped using the actual pulpit. His gleaming white teeth and boyish good looks gave him the discomforting appearance of a children's television presenter. "Welcome everyone! Welcome! How nice to see so many of you here this Christmas Eve."

Ernie's mind immediately wandered. The vicar's words echoed vacantly around the church. Ernie was no longer listening. His thoughts were elsewhere. The service passed deep in memories, only occasionally coming to when it was time to take to his feet to join in with the hymns. A few were comfortingly familiar. Most sounded like they had been written for the latest boy band.

At the end of the service Ernie noted that he felt less festive than he had at the start. He removed his glasses and rubbed his eyes, wondering why that might be, but he was unable to give himself any real answer. He got to his feet and shuffled to the end of the pew to join the queue for the door. The vicar shook his hand, grinning blankly, without making any eye contact.

Ernie walked back out through the graveyard. The rain had gone off and the long grass that covered the graves glistened crisply in the cold.

"Fear no more the heat o' the sun," he said aloud in a whisper to the graveyard at large. "Nor the furious winter's rages." He ran his hand across the stubble of his own cheek as he walked slowly along the path. "Thou thy worldly task hast done, Home art gone, and ta'en they wages."

Ernie stopped and turned back to look at the church steeple behind him, with the gravestones ancient and modern dotted around beneath the stretching reach of a yew tree and the chattering congregation mulling around the doorway. He took in a long, slow, deep breath, enjoying the damp English air. He closed his eyes a moment and those olive eyes smiled once again in his memory. A smile flickered across his lips. "Golden lads and girls all must, As chimney-sweepers, come to dust," he muttered and pushing his hands into the pockets of his overcoat, Ernie ambled towards the gate.

"Look around the hillsides, Through the mist and rain,
See the scattered crosses, Some that bear no name.
Heartbreak and toil and suffering gone,
The lads beneath, they slumber on.
They are the D-Day Dodgers,
Who'll stay in Italy."

About the Author

David Clensy is an award-winning writer, originally from Birkenhead, in Merseyside. He now lives in Wiltshire with his wife and two children.

He spent more than 20 years in regional newspaper journalism and was twice named South-West Feature Writer of the Year at the EDF Regional Media Awards. He has also worked as a magazine editor, sub-editor, communications officer and a senior copywriter.

David has written a number of both non-fiction and short fiction books, including *Island Life: A History of Looe Island* (2006), *The Mole of Edge Hill* (2006), *Walking The Wolds Way* (2007) and *Walking the White Horses* (2023).

In 2023 David won the Frome Festival Short Story Competition Local Prize. His short stories have also been long-listed in the Cranked Anvil Short Story Prize 2022, short-listed in the Wells Festival of Literature Short Story Competition 2022 and short-listed in the Yeovil Literary Prize 2023.

Prayer in Time of War is his debut novel. Reviews are important for authors, so if you enjoyed *Prayer in Time of War*, please take a moment to review the book on Amazon, Goodreads or similar platforms and play your part in letting the world know about it.

Connect with David Clensy on social media and sign up for his newsletter to be the first to find out about new work, by visiting:

www.davidclensy.com